DEATH HAS ITS BENEFITS

*Jim,
Thanks for coming out to support me. I'm looking forward to getting your input on Dawgy's Nite Out.*

DEATH HAS ITS BENEFITS

Ronald Aiken

2012

This is a work of fiction. The events described are imaginary. The characters and settings are fictitious. Any references to real persons or places are included only to lend authenticity to the story.

DEATH HAS ITS BENEFITS

FIRST EDITION

All rights reserved.
Copyright © 2012 by Ronald Aiken

Cover art: Carole Mauge-Lewis

This book may not be reproduced in whole or in part, by mimeograph or any other means, without permission of the publisher, except in the case of brief quotations embodied in critical articles or reviews.

ISBN: 978-0-9819572-7-2

Nightbird Publishing
P.O. Box 159
Norcross, Georgia 30091

Website: www.nightbirdpubs.com

e-mail :   info@nightbirdpubs.com

PRINTED IN THE UNITED STATES OF AMERICA

First Printing: July 2012

10 9 8 7 6 5 4 3 2 1

For the women whose love, support and belief in me never wavered: my mother, Eddie Lee Aiken; my mother-in-law, Mildred Jaye, who was like a mother to me; Cousin Sylvia Rolnick who always asked, "How's the book going?" and especially my wife, Herma Jaye Aiken.

Death Has Its Benefits

1

LEO RADIGAN AND I couldn't have been more different, and not just the color of our skin. I lived in the city. He was out in the 'burbs. I was a lawyer with a corner office. Leo was blue collar with dirt under his fingernails. No kids for me, two for Leo and his wife Trudy.

But when a guy saves your life, none of that stuff matters.

"Gimme two more, Leo," I yelled over the din of a typical Monday night crowd at Bay View Health & Athletic Club. "Come on, tough it out."

Leo grunted under the strain of the weight on the bar, and wheezed out another rep.

"One more to match me."

He pushed up the last rep and dropped the weight back onto the chrome uprights.

"You're strong tonight," I said. "You been juicing?"

Although Leo and I were about the same height, I packed an extra twenty pounds, mostly around the midsection. So usually, after he finished a set, I'd add another ten or twenty pounds to whatever exercise we were doing. But not tonight. He matched my load, rep for rep.

He smirked. "Naw, man. Just straightened out a little problem that's been weighing on me, and all's right with the world."

"What little problem?"

"Some shit I was dealing with at work." He stretched his arms, then cock-walked around to the head of the bench to spot me.

"It's good you took care of whatever it was, because you've been pretty much a dick the last couple a weeks. You must've been a real bundle of joy at home."

"Don't worry, I'll make it up to you."

"Oh, how?"

"You and me . . . we're hangin' out tonight."

"Can't. Gotta go straight home. Diana's got a honey-do list for me."

I toweled off the bench, lay down and lifted the bar.

"I don't mean hangin' out, like we're together, numb-nuts. I need you to cover for me. You know, just in case *somebody* asks."

I completed the set and said, "You mean Trudy, right?"

"Exactly. Trying to stay off her radar."

I threw the towel at him and he blocked it aside. "So, where did we hang out—just in case, you know, somebody asks?" I said.

"We went to that little bar over on Main Street and got shitfaced."

"I quit drinking, remember," I said, then squeezed a stream of orange Gatorade into my mouth.

To save my marriage, I'd stopped boozing about a year ago.

"Shit, I don't know. Make something up."

Leo paused to give it some thought, then tugged at his nose, morphed his face into a smirk and said, "You drank club soda and played grab-ass with the bar maids. Anyway, doesn't matter, it'll cover up any inconsistencies in our stories if Trudy asks."

"I don't have a story. I'm going home to my wife."

"Ah, yes, the lovely Diana."

"Eat your heart out, brother."

He tapped me on the shoulder, then pranced around like he'd just bagged some Hollywood starlet. "I'm screwing this dancer."

"Let me guess. She's with the City Ballet, right?"

He took me seriously and answered, "Naw, man. A Russian babe from the strip club."

"Oh, you mean Irena."

"How'd you know?"

"Isn't every Russian babe working a strip club named Irena?"

He added a couple of five-pound plates onto the bar, and started doing another set.

"I can't believe you're playing around," I said. "Trudy's smarter than you, makes more money than you, and looks a hell of a lot better than you deserve."

He pushed out the last rep, sat up, then said, "Here's a little fact of life for ya', bro. No matter how good looking a broad is, there's always some guy out there who's tired of putting up with her shit. Bank on it."

"Enlightening. So partying with strippers, that's your answer?"

"For now," Leo said.

"Wrong answer, man."

"I know you've got a perfect little life, but come down off your high horse for a minute. You don't have to deal with the shit I'm dealing with."

One of the several city cops who were club members ambled over and said, "You pussies done yapping, or what?" He was wearing a faded, blue NYPD T-shirt and sweatpants, I guess so we didn't forget he had a badge and a gun.

Without acknowledging the prick, Leo and I moved away from the bench.

"Thanks, girls," the cop said.

"Fuck him," Leo mumbled.

"We all have to live with the choices we make, Leo."

"I knew you'd understand."

"Come on, lighten up. You're getting laid tonight."

"Don't worry. All my faculties will be up and running just fine."

2

I'D MET LEO TEN YEARS AGO at Bay View. In the club parking lot, to be exact. Because of a rash of car break-ins, club members had been warned not to leave valuables in their cars. But that night a gang of bored rich kids from a nearby subdivision decided to step up their game, ambushing me on the way to my car. It wasn't enough for them to just take my credit cards and the paltry ten bucks I carried in my wallet. They decided to add to their evening's entertainment by using my dome to play whack-a-mole. Somewhere on my way to unconsciousness, Leo, my white knight, came running to the rescue, swinging a baseball bat like he was hitting cleanup for the Yankees. I can still hear the sound of the heavy maple crashing against bone, and the accompanying screams from the punks. When my head cleared, I saw half of the gang writhing on the pavement, limbs broken, blood everywhere.

"You always carry a Louisville Slugger around with you?" I said after the action was over.

"Just when I need it," Leo said.

"You saved my life, man. I owe you, big time."

"In spades."

Now, being a black man, it took a second to divine his meaning. But what the hell, he'd just saved my ass.

After I recovered, Leo and I worked out together twice a week—upper body on Mondays, lower body on Thursdays. He filled in the rest of the week with boxing and aerobics. You'd never believe the guy had a wife and two kids, because I didn't know any married men who spent that much time out of the house.

FROM THE JOGGING track at the top of the club, you looked out on the luxury yachts and sailboats tied up to the piers in Port Washington Bay. But in spite of the panoramic view, members called the place Horror View. Every week it seemed like something else would break down. Air conditioning one week, sauna the next. The place smelled of decaying vegetation, but sometimes during the spring, a breath of fresh salt air off the bay would deodorize the place. Surprisingly, members didn't seem to mind the disarray. It just gave the guys something else to bitch about besides their wives.

Like most clubs, Horror View had its own caste system. Hardcore muscle-heads, biceps and quads straining against the fabric of their tight-fitting gear, were usually grouped under the jogging track, preening and lifting big weight, putting on a show for each other. The young hip crowd, dressed in their color-coordinated designer outfits, was at the other end of the floor, occasionally lifting a dumbbell, but mostly just standing around bullshitting about how great they looked. Leo and I were marooned between the two groups, all faded T-shirts and baggy sweatpants, usually with a handful of other misfits.

We'd finished showering and were sitting on the bench in front of our lockers, getting dressed. It was late, so only a few other members were still around. Naturally, the locker room was as drab and messy as the rest of the place.

"I ever tell you 'bout my boss?" Leo said.

He'd slipped on a pair of jeans and a sweatshirt. An oversized baseball cap was turned backwards, and pulled down over his ears.

"Not really."

"I think he's connected."

I laughed, and slapped him on the shoulder.

Leo shrugged. "Laugh if you want, but I'm telling you, he's one really scary dude."

"Why're you telling me? So, don't work for him."

LEAVING THE CLUB, we ran into Eddie Hambrick, a muscle-head we both knew.

"Frick and Frack," Eddie said. "We starting to wonder about you two guys."

"Ha, ha," Leo said, brushed him off, and continued on to his car.

"Hey, what's the rush?" I said, catching up to him. "Irena will be there when you get there."

It was foggy and our breaths vaporized in the cold, damp air. Up ahead, I heard a car window breaking, the car alarm wailing a beat later. A man in dark clothes was rummaging through a car.

"Isn't that your old Chevy, Leo?"

"What the fuck?" he yelled.

The thief looked up, then jogged off towards a large sedan idling at the back of the parking lot, Leo in hot pursuit.

"Watch out, Leo. He might have a weapon."

The car's headlights flashed on, stopping Leo dead in his tracks. I shielded my eyes from the glare. The vandal stopped next to the car, turned and faced us. He was brandishing a crowbar.

I came up alongside Leo. "Can you see the license plate?"

"Can't see shit."

"How about the big-ass crowbar the guy's holding?"

It was a standoff. We weren't going after them and they weren't coming back at us. Thick chords of heavy metal guitar riffs screeched from inside the vehicle, the dissonance pushing us back a step. The guy dropped the crowbar, hopped into the car, and the driver sped out of the lot.

Eddie said, "What the fuck was that about?"

"Don't know, but goodnight, Irena," I said.

Leo turned away, muttering, "It's starting."

3

DIANA AND I used to go out regularly with Leo and Trudy, but that pretty much stopped when they had kids. However two nights after the incident at the club, Leo called and we met him and Trudy at the Foghorn Diner out in Nassau County.

The Fog, as the regulars called it, is a classic suburban diner, all chrome and blue neon. The owner paid homage to classic rock 'n roll with pictures of Elvis and other '50s teen idols covering the walls. A miniature replica of a '56 Chevy convertible hung outside above the entrance.

The Fog was noisy and chaotic. Every booth and table was taken, with an army of waiters shuffling back and forth to the kitchen.

A young blonde, dressed in black spandex jeans and strapless top, like Olivia Newton John in the movie *Grease*, scribbled Leo's name on the waiting list.

"Fifteen minutes," she said.

"So, I hear you and Leo had quite a time the other night, huh?" Trudy said. She laughed, but I could see the tension lingering just below the surface of her big toothy smile.

"It was cool, just shooting the breeze, watching the game," I said. "You know, guy stuff."

After about five minutes the hostess called Leo's name, handed us menus, and we followed her to our seats. Every booth had a vintage tabletop jukebox, and Elvis' hushed voice implored his woman to *Love Me Tender*.

"Leo didn't get home until two in the morning," Trudy said a second after we'd been seated. "And on a work day, no less."

The waitress took our orders—we all had burgers, fries,

and a soda—and almost before Trudy could continue grilling me, we were eating.

"What time you get in, Tony?"

"Come on, Trudy," Leo said. "We don't need to get into that."

I looked from Trudy to Leo, then said, "On Monday? I don't know, Trudy." I asked Diana. "Around twelve? I kinda lose track."

I caught a glimpse of Diana giving me the fish eye.

Time to change the subject. "Too bad about Leo's car, " I said, stabbing a forkful of French fries and stuffing them in my mouth.

"Yeah, with a thousand-dollar deductible, I lost all around," Leo jumped in. "I'm still picking glass outta my ass."

"They steal anything?" Diana said.

"Nothing to take," Leo said, around a mouthful of burger.

"How weird, though," I said. "A parking lot full of Lexuses and Benzes, and they pick on your old beat-up piece of crap?"

"I keep telling you it's a station-car," Leo said.

"That you take to the gym," I said.

A lot of suburbanites owned old junkers like Leo's for the sole purpose of getting to and from a nearby Long Island Railroad train station, but Leo drove his everywhere. A crazy love affair with his first car.

"You think it might've had something to do with that little problem you mentioned?"

"I told you I got that straightened out," Leo said. He'd been cutting a slice of tomato, then dropped the knife onto the table.

"What problem?" Trudy asked.

Leo's face reddened. "Uh, we're trying to unionize, and you know how the bosses hate unions. It's all good now, though." He cast a sidelong glance at me. "Teamsters don't give up easy."

Trudy looked at me, pointed to her chin and said, "Ketchup."

I wiped my face.

Leo continued elaborating on the bogus union conflict. After we'd finished off the burgers the women got bored with Leo's tale of the Teamsters' heroic stand, and headed off to the ladies' room to freshen up.

"Man, don't ever talk about shit like that around Trudy. That was between me and you."

"Hey, sorry. Didn't know."

"Next, you'll be telling her about Irena."

"Speaking of Irena, what'd you do the other night after you left the club?"

"We hooked up."

Leo had insisted upon keeping his date with Irena, but I didn't believe he'd actually go through with it. "Damn, Leo. With glass in your ass? That's some real heroic shit."

He'd been unresponsive most of the night, but now he was fired up, his face flaming as red as his stringy hair.

"Trudy thinks I was with the police, filing a report. Then you and me went out for a drink to calm him down. So don't fuck up my story."

Our waitress sauntered over and said, "Anybody save room for dessert?"

"Just the check please," Leo said, preempting any thought I might've had about ordering my favorite, apple pie à la mode.

She gathered up the plates and handed the stack to a passing busboy.

"Hey, don't blame me for your mess," I said after the table had been cleaned. "You really think Trudy believed that bullshit story about us hanging out the other night?"

"What Trudy *don't* know is just pure speculation, man, and if it's all right with you, let's keep it that way. Anyway, women don't want to know the cold hard facts."

"You threw yourself under the bus on this one, my man."

"Yeah, and guess who was driving the damn Greyhound?"

"Shit. I thought a little action on the side was supposed to make you happy."

Leo's demeanor suddenly changed. He became introspective, slumping his shoulders, staring at his hands steepled under his chin. "My life's in the shitter, Tony."

"Come on. Maybe a good hard workout will change your outlook on life. Let's get together tomorrow."

I reached across the table and patted his forearm. But he pulled back and said, "It's going to take a whole lot more than a workout to get my shit straight. I'm about ready to snap. Between putting up with Trudy's bullshit, the kids, bills . . . I can't think straight right now."

I sawed on a miniature air violin and said, "Boo, hoo."

"As always, thanks for your support, Tony."

"Come on, man. Suck it up."

He dropped his head into his hands. "The broad I'm banging—"

"Irena?"

"Yeah, she's bustin' my balls about me not spending enough time with her. She threatened to call Trudy and tell her everything. Probably doesn't matter. One of Trudy's girlfriends ran into me with Irena at the mall. She probably couldn't wait to get on the phone and tell Trudy."

He took a deep breath and exhaled. "And to top it all off, my boss is gonna kill me."

"Now, that's a novel approach to workforce reduction." I'd had enough of his little pity party. "Up to me, I'd just fire your lazy ass."

"No, I really—"

The waitress dropped the check onto the table. "Thanks, and come again," she said.

"The other night when that guy broke into your car, what'd you mean by, 'it's starting?' "

My cell phone rang. Our home security company showed on caller ID. "Hold on a sec. Gotta take this."

While the guy from the monitoring center filled me in, I

watched the women make their way back to the table. If you didn't know better, you would have thought Trudy and Diana were related, they looked that much alike—a slender five feet, four inches of Midwestern no-nonsense, with a hint of the rock singer Alanis Morissette etched in their angular faces and prominent chins—albeit two different shades.

Trudy stopped at a booth to speak with a woman, who, if her animated gestures were any indication, she obviously knew. Diana continued to walk towards me.

"We're on our way," I said into the phone. "Twenty minutes." Turning to Diana, I said, "It's that damn alarm system again." Then to Leo, "We've gotta go. The police are on their way to the house right now."

I handed Leo three, tens. "This should take care of our end. We'll talk later about tomorrow, okay, buddy?"

Leo was clearly discomfited and I wasn't sure he heard me, but he nodded, nevertheless.

Trudy came back to the table, and asked, "Everything okay?"

"Our security company," I said, holding up my cell. "Probably just another false alarm. We'll call you guys later."

Trudy hugged Diana, then me, holding on a beat too long. Diana mocked staring at us.

Outside, I noticed a large sedan parked at the far end of the parking lot. It looked an awful lot like the one I saw at the club.

4

NEITHER DIANA NOR I were worried about a break-in, but nevertheless we hurried back to our modest three-bedroom Tudor in the quiet Jamaica Estates section of Queens. The police had been cracking down on false burglar alarms and meting out hefty fines on homeowners with faulty security equipment. We'd inherited the alarm system when we bought the house five years ago, and the damned thing was a problem from day-one. But we were usually home when it went off and were able to stave off NYPD before they were dispatched.

"Leo was a little withdrawn tonight," Diana said, breaking the silence that had settled in between us. "Trudy says he's been like that for a while now. Did you know they haven't made love in forever?"

I snickered. "First, how would I know, and that's not what I hear from Leo."

"Let you guys tell it, you'd have every woman believing you're sex machines all revved up and ready to go at the blink of an eye."

She laughed, then turned on the radio to an all-news station. "Watch your speed, Tony."

I tried to think back on the last time Diana and I'd made love. It had been awhile, too, but oh how I loved to hear the sound of her laughter. It was happy music.

"You weren't with him the other night, were you?" she said, her accusatory tone a stylus skipping across the surface of an old vinyl record.

"Sure I was," I said, hoping the Mercedes' dark interior hid the rush of blood spreading across my face.

"Tony, I can tell when you're lying."

"Okay. You got me. He's fooling around." *That was easy.* "There, you happy?"

She turned off the radio. "That bastard. How long have you known?"

"I just found out the other day," I pleaded.

"And you've been covering for him?"

"No way."

"I can't believe you didn't tell me."

"I just did."

"But I had to drag it out of you. I'm going to tell Trudy."

"Why on earth would you want to do that? Besides, I think she already knows. The guy's been pretty reckless."

I turned onto our street near the St. John's University campus. Up ahead, I could see the lights on the athletic field blazing through the skeletal line of trees. Further ahead, two police cruisers were parked in front of our house, a security company minivan in the driveway. All the lights in the house were on, and the front door was wide open.

"Oh my God," Diana said.

I pulled in behind the minivan. The car was still rolling when Diana jumped out and ran to the front door. I was right behind her. A policeman held out a restraining hand, stopping us from entering the house.

"This is a crime scene, folks," he said. "Please stay back."

"This is our house, officer," I said.

A guy dressed in the security company uniform pulled aside the yellow police tape and said, "It's all right, officer, you can let them through."

"I'm sorry, Mr. and Mrs. Benson," he said. "I'm Jamison from Ace Security." He shook my hand. "Bastards left quite a mess."

"What happened?" Diana said.

I held her tightly around the shoulders, feeling a tremor working its way through her.

"Looks like it might've been kids," Jamison said.

"Why do you say that?" I said.

"We typically see this kind of vandalism with teenagers. It's usually some kind of prank. You got the college close by, fraternities and such."

"Fuckers," I said.

We did a quick tour of the house. Jamison was right—it was a total disaster. Chairs and tables overturned, seat cushions thrown about, paintings pulled off the wall. In the kitchen, utensils were strewn on the floor. Drawers emptied in the master bedroom. Diana took it all in, then broke down crying. I turned the living room couch upright, took Diana's hand, plopped down, and pulled her close.

"Take your time, folks. A detective's on the way. Let me know if anything's missing."

"You're kidding, right?" I said, taking in the chaos.

The security rep held up his hands, then backed away.

"WHAT-A YA DO FOR A LIVING, MR. BENSON?" Detective Williamson said.

He wore a black topcoat over a tan sports jacket, white shirt and blue slacks. A brown and green patterned tie was open at the neck. Nothing matched. It was as if other detectives in the squad had made a clothing donation.

"I'm a corporate lawyer, my wife's a teacher."

I'd placed the chairs upright, put the seat cushions back in place, and we sat around the cold fireplace. A flashing kaleidoscope of color from the cop cars' light bars sparkled on the frost-covered living room windows. Diana and I were side-by-side, holding hands. She'd stopped crying, but her focus seemed to be on some distant object.

"Maybe one of her students did this," the detective said.

"She teaches third grade," I said.

"You piss somebody off?"

"We pretty much stay to ourselves," I said.

"Beef with a neighbor?"

"This is a quiet neighborhood."

"Let me know as soon as you can if something's missing, so I can finish up my report."

Detective Williamson shook my hand and handed me his card. "I'll be in touch," he said.

A nod of the head, and he was gone.

5

DIANA AND I SPENT the next few days cleaning up the mess. We must have washed every dish, piece of silverware, and item of clothing at least twice. But we couldn't sweep away the image of the vandals' hands pawing over our personal belongings. The good news—nothing seemed to be missing. Somehow, the thieves had overlooked Diana's jewelry and the cash lying atop the bureau in the bedroom.

All the furniture, pictures, paintings, and knick knacks had been put back in place, and we were in our familiar evening positions in the living room—I was curled up in my favorite brown wing chair reading *The Black Angel*, John Connolly's tale of mysticism and mayhem. Diana, leaning over the small desk next to the fireplace, was working on a lesson plan for her third-graders.

"We have to move," Diana said. "I really don't feel safe here anymore."

"This is not exactly a good time to be trying to sell a house, not with the economy in the toilet. Besides, my guess is it was college kids, just like Jamison said. A fraternity initiation rite, something stupid like that."

"Where were our neighbors? The alarm screaming like a banshee and nobody saw or heard anything?"

"Damn system cried wolf one time too many," I said.

"So, we wait for some crazy person to break in during the middle of the night and kill us in our sleep? If we're lucky?"

"Tomorrow, I'll start looking for a new alarm system, okay?"

I knew Diana wasn't satisfied with that non-solution. Nothing short of leaving was going to satisfy her. She started to say something else, caught herself, then turned back to her lesson plan.

"Don't worry, we'll figure something out, babe," I said in the most assured voice I could muster.

I went back to my reading, and on the bottom of page 197 Charlie Parker blows away a religious nut job. I turned the page. A yellow post-it note, folded along the sticky strip, was wedged between the pages. I removed it and peeled it open. Someone had scribbled a word game puzzle on the note.

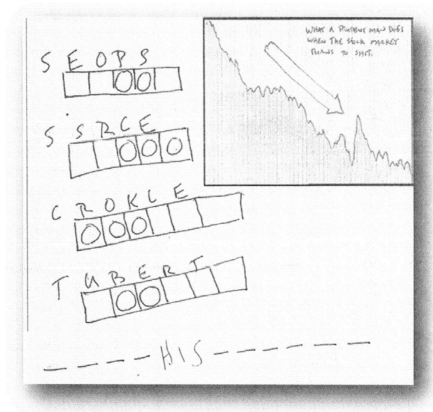

I held up the book and asked Diana, "You ever read this?"

"He's way too gory for me. Why do you ask?"

"I found this," and showed her the note.

"What is it?"

"A word puzzle. I guess someone used it as a bookmark."

"You figure it out?"

"Not yet."

Actually, I had. As a kid, my father and I used to do the word puzzle every day. To him, the game was brain exercise. He'd give me the first crack at unscrambling the letters and solving it, then help me out when I got stuck. When I got older, we'd compete to see who could solve the puzzle first, and it became my childhood obsession to best my old man. "You'll never be better than me at this, son," he'd joke. By the time I was sixteen, though, he couldn't win unless I let him—and then always by a second or two. He caught on, and that stopped our little *friendly* competition. But solving word puzzles remained a part of my daily routine.

I was at a loss now, however, trying to figure out how the note got stuck between pages 198 and 199. My "bookmark" theory was a non-starter, because the binding wasn't worn, nor were the pages. Had I bought it new?

Diana saw me inspecting the book, flipping through the pages, looking for other notes.

"Everything, okay?" she said.

"Book's a few years old. Just trying to remember where I got it."

"Tony, you know I can tell when something's wrong," she said, worry lines spreading across her face.

"Honestly, this damned puzzle is . . . well, it's puzzling."

But not in the way she was probably thinking.

Who was telling me to *cut my losses*, and what losses was I supposed to be cutting?

6

LEO INVITED ME OUT TO HIS HOUSE to watch the Super Bowl.

"I'm having a few of the guys over," he'd said.

Not wanting to be left alone, Diana gave me a hard time when I told her, and I couldn't leave until Janet, a fellow teacher and friend from school, came over to keep her company.

Leo's small house was the last in a line of similarly sized, box-shaped Cape Cods lining both sides of a dead-end street that backed up against the Parkway. In some ways, the house symbolized the way Leo felt about his life—trapped and going nowhere, while the world around him whizzed by.

What was supposed to have been a night-out-with-the-boys turned out to be just Leo and me.

Trudy greeted me with a hug and a peck on the cheek, and then I followed her to Leo's man-cave in the basement, the walls of which were paneled with a cheap brown wood veneer. The room had the damp, musty smell of an underground cavern.

"All for you," I said to Leo, holding up a six-pack of an imported beer. Trudy looked at me askance. "Other people enjoying a cold one doesn't bother me. One year, five days—" I looked at my watch, ". . . thirteen minutes and counting."

"Enjoy," Trudy said, then disappeared upstairs.

Leo shared the basement with his two kids, Hallee and Cody. A playhouse with white siding, and a red roof and trim took up most of the kids' half of the basement. Toys and stuffed animals were scattered everywhere.

Leo and I settled in to watch the game on a large-screen TV, the surround-sound speakers projecting the being-there feel of live action.

Taking it all in, I said, "You get a raise, big guy? Hit the lotto?"

"Something like that." Leo, wearing an oversized faded-blue Lawrence Taylor football jersey, kicked back in a brown leather recliner. An autographed Giants football helmet took up a prominent place on a nearby wall shelf.

As the game progressed, I took in the solitary ambience and said, "Man, you really know how to par-tay. So, where's everybody?"

"They'll show up," Leo said, then took a long pull on the beer he'd been nursing for most of the second quarter.

"What're they waiting for? It's almost halftime, dude. They're going to miss the big halftime show." I laughed at the thought of watching some old washed-up rockers trying to recapture the magic they'd lost thirty years ago.

Cody ran through the room, knocking over a bowl of pretzels.

"Cody, get back here and clean up this mess," Leo yelled after him. "Damn. Trudy!"

The boy crawled into the playhouse, hiding from his little sister, who came barging down the stairs, Trudy right behind her.

"How you guys doing down here?" Trudy said. Looking around, she said, "Nobody showed up?"

I raised my hand and said, "Present and accounted for, ma'am."

"Well, I guess you know who your friends are, Leo."

"Friend," I said.

Trudy grabbed the kids and hauled them back upstairs.

"Who all did you invite?" I asked.

"Some guys from work, couple of neighbors up the street. My boss said he might drop by."

"Why don't you call 'em, find out what's going on?"

He rolled the jersey's sleeves up above his elbows. "Fuck 'em. They coulda told me they weren't gonna show before I went out and bought all this food. What am I going to do with all this shit?" He crushed a bag of potato chips and threw it at the television.

"Take it to work. The guys'll love you, man and who knows . . . you might get off your boss's shit list."

"He's going to kill me."

"So why'd you invite him? To make his job easier?" I laughed, hoping it would be infectious, but no such luck.

"He overheard me talking to the guys. Had no choice."

"Okay."

"You're not listening, man. He *really* is going to kill me." Leo's face was crimson. His lower lip quivered. From the expression on his face, he appeared to be on the verge of tears—a heavy dose of fear mixed in.

"Shit, you're serious. Why?"

"Can't get you involved, man."

"Trudy know?"

"Only you . . . and him." He took a deep breath, then exhaled with a long whistling sigh.

"It's just said until it's done, Leo. Call the cops." I picked up the phone, and handed it to him. "Call 'em right now."

Leo started laughing, pointed a finger at me and said, "You just got punked, man."

"What? You asshole."

"Had you going, didn't I?"

I scooped up a handful of popcorn and threw it at him. "What's the fucking score, anyway?"

THE SECOND HALF WAS CRAZY, the outcome in doubt until the final seconds. Just the two of us enjoying each other's company, and thoughts of Leo's friends bailing out on him long forgotten. We'd made a small bet on the game, just to keep things interesting, but by the time it was over, we couldn't remember if the bet was straight up or with the point spread.

"Take some of this stuff home with you," Leo said.

"I thought you were taking it to work?"

"Fuck the guys at work."

I heard the telephone upstairs ring. In short order, Trudy shouted, "Leo, it's for you."

"Maybe some of your pals," I said.

Leo grunted as he picked up the phone. "Hello? Oh, hey."

The smile left his face, then a series of un-huh's followed.

"Just my friend, Tony. Yeah, Tony Benson . . . sure, maybe next time . . . yeah, see you in the morning."

"One of the guys who didn't show?"

"My boss. He's not going to make it."

"No shit. The game's over. Guess he'll have to kill you some other time."

7

DIANA WAS ALONE WHEN I GOT HOME.
"Where's Janet?"
"I sent her home. I was being silly."
"Wow. So, all quiet? Nobody tried to break in?"
"No, but I still want to move. Enjoy yourself?"
"Yeah, sort of. It was weird. Leo invited a bunch of guys over, but nobody showed up."
"So, how was it between Trudy and him?"
"They seemed to be okay."
"He's still seeing that woman?"
"It's none of my business, and I'm staying as far away from it as I can."
"Bull. You guys can't keep your mouths shut."
"Believe me, all we talked about was football. Want some chips?" I said, tossing the bag to her.
"No thanks. You figure out that puzzle?"
I knew by the tone of her voice that she'd solved it.
"Yeah."
"You think it means anything?"
"Who knows? But with all the turmoil in the office, I was thinking it could be some jerk's idea of a practical joke. Everybody knows I'm a word puzzle junkie."

Was I right? The puzzle a clue about my job security? Telecom Structures, the company I worked for, had cycled through so many management changes in my ten years there, I had to think a minute to figure out who my boss was. But I didn't complain. In a tough economic climate, I was lucky to still have a job.

"Come here, let me make it better," Diana said.

She wrapped her arms around my shoulders and kissed me, pressing her lips hard against mine.

"You were drinking!" she said, and released me in disgust.

"No. Leo knocked over a beer. I'm still sober. Want me to take a breathalyzer?"

She peered at me with an expression of skepticism, then said, "Speaking of your office, you got a call. I think you're going to be taking a trip."

8

I HAD TO RUN OUT TO THE WEST COAST for a few days to address a problem Telecom Structures was having with a cell phone tower installation. Seems the property owner was having second thoughts about putting the tower on the roof of his apartment building. Something about "concerns for the safety of my tenants."

I was sure his *concerns* could be alleviated by throwing some more money on the table, but boy was I proven wrong.

About fifty tenants were gathered in the lobby of the Crystal Towers apartment building in Century City, high above Downtown Los Angeles, to share their concerns about the tower. Looking out the windows, I could barely make out the tops of skyscrapers in the distance through the yellow smog.

The building's owner, a Mr. Stewart ("call me Stewie") and I stood on a makeshift platform, facing a barrage of outrageous comments from the *ad hoc* tenants committee calling itself "Fight the Tower."

"The government created cell phones to cut down the world population, but they didn't count on so many of those Wall Street crooks getting brain cancer, so they cut back on the microwaves," a shirtless twenty-something said, all LA cool in mauve cargo shorts and leather flip-flops.

"Yeah, even the folks at World Health say using a cell for a long time can fry your brain, man," said an elderly gentleman, brandishing a folded *Los Angeles Times*.

"This is LA, man. Everybody's on a cell phone all day, every day," another tenant chimed in.

And that was just the opening salvo. I had to suffer this nonsense, because Crystal Towers was a perfect location—

plopped in the midst of a densely-populated area with heavy traffic, and no zoning issues. It was primo real estate. So I needed to close the deal fast, before our competition swooped in.

Stewie, smelling like he'd taken a bath in a tub full of cologne, leaned over and whispered in my ear, "Bet you thought I was just another scumbag slumlord trying to squeeze another drop out of the tit, am I right?" He smiled, showing off a set of perfectly capped teeth.

"Yeah," I confessed.

"Now you see what I'm up against. Welcome to the party, pal." Bruce Willis in the first *Die Hard* movie—pure Hollywood.

"Look, folks, we're constantly being bombarded by radio waves coming from a lot of different sources," I said. "Your remote control or a low-flying jet airliner communicating with the control tower, just to name a few."

"So, we don't need any more radio waves," yelled the tenant who was wearing pajama bottoms. Yeah, he *had* to be the ringleader.

"This guy's a real *schmuck*," Stewie said, confirming my appraisal.

"You from New York?" I said.

"What gave me away?"

I shrugged.

"Been out here five years," Stewie said.

I turned my attention back to the crowd. "Right on, man. Power to the people." *Someone actually said that*? Surfer dude in volleyball shorts, of course.

Was LA just one big cliché?

My cell phone beeped. A text message from Diana. Leo had called and left a message. It was important he speak with me. He'd call back later. Diana was worried—Leo sounded weird, maybe on drugs.

Ignoring the protestor's babble, I texted her back: In meeting. Call u later.

After enduring the tenants for another hour, I said to Stewie, "Can we pull a couple of these guys off to the side and settle this thing?"

Stewie and I huddled with Pajama Bottoms and Surfer Dude, while the rest of the tenants wandered around outside and enjoyed the smoggy day.

"It's all about being *green*, man," Pajama Bottoms said. "Saving the planet, that's where it's at, man." Up close, he was older than he had appeared.

"Right on," Surfer Dude chimed in.

"Hey, look, I couldn't agree with you guys more. I live in New York, *comprende*? But I know you'd hate not being able to get a signal, especially when you're trying to close that *big* deal."

Ultimately, we settled the group's concerns by getting Stewie to make adjustments to the tenants' rent, and I bumped up his fee to cover any losses, plus a little extra.

No matter what people say, it's *always* about the green, as in m-o-n-e-y.

I CALLED LEO after I wrapped everything up, and, to my surprise, his home number had been disconnected with no forwarding information. I tried the operator, who informed me Leo had a new number, but it was unlisted. I tried his cell, and got: "The cellular customer you have dialed cannot be reached at this time."

Trudy called my cell.

"What's going on?" I said. "Leo cut off your phone."

"He's in the hospital," Trudy said.

"Is he all right?"

"He's had a breakdown."

"A breakdown? I just saw him and he seemed okay."

"I'm not sure what happened. Something at the club set him off. Leo can't tell me anything right now, and with the kids— "

"You okay?"

Stewie came up behind, tapped me on the shoulder and said, "Nice job, New York." He saluted me with two thumbs up. I nodded, thanks.

"My mother's here," Trudy said.

"Where's Leo now?"

"The psych ward at Mercy Hospital. I'm going to visit him tonight."

"I'm out in LA, but Diana and I'll get there as soon as we can."

After I hung up, I sent a text message to Diana: **Call Trudy. Leo in hospital. I nu something was wrong.**

9

I WAS APPREHENSIVE about visiting Leo. If he had cancer, or a heart problem I could deal with it. He'd have my unflinching support. But, mental illness? That was downright scary.

Leo was housed in the hospital's Behavioral Modification wing. I cringed—political correctness strikes again. I imagined a patient saying, "I'm not nuts. Just here to get my behavior modified."

The ward was locked down tight, as if it were a prison.

A burly gentleman with a shaved head and sporting all-white scrubs led Diana and me into the rec room. The walls were painted a washed-out green. Tables and chairs were arranged in small clusters. Patients and visitors sat around, mostly just staring at each other. Off in one corner, a television set had attracted a few patients, who watched an animated movie.

Diana and I waited for Leo at a table as far away from the crowd as possible.

A patient stood off in a corner, rocking back and forth and muttering under his breath, as if reciting a Jewish prayer. He punctuated his incantations by pounding his right fist into his palm.

"Is he saying the C word?" Diana said. "What's *his* problem."

Definitely not praying.

"Probably some broad screwed him over."

"Likely story."

"Good point, because otherwise this place would be as crowded as a Promise Keepers convention," I responded.

Diana playfully poked me on the shoulder.

The little guy drifted closer to us. Alarmed, I waved for help. An orderly approached the guy, took his arm, and tried to pull him away from us. But the little fellow jerked free and took a boxer's stance, ready to strike.

"How ya doin', Anthony," the orderly said.

"Take your fucking hands off me."

"Okay . . . take it easy, pal."

"I ain't your fucking pal, *pal*."

The orderly, big enough to crush Anthony, backed off and held his arms out like he was placating a child. The patient, mumbling obscenities, retreated and joined the group watching television.

"Sorry 'bout that," the orderly said.

I waved him off, no problem.

After a few minutes, I spotted Trudy leading Leo into the lounge. "God, he looks like shit," I said.

Diana shushed me.

Leo was wearing a short robe, exposing knobby knees and skinny, pale legs with prickly red hair. A straggly growth had started sprouting on his cheeks. His eyes were unfocused—nobody was home. He offered a limp handshake and sat down.

I had no idea what to say, so I offered a lame "Howya doing, Leo?" and received a blank stare in reply. "When you blowing outta this joint?"

Diana nudged me with a sharp elbow to the ribs.

I imagined the *old* Leo, saying, "How am I doing? You've got to be fucking kidding me. How's it look like I'm doing, asshole?"

I crossed my arms and leaned back, balancing myself precariously on the chair's back legs.

It was Leo who finally broke the awkward silence. "Wanna play cards?"

"Sure, great idea," I said, relieved. It wasn't much, but it sure beat trying to make small talk.

Leo dug a deck of playing cards from a pocket of the robe, started shuffling, and a few cards fell onto the floor. I picked them up and handed them back to him. Most of the cards were either bent or torn.

"He means *Go Fish*," Trudy said. "You guys know how to play?"

"Nah, not really," I said.

"Me neither," Diana said.

"We each get five cards," Trudy said, then explained the game's rules.

"I think I can handle that," I said when she'd finished.

"Whoever collects the most books, wins. It's a simple game, really. Leo, can you deal?"

Leo shook his head and handed the deck to Trudy, who dealt out the cards.

"Tony, why don't you lead," Trudy said.

"Okay. Leo, got a Jack?"

"No, go fish," he droned.

I drew a card and we continued around the table. The women tried hard to let Leo win, giving him hints he didn't understand. It was surreal. I was a character in *One Flew Over the Cuckoo's Nest*.

We'd played a few hands when Eddie Hambrick dropped by. His right hand was wrapped in an Ace bandage. Before I could ask what the hell happened, Trudy started giving Eddie an abbreviated version of the rules, and just like that he joined in. But not before turning to Leo and saying, "Hey, bud. Rough week, huh?"

He sounded about as comfortable as I was.

After a few plays around the table, a bell sounded, signaling visiting hours were over.

My immediate thought? *Thank you, Lord.*

"That's it, Leo," Trudy said. "We gotta go, babe."

In unison, we all pushed back from the table, except Leo, who didn't move.

"Come on, hon. Say goodbye to everybody. Thank everybody for coming."

Leo stood, bumped into the table, knocking the cards onto the floor.

We headed towards the exit, Trudy dragging Leo along behind her.

One of the staff guarded the door, careful not to let any of the patients escape.

Trudy dug her chin into Leo's chest and hugged him tightly. "I'll be by tomorrow, hon. I love you." She pecked him on the cheek. Seemed like he didn't have a clue where he was.

As Eddie waved goodbye and double-timed it towards the door, I swatted Leo on the back, shook his limp hand, then said, "See ya' later, partner. Hang in there."

The door closed behind us, Leo's somber face framed in the door's window.

ONCE WE'D SAID OUR GOODBYES to Eddie in the main lobby, Trudy, Diana, and I headed to the cafeteria. Large glossy color photographs of happy families on vacation at picturesque nature spots lined the pink pastel walls. Hospital staff, dressed in dark blue scrubs, sat around enjoying a coffee break. A table of *civilians*, all looking as dazed as I felt was engaged in what appeared to be a serious discussion. As a violin-syrupy version of "Strawberry Fields" played over the PA system, a steady stream of pages cut into the music, breaking up the Beatles' mournful melody.

"Anybody for a cup of coffee?" I asked.

Both women declined.

"I'll be right back."

From the checkout line, I watched Diana, fighting back tears, give Trudy a sympathetic hug.

When I got back, I said, "You girls okay?"

Diana nodded, then said, "We're sorry we couldn't be there for you, Trudy. You know, what with Tony out of town and that *thing* at the house."

She still had a problem giving voice to the word "break-in."

"I never imagined I'd be sitting here, in my mid-thirties, with two young kids, and a husband in a psych ward," Trudy said. "To be honest, I have absolutely no idea how I'm going to keep it all together." She dabbed her eyes with a table napkin.

"Just let us know what you need," Diana said.

Trudy bobbed her head.

"So, what's the story?" I said.

She cleared her throat, then said, "Leo had gone to work out with Eddie at the club. Next thing I know, I get a phone call from the general manager. He said there'd been some trouble. Leo hadn't been arrested, but the police took him to Mercy for observation. That's all I know."

Neither Diana nor I spoke as we struggled to grasp what Trudy had told us.

Finally, she said, "He thinks his boss is going to kill him."

"Oh, shit," I said, spilling some of the hot coffee onto the table. "He said something like that Super Bowl Sunday. First, I thought he was goofing around because his boss didn't show up. But he kept insisting and when I pressed him to call the cops, he said he was just kidding around. Punking me, that's what he said. Truth is, he'd been acting kinda weird—"

"It's not your fault. He's delusional," Trudy said.

"I don't know. Maybe I could've said something, or done something. Then again, I didn't know what to believe."

"Any idea why this happened now?" Diana asked.

Trudy shrugged, then said, "He's undergoing counseling."

I had a real good idea why *now*. The dreaded yolk of responsibility got too heavy for him to carry. Trouble at work, trouble at home, a mountain of debt, and a little action on the side.

"Hopefully, the electroconvulsive therapy will work," Trudy said.

"Shock therapy?" Diana said.

"Yeah, they think he's schizophrenic."

Diana and I exchanged looks of disbelief.

"They still do that?" I said.

"I know what you're thinking, but it's not like in those old horror movies. The doctors say it's like rebooting a computer." Trudy paused and took a deep breath, then said, "The treatment only lasts for about a minute. They've scheduled six sessions, then they'll re-evaluate him."

You've got to be shitting me? I rephrased my mental question. "How does sending a jolt of electricity through someone's head make them better?"

Diana admonished me with a sharp turn of the head.

Trudy took notice. "It's okay. It only takes a few seconds to induce the seizure. They don't know how it works, but somehow that electrical jolt snaps patients out of their doldrums. So, I'm hoping—"

She crossed her fingers, looked at her watch.

"Oh, well, gotta get going. Mom's looking after the kids."

After Trudy left, I said, "Leo's a goner."

"Don't say that, Tony."

"Shock therapy? Come on."

10

I WORKED IN ONE OF THE LARGE OFFICE park complexes centered around the Route 110 Exit on the Long Island Expressway.

That's where I was a week after seeing Leo that first night, sitting in my two-hundred-square-foot office overlooking the parking garage connected to Telecom Structures headquarters. The office was spacious by corporate standards, but rather modest when you compared it to a partner's office in one of the big white-shoe law firms in Manhattan.

Across the way, I saw a young woman on the garage's top level struggling as she tried to get a kid—both arms and legs flailing—into an infant car seat. The sun's glare obscured the frustration she surely felt.

I turned back to the stack of applications atop the desk awaiting my attention, but I was reluctant to dig in. I didn't relish going through a bunch of requests from every greedy bastard in the country with a high perch looking for "mailbox money."

As a senior vice president, I headed up Telecom Structures' contracts department, such as it was. My paltry staff consisted of a young attorney fresh out of law school, a transmission engineer, and a technician. Normally, they would have been doing the preliminary screening, but the engineer was on vacation and the tech out with the flu. Shit, out of the whole stack, fewer than five percent of the properties would meet our clients' specifications. That, or some dumb shit would screw up the application.

Little did I imagine when I entered law school that I'd wind up being a desk jockey in a corporate law office, negotiating pro forma licensing agreements. Occasionally, I'd get a real hard-assed case like the cell tower in La-La land. But more often than not, negotiating meant cutting and pasting the name and address of the licensee into the new contract.

There was a time when I'd pictured myself being the firebrand, anti-establishment legal voice of the little people, someone like the character Al Pacino played in the movie, *And Justice for All*. But midway through law school I lost that dream and found myself trapped in a legal netherworld—too far in to drop out, too far to go to muster up what little passion I still had left to be committed.

So, I coasted to the finish line, and with no other marketable skills, opened a small practice after I was admitted to the bar. And what drudgery, preparing wills, DUIs—my bread and butter—real estate closings, occasionally defending some scumbag criminal.

I had a title—Anthony Benson, Attorney at Law—but not much else.

"Oh, he's a lawyer," the mothers of the women I dated would say, like that was some big fucking whoop, giving more weight to my potential as an earner than the sleaze factor that came with it.

"The only thing lower than a lawyer is a lawyer who's a politician," Diana's father told me on more than one occasion. He was right of course but *gee, thanks, Dad.*

A friend from law school threw me a lifeline steering me to Telecom Structures' corporate legal department. God, that was ten years ago.

The intercom buzzed.

"Mr. Benson, you have a visitor," my secretary, Jill DaRainey, said.

I punched up Outlook and checked my schedule. "I'm not showing anything, Ma," I said.

Jill was a big blues fan and loved the '20s singer, Ma Rainey, so I took to calling her Ma—Ma DaRainey. And, Jill was the glue that kept the office running, thus giving me another reason to call her Ma.

"The gentleman doesn't have an appointment. Says his name's Eddie Hambrick, that he's a friend of a Leo Radigan's. Says you know him."

"You can send him back. Thanks, Ma."

After a few seconds, I recognized her syncopated tapping on the door, then Eddie stuck his head in the room, and said, "Hey, Tony."

"Come on in. How'd you know I worked here?"

"That any way to greet a friend?" When I didn't respond, he said, "Leo told me."

"Leo doesn't know where I work."

"I don't know. Must a heard somebody at the club mention it." He pulled out a chair and sat down. "Hope you don't mind me popping in like this."

"What brings you here, Eddie?"

"I was in the area. You see Leo again?"

"Yesterday."

"How's he doing?"

"About the same," I said.

"He didn't look so good, did he? And that stupid card game? How fuckin' weird was that?"

No weirder than you, all puffed up like the Michelin Man with a bad tan. Word around the club was that Eddie had been a competitor in the Mr. Universe Contest, back when.

"What's your point, Eddie?"

"You know what happened with Leo, right?"

"Not really."

"Fucking guy went all Cujo and shit," he said, holding up his bandaged hand. "Did everything 'cept foam at the mouth. Fucker damn near bit my finger off."

"Kind of hard to believe, seeing how you're twice Leo's size, Eddie."

Sensing my impatience, Eddie laughed it off. "Gotta excuse my language, Tony. This shit with Leo's got me rattled."

Eddie stood, and started pacing around the room as he filled me in. He and Leo were with the club's kick boxing trainer. About half-way through the session, Leo became agitated, flailing away on the heavy bag one minute, collapsing in exhaustion the next. He did that a couple of times and then started confronting other club members with grunts and strange noises. The staff, fearing he was going to injure himself, or others, tried to calm him down, but their efforts only incited him more.

"One of the Nassau County cops—you know, the guy that's poppin' that hot little blonde trainer—had to tase Leo's crazy ass. Let me tell ya, that looked like some real hurting shit, the way Leo was bouncing around on the floor."

Eddie started fidgeting almost as if he was ready to go a few rounds.

"So, what'd you want, Eddie?"

"Fucking guy," he said, then held out an envelope. "There's a grand in here. The boys at the club chipped in to help out Leo's family. Nobody knew how to reach the wife, but I know you and him's close, so here ya go."

I took the sealed envelope, and then shook his hand.

"Hey, thanks," I said. "Sorry for being such an asshole."

"No problem. This Leo thing's got everybody acting a little nuts, including Leo." The big man controlled a snicker. "Nice office, by the way. What's with all the elephants?"

A colorful herd of glass and ceramic elephants stampeded across the top of my desk.

"I collect them. They're a good luck symbol."

"Elephants should face the door with their trunks pointed up, right?"

"Yep."

"Didn't know you were a superstitious guy, Tony."

"I'm not. It's just a thing."

"Good, 'cause that one's got his trunk turned down," he said, pointing to the red and orange ceramic elephant with a psychedelic design that Diana bought in San Francisco a few years ago—a birthday present.

Eddie stopped fidgeting long enough to say, "Well, gotta get going."

"I'll make sure Trudy gets this right away," I said, holding up the thick envelope.

"See you 'round the club."

After Eddie bobbed and weaved his way out the door, I took the psychedelic elephant off the desk and buried it in the bottom drawer.

11

THE PSYCH WARD was on my way home, so I tried to see Leo at least once a week. Over time, he'd become attuned to the world around him, but still his progress was slow. He became more and more isolated as friends first distanced themselves, then disappeared. After awhile, I think I was the only one who dropped by to see him.

I met Leo at our usual spot in the game room. A chessboard was set up, but some of the pieces were on the wrong squares—black pawns where the bishops should be, a white rook taking up the queen's square.

Leo was sprawled across a couch, leafing through an old copy of *Field & Stream*.

"Didn't know you liked fishing." I said.

"Don't." He threw the magazine on the table, knocking over a few of the chess pieces. I picked them up and put them on the right squares.

Trudy had bought Leo some clothes, and now he looked more like a guy in for an appendectomy instead of undergoing shock therapy. He had on the same Giants jersey he wore the night of the Super Bowl party, and faded jeans.

"You're in damn good shape for a guy that's been sitting around on his ass," I said.

"They got an exercise room."

"Not very chatty today, huh?"

"I'm sorta sick. Got a fuckin' headache. What day is it?"

"Saturday."

I had Googled shock therapy, and knew from my research that Leo seemed to be exhibiting some of the common side effects of electroconvulsive therapy. Maybe he'd had a treatment earlier. Physically, he didn't look much different than he did when we were back at the club working out. But the darting eyes were a dead giveaway. All of his systems most definitely weren't *go*.

"Don't mean to pick your brain or anything," I said, "but that shock treatment—what's it like?"

He bolted upright, leaned in close and said, "That's got to be the dumbest fuckin' question anybody's ever asked me. Pick my brain? Tell you what—let me clamp jumper cables to your ears and your balls, turn up the juice, then *you* can tell me what it's like."

I knew that wasn't the way the treatment was administered, but I said, "Good to see you're feeling better."

He slumped back in the chair, then started shifting around on the cushions—head tilted back, his eyes closed. Maybe a calming exercise he'd learned in therapy. Finally composed, he said, "You know . . . I can get out of here anytime I want."

"So, why don't you?"

"You kidding me? I'd be dead before I got home."

"Your boss."

He nodded, then stuffed his hands in his jeans pockets.

"You plan on staying here until when? Forever? Or maybe until he dies?"

Leo shrugged, deflated. "Depressing, isn't it?"

"Honestly? I don't think you're ready to get out of here, not just yet."

"As always, Tony, thanks for your fuckin' support."

Out of the corner of my eye I caught movement coming at us. "Hey, look who's here," I said.

Trudy walked in with the kids, who ran over to Leo, climbed onto his lap and squeezed their little arms around his neck.

When Trudy noticed how depressed he was, she said, "Leo, what if you're wrong and you're going through all of this for nothing. Just take the opposite tact. You might save your life thinking that way. Try it, see what happens."

As if you can reason with a crazy man. Seeing that Leo was getting agitated, I said, "I'll bet you're glad we came."

"Why don't you take the kids and get them a soda or something?" Trudy said to Leo.

"Sure, what's up?"

"Just want to talk to Tony a minute."

Leo eyed us suspiciously, frowned, then said, "Okay."

After Leo and the kids had gone, Trudy said, "The envelope you gave me. How much you say was in it?"

"Eddie told me a grand. There a problem?"

"I don't know, but it was only five-hundred."

"It was sealed, so I didn't count it," I said.

"Maybe you heard him wrong?"

"I don't think so, but I'll find out."

"Forget it, Tony. It's no problem."

But there was. She thinks I stole it.

"Believe me, every little bit helps. I wouldn't have been able to pay the mortgage without that money. When you see the fellas, tell them thanks for me, will you?"

"Sure, but I'll talk to Eddie."

"I called Leo's boss. You know, the guy Leo thinks is going to kill him?"

"Oh?"

"I needed information about Leo's coverage, but he wouldn't talk to me. I figured he was trying to avoid paying workman's comp. You won't believe what he did, though. He goes and writes a letter to the hospital, with copies sent to just about every mental health department in the state, saying Leo's dangerous, that he's calling and harassing him and his staff. He says Leo even threatened to kill him."

Dumbfounded, I said, "Hell, Leo can barely string two complete sentences together. This guy sounds like maybe he should be in here, too."

HEADING BACK TO my car, an attractive young woman stepped from behind a minivan, blocking my path.

Maybe forty, but she could've been thirty. Hard to tell with the heavy raccoon makeup around her eyes.

"Are you Tony Benson?"

"Who's asking?"

She wore a tight red miniskirt over dancer's legs. I would've easily spotted her even if she had been at the other end of the parking lot.

"I'm Irena, Leo's friend. He talked about you a lot."

She trailed alongside me, her heels clicking on the pavement.

"Funny, you don't sound Russian."

"I'm not. I'm from the Bronx."

"Leo told me you were from Russia."

"For some reason, you guys like Russian girls. Think they're sexy, so you give them big tips." She shrugged. "So, I'm Russian, too." She laughed.

After spending an hour with Leo, it was music to my ears.

Okay, she wasn't Russian, but she was hot all the same. I had no idea what she saw in Leo. Icy blue eyes, bottled blond hair with streaks of wheat. Carrying a lot up top, too—I'd bet most of it surgically enhanced.

I stopped in front of my car and said, "What's your real name, Irena?"

"Demi Shadow."

I pressed the keyless remote, opened the door, and swung in behind the wheel.

"You're kidding me, right?"

"Shadow's an Anglicized version of Shadowski. And my mother liked the Hollywood actress."

"Your mother couldn't be that old."

She leaned against the fender. "I'm that young."

I closed the door, started up the car, and opened the window.

"Okay, now that we've got the history lesson out of the way, what do you want?"

"Leo's dead." She swayed from side to side on those impossibly high heels. "He just doesn't know it yet."

"I just left him," I said, hiking my thumb back towards the hospital entrance. "Did you see him?"

"No. Might run into the wife. Besides, it's you I came to see."

"How'd you know to find me here?"

"Lucky guess."

"Bullshit. You been following me?"

She shrugged.

"What do you want?"

"Shit happens. Hope when it does, it doesn't happen to you."

And then she turned and walked away.

12

TOO MANY DAMN MYSTERIES. First the word puzzle, then the missing money. Now some broad named Demi Shadow with her "shit happens." But the money was one mystery I could solve. I drove right out to the club hoping to find Eddie, and he didn't disappoint. He was standing in the middle of a circle of fellow muscle-heads near the rack with the fifty-pound dumbbells. Eddie was wearing a shredded wife-beater and black cutoff sweat pants. Thick veins coursed down his biceps and Popeye forearms. I couldn't hear what his buddies were saying, but they stopped talking as I approached, one of them dropping a set of weights onto the floor for punctuation.

"Guys, what's going on?" I said.

"Everybody's still talking about Leo," Eddie volunteered.

A large hole was punched in the wall near the door to the men's locker room.

"Looks like someone was in a hurry to leave," I said.

"Your boy, Leo."

"They're not exactly Speedy Gonzalez on repairs around here, so that hole'll still be there next year," one of the muscle-heads said.

"You give Mrs. Leo the envelope?" Eddie said.

"Yeah, and she wanted me to thank all you guys. Very thoughtful."

"No need. Glad to help out. Leo was a nut, but he was our nut."

Eddie's minions laughed and exchanged high fives.

"Eddie, can I talk to you a minute?" I said.

"Sure."

I moved a few feet away from the crowd, Eddie followed me. "What's up?"

"How much you say was in the envelope?"

"Five-hundred."

"I thought you told me a grand."

"You must've misheard me, Tony, because I said five-hundred. That's what me and the boys got together. Besides, I don't ever say *grand* when I'm talking about money. And if I did say grand, I would've said half-a-grand. Five-hundred dollars. Maybe you didn't hear me say *half a*, and just heard me say *grand*."

"So which is it?"

Eddie casually flexed his biceps, then went through a series of poses, showing off as if he were competing in the Mr. Universe contest.

I quickly dropped any thought of taking our discussion any further. "I guess you're right, Eddie. I must of heard you wrong."

Why was Eddie jerking me around? I'd swear on a stack of Bibles he said there was a grand in the envelope. Give five, take five? The dots weren't connecting up.

"Hey, no problem. Why don't you go get dressed and come work out with some real men."

My meek refusal was followed by another chorus of laughter from his buddies.

Eddie fist-bumped me. His right hand wasn't bandaged, and I didn't see any sign that Leo had damn near bit his finger off.

13

LEO WAS RELEASED IN EARLY SPRING when his insurance ran out. Apparently, lapsed coverage is the best cure for what ails you. Better than shock treatments or antidepressants.

I arranged my schedule so Leo and I could go bike riding on weekends in hopes of helping him get his life back on track.

We'd finished a brisk ride through Bethpage State Park on one of the many off-road trails winding through thick woods. It was a perfect spring day—sunny, the humidity low. All seemed right with the world. Just two guys out having fun, anything but a therapy ride. The bikes' fat tires had kicked up a lot of dust and rocks, and we were covered in dirt and grime.

Walking the bikes back to Leo's car, I said, "You wanna stop at the deli and grab something to eat? My treat."

He squeezed a jet of water from the bottle over his head. "Sounds good."

"Looks like you're getting back to where you were before—"

"—I took a detour, right?" Leo said.

"Yeah, that's what I meant to say."

I nodded and helped put the bikes on the car's roof-mounted rack.

At the deli, we got sandwiches and bottled water, then sat at the picnic benches at the edge of the parking lot behind the deli.

Leo was pleasant enough, even good to be around. As long as I avoided the "Boss" subject.

Stupid me. "You ever hear from your boss, again?"

"No, but I know he's watching."

I rolled my eyes. "So, I take it you're not going back to work for him."

"You take right."

"What you got planned then?"

Trudy had asked me to prod him to get back to work, and fast. As a freelance graphic artist, she couldn't make it on her salary alone and, as she told me, "I'm not going to take care of three kids."

"Chill out for awhile, get my head together before I start looking for work," Leo said.

"How long you think that'll be? You gotta be hurting for money."

"Long as it takes." Leo said.

"This was fun. We'll do it again next weekend, okay?"

He took a last swallow from the bottle, and tossed it into a trash can, then started in on the sandwich.

As an afterthought, he said, "Yeah, if I'm still alive."

"Then how about putting me in your will and leaving me that nice bike of yours?" I pointed to his orange, four-thousand-dollar mountain bike complete with top-of-the-line components.

"You know, you wouldn't be such a prick if someone was about to kill you," Leo said, sourly.

I'd had enough of Mr. Doomsday, so I decided to ask the million-dollar question. "Okay, you got me. Why does your boss want to kill you?"

Leo dropped his chin, but didn't answer right away. Then, just when I thought he wouldn't respond, he raised his eyes and said, "I'd been chipping off a little here and there for years. You know, nothing to draw attention, at first. But I got a little greedy." He paused, then said, "I took five-hundred bucks and some electrical supplies from a job I did before all, um . . . before all this shit happened."

"You? Stealing?" I said, surprised by the revelation. "That doesn't sound like you. Why?" *Like the big screen TV with surround sound, and the expensive bike?*

"I needed to finish up a few things around the house. Build a playroom for the kids. In case you haven't noticed, the damn house's just one big playground."

"Hey, I could've of helped you out. All you needed to do was just ask."

"And I appreciate that, Tony."

"Trudy know about the money?"

He stared off into the distance, shook his head.

"I fucked up."

"This doesn't make sense. A legitimate businessman killing you for what? A few hundred bucks? Or any amount, for that matter. Why not just fire your ass or have you arrested?"

I bounced my bottle off the trash can, and it rolled into the parking lot.

"You're naïve, Tony," Leo said. "With this guy you gotta give an arm to keep a leg."

Another bite of the sandwich, then he spilled out the whole story. "Couple of weeks ago, I was having lunch in the office. The boss walks over, sits across from me. We chit chat, you know, small talk. Then out of the blue, he asks me if I knew what he'd do to somebody who stole from him. I don't know what the hell to say. But the way he said it, I got a real bad feeling. Then he says, 'Nobody fucks me over. I'd fuckin' kill'em first.' "

Leo paused and opened his mouth, took a slow trip around his lips with his tongue, and then said, "He didn't sound mad when he said it. Real low key, matter-of-fact. I got to tell ya, he scared the livin' shit out of me. Then he says, 'But before I kill the sonofabitch, I'd make the fucker suffer. Wanna know how I'd do it?' "

"What could I say? So I said, 'Sure.' He says he'd learn everything there was to know about the guy—his family, friends, business acquaintances. Then he'd get to every one of 'em; tells 'em what he was going to do to the guy, and how they'd better keep out of his way, or else. The scary part? He's saying this like we were talking about ball scores or something. I knew he was talking about me."

Looking at Leo's ashen face, I had no doubt in my mind he believed every word he uttered. Of course he did—Leo was crazy.

"Didn't they give you meds, ah . . . for this kind of thing?" I said.

"That shit only works if you're delusional. What I'm telling you is *real*."

I said, "If he wants to kill you, why go through all that trouble? This sounds way too complicated. Who is this guy, Oliver Stone?"

"Name's Muertens."

"What the hell kind of name's that?"

"Joe Schmo, what the fuck does it matter? Don't you get it? The guy's going to kill me."

Playing along, I asked, "Then why don't you just go to the cops?"

"Because he'll tell 'em about the money I stole. Then who'll believe me? Besides, the cops are in on it, too."

"Now you're really off your rocker."

"You think I actually volunteered to put myself in a loony bin?"

I walked over to the car and played with his bike's gear shifter. Over the shoulder, I said, "That's what I was told."

"It's bullshit. That's what *he* wanted me to do," Leo said.

O-kay. "How does he know who your friends are?"

"We'd be talking, see, and he'd ask these seemingly innocent questions, like who I hung out with. Do I know a good lawyer. Who're the guys I pal around with. Shit like that."

"How 'bout me?" I said, wearing a big grin. "Like, who's your best friend?"

"I never mentioned you."

"Why not?"

"You're not my best friend."

"So, why am I here?" I said.

Again, Leo shrugged.

"How do you know who's part of this *grand* conspiracy?" I said.

"Take Dave Schoolkraft, my lawyer? I know Muertens got to him, 'cause fat Dave gave me the code."

"The what?"

"Say I call him; no schmoozing. 'Howya doing, how's the wife.' Instead, Schoolkraft'll just say, 'I don't do divorces,' then hang up. That's the code. 'I don't do divorces.' Muertens got to him."

Yes, my buddy had definitely gone over the edge. I started to respond but he barged ahead.

"Muertens is really a sick fuck. He said he'd push the poor bastard so hard, the dude wouldn't know which end is up. What's coming next, when it'll stop, or maybe it would never stop until he kills himself. He talked about pushing up on a guy's wife, even his kids if the *thing* didn't move along fast enough to suit him. Whatever it took. See, it's all just one big game to Muertens. And I know he's got Eddie Hambrick from the club spying on me."

When I didn't jump to the bait, Leo said, "I'm telling you, this guy's connected."

"What's in it for this Muertens character? He kills you, you kill yourself, he can't get his money back."

"He said he took out a life insurance policy on me."

Yes, Leo definitely needed medication. To placate him, I asked, "Tell me you didn't sign anything?"

Leo spun the bike's front wheel, the spokes making a whooshing sound.

"I don't know. I remember signing something. Said he needed it because I was his key man. Yeah, that's what it was. Key man insurance."

"You're an idiot. I thought you were smarter than that. Anyway, he can't collect a dime if you commit suicide within the first two years. When'd you sign whatever it was you signed?"

He thought about it then said, "A while ago. I don't remember when exactly. Anyway, I think he said he paid extra to get that waived."

"If you were an insurance company, would you waive the suicide clause?" I said, shaking my head. "There'd be a lot of dead assholes out there before the ink dried on the policy."

A woman pulled into the space next to Leo's car, and we went quiet until she'd grabbed a cart and rolled it inside the deli.

Only then did I shake my head in disbelief. "You've got to be shitin' me?" When Leo didn't add anything further, I asked, "How much?"

"Half-a-mil."

With the script well developed in his head, Leo had a ready answer for every outrageous plot twist in his tall tale.

"He's got pictures of me jerking off at a peep show," Leo said.

I laughed, as much at the absurdity of Leo's story as the mental picture I formed of him playing with himself. "Jacking off? Now that's the first thing you've said I actually believe."

"This isn't funny, asshole. He's showing them to my neighbors, passing them around at the club. It's just a matter of time before Trudy sees 'em."

"Come on, Leo," I said, still laughing. "How can he follow you into a peep show without you spotting him?"

"I saw the door slide open, and a flash go off."

"No, the flash you saw was from all of the little blue and white pills you've been taking."

But I wondered—if only for a nanosecond—was Muertens' code the reason none of Leo's friends showed up at the Super Bowl party?

"Tell me. What if I Googled this guy?" I asked.

"You're not gonna find the man I'm talking about on the Internet."

"I didn't think so."

Leo got into the car, and I slid into the passenger seat. I'd barely closed the door before he sped off.

"By the way, I ran into your stripper girlfriend," I said.

Leo perked up. "Irena? Where? At the club?" He brushed a strand of hair away from his face.

"In the hospital parking lot."

"She never came up to visit."

"She didn't want to chance running into Trudy. Besides, she was looking for me."

"You? What for?" he said, locking on me with an icy stare.

"Don't worry. I'm not trying to steal her from you. But I gotta tell you, she is one fine looking woman. You know she's not Russian, right? She tells everyone that because the guys give the Russian girls bigger tips. Anyway, she told me—"

"You seeing her again?" Leo was now grinning from ear to ear, his emotions changing like my stock portfolio—up and down, then down some more.

"Dammit, Leo. She told me that you're a dead man, that you just don't know it yet."

"What?"

He jammed on the brakes, the car screeching to a stop. All I could do was brace myself, anticipating his junk Chevy getting rammed from behind.

"Damn!" Leo slammed both fists on the steering wheel. "Muertens got to her, too. She's his Judas goat, warning you to cut your losses, to jump ship. You gonna jump ship, too, Tony, like the rest of the rats?"

When I didn't respond, unable to wrap my mind around his lunacy, he shouted, "Well, fuck you, Tony . . . with interest."

I ignored him, my head swirling. With one absurdity after another, one in particular finally dawning on me—*cut your losses*, the answer to that word puzzle.

"Cut your losses, is that one of your codes?"

Leo glared at me, said, "You figure it out, smart guy. Call your broker."

Cut my losses? Muertens, or no Muertens, that sounded like damn good advice to me.

14

I WAS BECOMING UNNERVED by all of the seemingly disconnected people and events surrounding Leo's disintegration—Eddie, Demi Shadow, the mysterious puzzle, Leo's crazy code. *Cut your losses.*

As soon as I got in my car, I called my broker to check on my stock portfolio.

"Market's up about two-hundred points right now, Tony. It holds like this, we'll recover a little bit of our losses."

Our losses? Code, my ass.

I TOLD DIANA about Leo's bizarre tale.

"So now he's a philanderer *and* a thief?" she said.

"That's harsh."

"Tell me what I said that wasn't true?"

"The guy's got problems."

"Yeah, but what if he's right and his boss is going to kill him? I don't want you getting caught in the crossfire."

"You've gotta be kidding. Leo's story is pure fantasy."

"Just in case, be careful."

15

AFTER WHAT WOULD PROVE TO BE our last ride together, I told Leo I couldn't make it out the following week.

"See you in two weeks, Smiley." I'd dropped the nickname on him once he'd become even more moody and depressed.

And, for the umpteenth time, he replied, "If I'm still alive."

"Damn. You've been saying the same shit for a month now."

"Don't worry, it's getting close. You'd feel that way too if you had a death sentence hanging over your head."

He paused, then started talking about suicide being his only way out. "At least I can protect Trudy and the kids," Leo said.

"You taking your meds?"

"Like you give a shit?"

"Maybe your shrink should increase the dosage, because the only person I see trying to kill you is you. You need to get yourself a job, brother."

"Too bad I'm going to have to get my fuckin' brains blown out before people start taking me serious."

16

I SPENT A FEW DAYS at my brother's house in Atlanta. His daughter was auditioning for the ASO Youth Orchestra. I didn't play an instrument, but I told her I'd be there for moral support.

My last ride with Leo had left me with a bad feeling about his future. I called him on Sunday morning from my brother's house. No one answered, so I left a message. Later that evening, I called Diana.

"Leo tried to kill himself yesterday," she said.

"Why didn't you tell me when we spoke last night?"

"I didn't want to ruin your trip."

"How?"

"Overdosed on sleeping pills. Trudy came home and found him disoriented, incoherent, foaming at the mouth. The kids were with her, too."

"He leave a note?"

"I don't know."

"Shit. What a coward."

"He's at Brunswick Hospital, out in Amityville. He's under a twenty-four-hour suicide watch."

I was stunned, although I don't know why. Leo was going to get Leo, one way or the other.

I GREW UP IN DA' VILLE, as we called Amityville back when I was a kid, and had a little history with Brunswick Hospital. So, on the way out to visit Leo, I decided to swing through the old neighborhood, which was close by. I guess Leo's suicide attempt had me seeking the comfort of some pleasant old memories. I drove past the Shanghai Motel, where I had some of my earliest sexual conquests—

all one of them.

Back then, da' Ville was being systematically ravaged by drugs. The house I grew up in was only a couple of blocks from the most notorious drug corner in Suffolk County. Although the war on drugs had been won, the neighborhood still showed the battle scars.

I pulled into the hospital visitor's parking lot, my nostalgia itch scratched. Brunswick hadn't changed much in the twenty-five years since I'd last been there. It still looked old, institutional and drab. I remembered when my mother took me to the emergency room, thinking the pain in my lower abdomen was from a hernia.

A hospital volunteer directed me to the second floor. Brunswick didn't have a Psych ward, so Leo was mixed in with the hospital's regular patients, sharing his room with an elderly gentleman hooked up to an IV. A big-boned black nurse sat quietly in a chair at the foot of Leo's bed. The suicide watcher.

Leo's mood was bizarre, to say the least.

"I swallowed over a hundred pills, man," he said, way too gleefully, as if he was the winner in a pill-swallowing contest.

"What were you doing, counting them as you chugged them down?"

"Nah . . . just saying."

Leo was on his back, thick straps pressed tightly across his chest and ankles, his hands restrained. I dragged a chair across the room to the head of the bed, and sat. Black smudges were on Leo's cheeks and nose.

"Can't even kill yourself right, you pussy," I said.

"I didn't have a choice, Tony. I'm in a box."

"Then do it like a man—blow your fuckin' brains out or jump off a building. I can't believe you let Trudy and the kids walk in on you foaming at the mouth like a rabid dog."

When the nurse coughed theatrically, I turned towards her, and said, "Sorry ma'am."

She frowned at me. "Sir, please watch your language, or

I'll have to ask you to leave. This man's sick."

She had a honey-sweet voice, with a touch of southern twang. I noticed she was holding a well-thumbed Bible in her lap, no doubt praying for Leo's soul.

Apologetically, I nodded. "Just blowing of a little steam."

Leo wasn't getting better, in fact, he'd gotten a whole lot worse. My friend, as I knew him, was gone, and it didn't look as if he was ever going to come back. "So, what happened?" I asked him.

"I've been pissing charcoal briquettes for a while. They're trying to get my system cleaned up."

"I mean why'd you try to kill yourself?"

He motioned for me to lean in closer, whispered, "I don't want her to hear. Muertens. He told me to do it, or else he was gonna hurt the kids."

"I'm going to the cops," I bluffed.

"You can't do that. He'll kill 'em all. And I told you, the cops are in on it, too."

"You've got to stop with this Muertens shit, Leo."

"Don't you judge me, Tony. You think it's that easy? Just stop talking about Muertens and, poof, he'll just disappear? I'm doing this for Trudy and the kids, man."

He turned away from me. A framed eight-by-ten color glossy of Trudy, Leo, and the kids at an amusement park leaned against the window.

"Well you're doing a pretty shitty job of it," I said.

Leo struggled against the restraints, his furrowed brow showing the effort.

A younger, trimmer version of the duty nurse entered the room, and Leo relaxed. The new arrival could have been the older woman's kid sister. The nurses huddled and occasionally glanced back at us. I knew they were talking about me, and imagined the nurse was warning her replacement, "Keep your eye on that one." The duty nurse left the room, the changing of the suicide guard completed.

"Now boys, play nice," the young nurse said.

"I don't need your bullshit. Get the fuck outta here," Leo hissed.

"What happened to that guy I met ten years ago? Leo the fighter? You can't just give up. That's not you."

The young nurse shushed me and then said, "Sir, I'm afraid I'm going to have to ask you to leave. I don't want to have to call security."

"What do you want me to do?" I said to Leo.

He turned his head away from me. "Leave me be for now. I'll figure something out."

I DECIDED TO DRIVE to the club and work off some of the built-up frustration caused by Leo's latest setback. I still felt obligated to stand by him. After all, I owed him.

I entered the locker room. Eddie Hambrick was sprawled across a bench reading the *New York Times*. As usual, the place was a pigsty—lockers hung open, and the floor wet from guys tracking their way back from the showers.

"Since when did the *Times* add a comics section?" I asked Eddie.

"Wiseass," Eddie said. "You ever get that thing with the envelope squared away?"

"Yeah, Eddie. Everything's hunky dory."

"I heard your boy Leo tried to kill himself. Tell me, smart guy, what kind a man tries to kill himself with pills, and fucks it up?"

"A pussy?" one of Eddie's sycophants said.

"You serious, Eddie, or you just being an asshole?" I said.

It happened quickly. Eddie dropped the paper, bounded off the bench, grabbed my arm, spun me around and got me in a headlock—my head a walnut in a nutcracker. I flailed my arms, trying to get free, but my futile effort only encouraged him to squeeze harder.

"Don't struggle, Tony, just listen up," Eddie said, relaxing his grip, but not that much. It still felt like my head was going to implode.

"You're going to drop this thing with the envelope, got it?" He squeezed again to emphasize his question, his rock-hard bicep digging into my ear. "Nod if you and me got a understanding."

I guess I nodded, because Eddie released his grip and I fell to the floor. My right ear was ringing, and I wondered if he'd ruptured my ear drum.

I pushed myself up on to all fours and crawled towards the door, having a hard time getting traction on the wet floor. That's when Eddie planted his foot onto my butt, pushed hard, as if he was working out on a leg press machine, and sent me sliding across the tiled floor.

"Now get the fuck outta my locker room," he said.

I couldn't let Eddie punk me. Not in front of the guys. Had to go back at him. Pray that someone would jump in, hold me back, and avert a good old-fashioned ass kicking.

I scrambled to my feet and said, "You cocksucker, I swear to God I'm going to kill you."

And then I charged him. Problem was no one jumped in and grabbed me. All of which propelled me directly toward Eddie's big right fist that landed squarely on my unprotected chin, and sent me bouncing first off of the lockers and then onto the wet floor. Eddie stepped forward and stomped on my back, leaving me splayed on the floor, pinned beneath his shower shoe.

I heard him hiss, "Stay down, motherfucker, or next time I'm gonna put you down permanent."

17

I STAGGERED INTO THE HOUSE and checked myself in the mirror. My chin had turned black-and-blue during the twenty-five-minute drive home from the club. Eddie's forearm had left a red welt across my nose. The front of my pants and shirt were wet and covered with white foot powder.

"You okay?" Diana said.

"Would you believe I was out at the club and tripped over my own damn gym bag? Then slid across the floor and bumped head-first into a locker?"

"You're lying, Tony."

It's not a lie if you frame the lie in a question, right?

I laughed. "No. Really. You know how Horror View is."

"Don't sit there," Diana said, as I started to plop down in my favorite chair. "Take that stuff off, and go jump in the shower."

She pointed me out of the room, as if I was one of her unruly third-graders being sent to the principal's office.

A quick glimpse in the mirror confirmed my earlier prognosis. My chin looked as if I'd sprouted a tropical disease.

"I don't know why you keep going all the way out to the Island when there are lots of clubs much closer than Bay View. And they're a whole lot cleaner," Diana yelled.

"It's the guys," I yelled back. "I go because of the guys. You don't just find Horror View's vibe at any old club."

I stripped off the soiled clothing and was about to drop them in the clothes hamper when Diana appeared and said, "Let those dry out first, Tony."

After I'd toweled off and dressed, Diana gathered up the clothes and said, "You should sue those bastards."

"No harm, no lawsuit."

"Still—"

The telephone rang and I answered. It was Trudy.

"I've got a salvage company coming over tomorrow to clean out the garage," she said. "Is there any of Leo's old sports things you'd like to have? You can take whatever you want."

"Leo had an old Louisville Slugger. I'll take that if you can find it."

"What's a Louisville Slugger?"

"A baseball bat."

"Hold on. Let me go take a look."

Silence, then I heard her kids playing in the background. Seemed like all they ever did was play. Too bad none of that playfulness rubbed off on Leo.

I cupped the phone's mouthpiece and said, "Trudy's selling off all Leo's stuff."

"Well, she needs the money. Practicality trumps sentimentality."

After a minute, Trudy came back on, and said, "I found two bats. One's wooden and the other's metal."

"Yeah, the wooden one," I said.

"It's yours, but what's so important about an old baseball bat? This thing looks like something chewed on it."

"It saved my life."

I told her how Leo had come to my rescue ten years ago, wading into a gang of teenagers who were beating the hell out of me, wielding the bat like he was Hammerin' Hank Aaron.

"Leo never told me about that," Trudy said. "Did he hurt them?"

"Never heard anything, one way or the other. But I got to tell you, no matter how crazy . . ." I hesitated, then finished, "I mean, no matter how much trouble Leo's in, he's my boy. Just hold on to it for me. I'll stop by and pick it up after work, tomorrow."

"Okay. Is there anything else you'd like before all this

stuff gets picked up?

"Maybe Leo's bike?"

"Sorry, Tony. It's on eBay."

18

AFTER A COUPLE OF DAYS at Brunswick, the Department of Health found a bed for Leo and transferred him to Pilgrim State, out in Suffolk County. He'd made it to the "big house" of psychiatric treatment centers, the last remnant of New York State's Draconian mental health system.

Although I was still visiting him as often as I could, I was growing more and more resentful with each trek I made. Sure, I owed him one. And, as he said, in spades. But the price was getting to be too high. Indeed, it was time to cut my losses.

Driving north on Sagtikos State Parkway, Pilgrim State's two, dingy red-brick monoliths emerged from above a line of pine trees. I exited the Parkway and turned onto the hospital grounds.

Pilgrim State had once been the largest hospital in the world, housing almost 20,000 patients. But now the expansive campus was littered with the rubble of demolished and abandoned buildings. Apparently, a big-time developer purchased the property from the state, but hadn't realized at the time that most of the buildings were contaminated with asbestos. High cleanup costs made it way too expensive for the mixed-use project he'd planned. The economic meltdown didn't help either.

A hawk circled high above the grounds. I followed its lazy corkscrew descent onto a pile of bricks strewn near the old laundry building, easily identifiable by the rusted washing machines and dryers piled on the loading platform.

I pulled into the parking lot outside Building 80, then walked across the pockmarked lawn to Leo's new home—Building 82—one of the two tall towers I saw on the way in.

Nearby, several patients were playing basketball on an outdoor court cocooned inside a high, black chain-link fence.

Once inside the building, an armed state trooper ran me through the security protocol. I entered through a sally port—one door opens, another door closes—passed through a metal detector, signed in and left my driver's license with an armed guard. All quite necessary, because Pilgrim State was home for the more severely damaged patients, including the criminally insane. The inmates, in both appearance and body language, were, ah, several cards shy of a full deck. It was typical to see patients orbiting each other, playing a game only they knew.

When I first visited Leo, patients immediately gravitated towards me as soon as I entered the large ward. A few of them followed Leo and me into the game room, all the while trying to touch the shiny new toy.

If Leo didn't talk about Muertens, he seemed normal. A recurring topic of conversation between us concerned the government's war on terror. Leo liked to argue, "If we don't fight the terrorists over there, we're gonna have to fight them at home. So, which would you prefer, here or there?"

Once, a hefty patient interrupted me before I could go into my usual spiel.

"Where you from?" the guy said, hovering over me. He smelled like a man who couldn't control his bladder.

"Ignore him," Leo said. "He says that to all the visitors."

I did, but the guy persisted. "You look familiar. You from 'round here?"

"No," I said, hoping it would satisfy him, that he'd wander off.

"So, what'll it be—here or there?" Leo said, picking up the conversation again.

"Neither," I said.

Finally, our piss-soaked intruder slinked away, trapped in his own bizarre little world where everyone he met looked like someone he knew from some dark and distant part of a faraway universe.

I asked Leo, "You wanna stay in this place? If you weren't crazy when you arrived, you certainly will be by the time you leave."

"It's okay," he replied, "I feel safe here. Just have to watch they don't inject me with AIDS or something. Muertens has got people in here, too, spying on me."

I'd learned to ignore Leo's wacky allegations, so when I didn't respond, he doubled down, and said, "He can reach inside these walls, no problem."

I watched the same patient who'd accosted me corner a panic-stricken visitor.

I pondered that piece of insanity for a moment, then said, "Seeing how Plan A's worked out so well, Leo, what's Plan B?"

"I've been thinking about that," Leo said. "Way I see it, I might be safe if I ran away, just disappeared. Leave Trudy and the kids behind."

"Plus the mortgage, and all the other bills."

"It's not like that."

"Won't you be putting them in jeopardy?"

"Naw," he replied.

"You said Muertens was all about revenge. Wouldn't he just pressure Trudy to find out where you went?"

Leo tapped his knuckles on the edge of the table. "Well, maybe one time, then he'll leave her alone."

If there was any doubt about Leo's sanity tucked away somewhere in my brain, he'd just terminated it. In the past, every time I'd pointed out an inconsistency or an improbability in his wild tale, he had a quick, ready rejoinder. Now he was making up shit on the fly.

"You mean you'd expose Trudy to that maniac even once?"

Leo's face seemed unfocused. He opened his mouth to reply, but kept his silence. Finally, he said, "She'd be better off without me."

"No argument from me there, pal."

I was pissed. My so-called friend had buckled under the

responsibility of maintaining a family. He was taking the easy way out, concocting a bullshit my-boss-wants-to-kill-me story so he could cut his losses—start over with a clean slate and a clear conscience.

No wife, no kids, no debt. Blue skies, baby.

19

I BATTLED EARLY RUSH-HOUR TRAFFIC to get out to Trudy's and retrieve the bat, but it was a good ride that I really wanted. Cycling with Leo had reinvigorated me, and reminded me how much I'd missed challenging myself aerobically. Weightlifting alone didn't give me all I needed, mentally or physically. The solitary rides allowed me time for introspection, my rapidly beating heart the only reminder of my mortality.

Leo's little house seemed more drab than I'd remembered it from the night of the Super Bowl party. I sensed an air of desperation emanating from every brick. But then again, it might have been my imagination playing tricks on me.

"Mind if I take Leo's bike out before some lucky stiff takes it off your hands?" I said to Trudy.

"No, but you know the bidding's still open."

I threw on some of Leo's outdoor clothes, put the bike on the rack and headed for the greenbelt trail we used to ride.

I pushed myself for an hour, the gears shifting easily at my command.

When I returned to Leo's, Trudy offered the use of their shower, which I gladly accepted. After I'd cleaned up, we sat in the living room. The kids were running around, making lots of noise.

"How're they doing?" I said.

"Fortunately, they're too young to understand what's going on. I take them with me when I see Leo. They think daddy's staying in a hotel with a lot of funny people."

"That's good. How about you? How're you doing?"

"Hanging in there. I don't know what I'd do without my

mother, though. She's been a Godsend. But this has been hard on her, too, and it's because of her and the kids I'm doing this."

Trudy paused and handed me an envelope.

"What's this?" I asked.

"A separation agreement. I just need him to sign it. In a few months, it'll be over."

A lone tear slowly tracked down her cheek. She started crying, then reached for a tissue. I put my arm around her shoulders and lightly rubbed her back. She dabbed the tissue on her face.

I took a cursory look at the agreement, then handed it back to her. "Leo know yet?"

"I told him yesterday. He seemed to understand."

"This sucks, but I know you've gotta do what you gotta do to protect yourself and the kids."

"Things weren't great before, but I never imagined this." She fanned herself with the agreement.

I wondered if a paranoid schizophrenic had the mental capacity to legally agree to anything. But divorce? It seemed too contrived—as if it's what Leo wanted all along but didn't have the balls to initiate. Even his suicide attempt seemed bogus, which got me wondering just how many pills he'd actually swallowed—or if he'd swallowed any at all.

"Well, I've got to get going," I said. "I'm sure he'll sign. Thanks for the bat, and the ride."

Trudy stood and we embraced. And then, in my own moment of insanity, I bent over and kissed her hard on the mouth.

I don't know what I was thinking, or if I was thinking at all. As long as I'd known Trudy, I'd never thought of her in a sexual way. She was just Leo's wife—a friend.

But in that split-second before I kissed her, I sensed her vulnerability, which attracted me—much as a predator would in sensing the weakest in the herd and singling it out for the kill. I'd thought Trudy had held my friendly embrace a beat too long a few times before, but I never fantasized something like this coming out of those close encounters.

I was just about to apologize for my stupidity when Trudy pressed her slender hips into my groin.

We disentangled, then Trudy said, "Hey, kids, why don't you go downstairs and watch cartoons for a while, okay?"

Now Trudy's a petite little thing, and I lifted her with ease, and carried her into the small bedroom, then bounced her onto the queen-sized bed.

"Close the door," she said in a husky voice.

We grappled, clothes flying. Finally unencumbered, her hunger sucked me in deeper. I was her safe haven.

Afterwards, Trudy lay in my arms, holding me tight, not saying a word.

For the first time, I took notice of the room. It was all frilly pinks and white; the comforter, pillows, drapes. Except for the autographed baseball in a Lucite display case on top the bureau, there was nothing to indicate Leo had ever lived here.

Trudy wasn't his anymore.

I checked my reflection in the gilded mirror above the bureau, suddenly feeling utterly disgusted with myself. Betraying not only Diana, but also a friend—taking advantage of Trudy's vulnerability when what she really needed was sympathetic understanding, someone she could lean on and help stop her world from spinning further out of control.

But as the old maxim goes, a man's libido has no conscience, feels no guilt. I'd never given my penis a name like some guys do. But if I did, at that moment, I would have called it Arnold, as in *Been-a-dick* to my friends. I'd always considered myself a good guy, but as I felt Trudy's steady heartbeat drumming against my chest, I knew that was no longer the case. It's said the difference between a faithful man and unfaithful man is opportunity. Well, opportunity knocked, I kicked the door wide open, and let it storm right on in.

I was the lowest of the low, but I wasn't feeling stupid. Diana would be like a bloodhound sniffing out Trudy's perfume on me. So it was back in the shower again, but this time not alone.

THUS A ROUTINE BEGAN. Drive out to Trudy's. Take the bike out for an hour or so, shower, then ride Trudy. Each time the guilt would come flooding back, but eventually it would go away.

Especially before our next rendezvous.

20

IT WAS LATE IN THE AFTERNOON and the Metro Tech Center's steel-and-glass caverns were deserted and deep in shadows, most of the thousands of workers having long since headed home for the weekend. A financial services company was looking to lease space on its nationwide network of microwave towers, so Rick Meyerson, Telecom Structures head of security, and I had spent the afternoon attending the bidders conference at the large business and educational complex in downtown Brooklyn.

Just before I'd left for the conference, Rick had decided to tag along, saying, "I heard about the little *difficulty* you had out in California. If I'd known you were going to have so much trouble, I would've gone with you."

"Uh, thanks, Rick, but isn't the head of security supposed to know about trouble *before* it happens?"

"I figured a tough guy like you could handle a bunch of Hollywood pussies." He laughed. "Hey, I was wrong."

"Actually, the ringleader was quite fetching in Harry Potter pajamas."

"You get her name?"

"Butch."

So, feigning concern for my safety, he'd decided to tag along this time, and keep me out of trouble. And maybe we'd break a rack or two, afterwards.

Rick had been with Telecom Structures about as long as I had, and he and I had become fast friends through a shared interest in billiards. But it was a workplace friendship. We never got together outside the office with the wives.

Word was Rick used to be a cold war spook and had been involved in *wet* work. If that was true, you couldn't tell it by looking at him. He wasn't physically imposing—average height, average weight—and he exuded a mild-mannered demeanor, full of good cheer. In short, he didn't appear to be a cold-blooded killer.

I'd probed him about his military experiences from time to time, but he neither confirmed nor denied the wild stories I'd sometimes hear swirling around the office. I had a suspicion he'd started most of them himself just to burnish his aura of mystery.

"I'll bet you find this glorified security thing really boring, right?" I asked on one occasion.

"This place suits me just fine," was his dry response. "I know where I'll be tomorrow, and my family likes knowing, too."

That was as close as I ever got to squeezing a revelation out of him. Just name, rank and serial number.

After the conference was over, I called the limousine service Telecom Structures used, but the ETA for a car was an hour, which meant it was more like two. So, we decided to walk over to Flatbush Extension and take the subway to the Brooklyn LIRR station.

Entering the Commons, the public space at the center of the Metro Tech complex, I watched two young men emerge from behind an outdoor sculpture piece and head in our direction. Telling by their long purposeful strides, they were definitely on a mission. When they drew closer, they slowed to a ghetto swagger, then stopped a few feet in front of us.

With a black hoodie and baggy black jeans, the taller of the men looked like an urban ninja. I couldn't see his shoes, because the jeans rested low on the hips and were bunched around his ankles.

"Mayday, mayday," I said.

"You're not profiling are you, Tony?" Rick said.

I wanted to tell him *it's not profiling when someone you thought might be trouble has a gun in your face,* but got lockjaw the instant the ninja pulled a pistol from beneath his hoodie. He held the weapon sideways, *gangsta* style, sighting along the length of his arm, like the fake gangstas in rap videos do. Nothing fake about the big shiny black cannon he pointed at us, though.

Rick stopped, then inched forward. "Evening boys," he said, as if he was greeting a couple of his old CIA pals.

The other kid, holding a knife, sported a purple NYU T-shirt, khakis, and white sneakers. He looked like Joe Ivy League home for spring break.

"Who you calling *boys*?" the punk holding the gun said. "Give it up, old man."

"What?" Rick said, cupping his right hand behind his ear.

"Them briefcases and the *chedda*, that's what."

"Afraid I can't do that, boys," Rick said, his voice dry and brittle as autumn leaves.

"Why's that?" the kid with the gun said, rolling his shoulders, ready to rumble.

"Because then I'd have to hunt you down to get my stuff back, and that's way too much work for an old man." Rick paused a beat, and then added, "Oh, almost forgot. Then I'd have to kill you. Messy business, that."

"Listen to this crazy mother —"

I don't recall if the punk actually said "motherfucker," or if I knew that's what he wanted to say, because the next few seconds flew by in a flurry of arms and legs. It was like I was watching a kung fu movie. Rick came up hard and fast with his polished aluminum briefcase, knocked the weapon free, then stepped forward and crushed the punk's left knee with a heel kick. The punk screamed and fell to the pavement, clutching his hyper-extended knee.

Joe Ivy League was slow to react, obviously as stunned by Rick's lethal quickness as I was. Wide-eyed and panicky, he lunged at Rick, slashing with the knife. That was his second mistake, because Rick caught Ivy League's wrist, redirected the four-inch blade and buried it up to the hilt in the kid's thigh. Ivy League fell alongside his partner in crime, and howled like a wolf, but even with both of the attackers disabled, Rick wasn't through. Frenzied, he kicked and stomped on them until I swore I heard bones snapping.

Stunned in horrified disbelief, I finally yelled out, "Rick, you're gonna kill'em, man." When I grabbed his arm, he turned on me as if I was a third attacker to be dispatched. "It's me, Rick," I pleaded, and backpedaled least I joined the two guys writhing on the ground.

I'll never forget the murderous rage etched in his crimson face. I didn't know the man standing in front of me, but when he recognized me as friend, not foe, my old buddy reappeared, his smile could only be described as borderline insane.

Releasing a deep sigh, he said, "Let's get out of here. Maybe grab a beer."

"Grab a beer?"

Still dazed by the mayhem I'd witnessed, I couldn't move.

"Come on, we've got a couple of spectators at ten o'clock," he said.

I started to bolt, but Rick gently took hold of my arm and said, "Be cool. Walk normal, and keep your head down. There're surveillance cameras everywhere."

He nudged me on, once again the Rick I knew.

Only when we'd put some distance between us and the carnage, did I have the nerve to ask, "You think those guys are okay?"

"I'm supposed to give a shit? If you're really that concerned, why don't you call the morgue when you get home?"

"You think you killed them?"

He shrugged, then said, "Your guess is as good as mine, but if I didn't, they might want to seriously consider a career change."

WE STROLLED OVER TO ATLANTIC Terminal—carefree, two businessmen going home after a tough day's work. No one pursued us, called for help, or pointed us out to the police. It was like the *thing* didn't happen.

"That punk shouldn't have called me *old man*," Rick said, matter-of-factly, as we sat in the Terminal's waiting area, going through a sort of post kickass cool-down.

"What'd you have in that briefcase?" I said.

"Nothing."

"Nothing?"

"It's titanium. Strong and light. You never know when it'll be more useful—empty or filled with useless crap. Today, empty worked fine."

"So that stuff floating around the office . . . ah, it's true, isn't it?"

"Don't know what *stuff* you've been hearing?"

"That you were a CIA assassin."

"Back there?" He laughed, hiking his thumb over his shoulder. "I studied martial arts when I was a kid. I made it to brown belt before I quit. Muscle memory, that's all."

"You've got some memory."

"Like riding a bike." He chuckled, then said, "I have a theory."

"About?"

"In your garden variety street mugging, like that little episode back there, the mugger and the victim both assume a certain risk."

"Meaning?"

"You're a lawyer—waiver of liability. Like if you go to Yankee Stadium, you can't sue the Steinbrenners if you get hit by a line drive. You assumed the risk that might happen before you even took your seat."

I mumbled, "I hated torts."

He flashed that haunting smile once again. "Same thing in our situation. The mugger's risk is the victim might get brave, overwhelm and beat the shit out of him, in which case he ends up in jail. But if the victim's counterattack fails, he could make a bad situation a whole lot worse, like being killed. See what I mean?"

"But I didn't assume anything back there."

Nor did I mention the mugging where the guy holding

the gun kills the passive victim just because he either didn't have enough *chedda* or for the thrill of it. But why ruin Rick's theory? Anyway, he'd probably just say that was the risk you took if you did nothing—justifying his convoluted theory and why he could have or should have killed those two assholes.

"I couldn't have done it without you, though, Tony."

"You trying to make me feel better?"

"I thought you were going to shit your pants when the kid pulled the gun. But that was good, because they thought they were sitting in the bleachers. Nobody gets hit way up in the nose bleeds."

I think he was running on like that to help calm me down, making sure I wouldn't freak out later. He'd gulped down three beers, while I worked on my second club soda. I'm sure he had some issues to work out, too.

During a lull in his narrative, I said, "I'm having an affair."

Rick took a sip of his beer, then said, "Show me a guy who hasn't, and why're you telling me? Do I look like Father Rick?" He laughed again. He'd been doing a lot of laughing.

"After tonight? A near-death confession, I guess."

"More likely the reaction to a midlife crisis."

"Boy, you're a cynical bastard."

"I've seen a lot of shit in my time. My advice to you, my friend? Juggle too many balls, some of them are going to get dropped. And what I know of you, you're a shitty juggler."

Rick's train was announced over the public address system. He put his drink down, turned and faced me.

"This . . . thing?" Rick said.

"What *thing* are you talking about?"

"It didn't happen." No smile, no playful punch to the shoulder. Only a raspy voice, saying, "I really don't want to hear anything about this circulating around the office. Not at home, nowhere. Understood?"

I nodded. I'd seen Rick Meyerson in action, and no way did I want to be on his bad side. I could get hurt, and that was a risk I wasn't willing to assume.

MOST PEOPLE GO THROUGH their entire lives without experiencing a single act of violence firsthand. Somehow, I'd managed to live through two muggings—in both of which I'd been saved by a white knight.

I didn't want to rely on a hard charging savior to survive a third time. I had a target permit for the SIG P220 I'd purchased back during the '93 LA riots, when it seemed the whole country was going to hell. I took it from the lockbox hidden on the top shelf in the bedroom closet, cleaned, and loaded it with a full clip—with one in the chamber, just in case.

21

ALTHOUGH RICK INTIMATED I shouldn't call the morgue, I still wanted to know if the punks had survived the beat-down. A tech had my computer apart doing some upgrades, so I walked into accounting and asked, "Anybody got today's paper?"

"I got *Newsday*," the department manager yelled out.

"I need the *News* or the *Post*. Preferably the *Post*." This sensationalist rag was the most likely to have a story trumpeting urban violence.

One of the clerks handed me the newspaper and I took it back to the office, paging through it until I found the story in the NYC Local section, the headline screaming, "Metro Tech Mayhem." Rick hadn't killed the muggers, just left them in critical condition.

"They got busted up pretty good," said a police department spokesperson.

Witnesses reported seeing two men in business suits walking away from the scene headed towards Flatbush Extension. And because the punks' weapons were found near them, the spokesperson speculated, "Looks like it might have been an attempted robbery gone bad, and the intended victims turned the tables on the bad guys."

Yeah, more like turned it over, picked it up, and beat them senseless.

The spokesperson concluded, "But unless we can find out who the real victims are, we don't have much to go on."

I called Rick and asked him to meet me in the company rec room. I no more than set down the phone when Ma tapped on the door, then entered followed by Ted Barr, the young lawyer on my staff.

I stuffed the newspaper in a desk drawer.

"You've got company," Ma said, then whispered, "I tried to keep him out."

"Hey, Tony," Ted said. "Got a minute?"

"My door's always open, Ted."

"Then why's it always closed?"

"Figure of speech."

"By the way, nice job in California."

"That was a while ago, Ted."

"I'm due for a raise, so I thought I'd do a little retro sucking up."

Ma said, "I'm leaving you boys to do whatever," handed me an application, and left the office.

Ted was wearing an old sweatshirt and jeans.

"Did I miss the memo on Casual Tuesday?" I said.

"Oh, I'm going out in the field."

"What do you need, Ted?"

"Weren't you at that big bidders' conference out at Metro Tech yesterday?"

"Yeah."

"And Rick Meyerson, he went with you, right?"

I nodded.

"You hear about what happened?"

"No."

"It was on the local news. Two suits beat the shit out of a couple of muggers. How cool is that?"

"What's your point?"

"Rick's a real badass," Ted whispered, "so I thought about you guys, you know, being out there and all."

"I'd hate to tell Rick you're spreading rumors around the office—"

"Me?" Ted said, the epitome of innocence.

"—especially with him being such a badass *and all*."

"Hey, just wondering if you guys saw anything," Ted said, now nervously rubbing his hands together.

"I can ask Rick, see if he remembers anything unusual about yesterday."

"No, no, Tony," he spread his arms. "My curiosity's been totally satisfied."

I retrieved Diana's birthday elephant from my desk and handed it to Ted.

"Here, have a lucky elephant."

He took it and said, "Shouldn't the trunk be raised?" then gave it back to me.

Ma's voice sounded through my phone's intercom, "Mr. Benson, I have two detectives from the Nassau County Police Department here to see you."

My first thought was something had happened to Diana. "Okay, send them in, Ma."

"What's up?" Ted asked.

Bewildered, I shrugged.

It was as if my office had a revolving door. Ted exited one second and two detectives escorted by Ma entered right behind him.

Filled with apprehension, I asked, "Is my wife okay?"

"Didn't mean to alarm you, Mr. Benson, but we're not here about your wife," the younger of the two detectives said.

I let out a sigh of relief. "Thank God. You had me worried there for a second, detectives. Please, have a seat," then to Ma, "Thanks, and please hold my calls."

The cops showed me identification, shook my hand, and introduced themselves as Lieutenant Stiles and Sergeant Riley.

Both wore sport jackets, baby blue dress shirts, and co-ordinated ties. Riley, the older cop, was smartly dressed. His brown tweed jacket—with the obligatory elbow patches—looked expensive and fit snugly over his slender frame. His nails were manicured, and he gave off a ready smile, displaying an even set of white teeth. Stiles, on the other hand, looked rumpled, the creased jacket a size too big. He wore a bushy, unkempt mustache, that couldn't quite hide a baby face.

"Sorry 'bout that, Mr. Benson," Riley said. "Guess you

got to figure when we come a knockin' we're not exactly the bearers of good news, huh?"

I tensed. *Oh shit. Was this about Metro Tech. No, think. They're Nassau County cops.* "How can I help you?" I said, trying to keep my growing tension under control.

"You know Eddie Hambrick?" Stiles asked.

"Yeah, he's a muscle-head works out at the same club I do."

"You friends?" Riley said.

"Not exactly."

"Enemies?" Riley, again.

"I wouldn't say that. What's this about?"

"We'll ask the questions, Mr. Benson." Riley said.

"We understand you had a run-in with Hambrick," Stiles said, picking up one of the elephants, inspecting it, then rotating it in his hand. "That right?"

"If you can call Eddie almost cracking my head wide open a run-in . . . yeah, I guess so. Why? He say different?"

"What was this, uh, *run-in* about?" Stiles asked.

"Do I need a lawyer?"

"Do you?" Stiles said.

"You're a lawyer yourself, right?" Riley said.

"Yeah." I pointed to the framed diplomas on the wall to my right.

"What's that saying?" Riley said. "Man representing himself has a fool for a client?"

"Abraham Lincoln," I said.

"If you follow old Abe's counsel, counselor," Stiles said, "we'll have to continue this conversation at the precinct." Stiles said.

An awkward silence ensued as they waited for me to decide what I was going to do.

"I think Eddie stole part of the money the guys at the club raised for a sick friend of mine."

"That friend Leo Radigan?" Stiles asked, putting the elephant back onto the desk. He picked up another one and gave it the same massage.

"Yeah, Eddie told me he'd raised a grand. But when I gave the envelope to Leo's wife, there was only five-hundred dollars."

This time, something about saying five-hundred dollars triggered an *ah-ha* moment. Leo stole five-hundred dollars from Muertens; Eddie stole five-hundred from the money raised for Leo; Leo said Eddie was spying on him for Muertens. Was Muertens behind this. Payback? Leo had tried to kill himself, and the cops were asking me questions about Eddie. Muertens? Stop. This was crazy.

"So, you confronted Hambrick about the discrepancy," Stiles continued.

"Sorta. We had a few words, then he jumped me. What's going on, detectives?"

"Hambrick was murdered last night," Riley said.

"Murdered? I just—"

Remember you're a lawyer. Don't give up more than you're asked.

"He was found lying near his car in the parking lot at Bay View," Stiles said.

"How do you know it was murder?"

"The back of his head was bashed in with a dumbbell," Stiles said, then put the elephant back on the desk.

I let out a nervous laugh, sort of like a *ka-choo*.

"What's so funny, Mr. Benson?" Stiles again.

How ironic, a dumbbell killed with a dumbbell. "Eddie's a pretty big guy. I just can't imagine—"

"Several people said they heard you threaten to kill Hambrick," Riley said.

He leaned forward and rested his forearms on the desk.

"Whoa . . . you don't think I—" Again, the nervous laughter. "I wouldn't exactly call it a threat. You know how it is—"

"No," Stiles said. "Why don't you tell us."

"You get into a scrape with a guy, there's always a lot of loose talk. Posturing, really. 'I'm gonna do this. I'm gonna do that.' It's just a little macho game guys play."

"Yeah, but sometimes those little macho games, as you call it, play out and somebody winds up dead, like Eddie Hambrick," Riley said.

"That's certainly not me," I said, becoming irritated with his implication.

"Where were you last night between, let's say, eight and ten?" Stiles said.

"Last night? I was with a friend."

"I suppose you can verify that?" Stiles said.

"That way we can eliminate you from our investigation," Riley said. "Otherwise, you're our starting point."

And ending point.

"Why don't you give us *his* name, where *he* lives, *his* phone number and we can clear this thing up, nice and simple, Mr. Benson," Riley said.

Riley's sarcasm told me the detectives had seen plenty of situations like mine, where a straying husband got picked off base by a totally unrelated incident. So, like an idiot playing further into their hands, I hesitated, further incriminating myself, I'm sure—and then gave them Trudy's contact information.

"Can you keep my wife out of this?" I whined.

"We'll see what we can do, Mr. Benson," Stiles said. "One of us'll get back to you."

WHEN I ENTERED THE GAME ROOM, Rick was shooting pool. I plopped into a lounge chair and threw my legs across one of the overstuffed armrests. Four guys from tech support were in one corner playing bridge. I heard them calling out their bids, "Three, no trump, four, spades."

Rick walked over, and shook my hand, then said, "Heard you had visitors."

"Yeah, couple of cops."

"Should I be worried?"

"What, you worry?" I said, even though his flat stare told me otherwise. "Nah. Just a guy I know was murdered last night."

"So, why're they talking to you?"

"The dead guy and I had a beef. I threatened to kill him. Just talking trash."

A smile crept across his face, like I'd gained some new level of respect in his eyes. "Of course," he said.

"But you, on the other hand, throw out the trash," I said.

"Me? I'm all mouth."

His laugh was without mirth, but I sensed the tension easing.

"You've got chalk on your forehead," I said.

He wiped his hand across his face, then said, "Hanging around you can be hazardous to my health."

"But that's not why I wanted to meet up with you."

"So, what's up?" Rick said.

"I checked on those guys."

Rick shook his head. "Yeah, and?"

I removed a pool cue from the wall-mounted rack, rolled the stick along the table's red felt-covered slate, checking the balance.

"They're not in the morgue, but you messed 'em up pretty bad."

He rubbed his bald head like he was polishing an apple, leaving another streak of blue chalk on his forehead, and said, "Damn, I'm slipping. Once upon a time—"

"You think this is funny, Rick?"

"Yeah, Tony, actually I do." He yawned. "You play the game, you got to know the rules. Those clowns weren't prepared. Either plain arrogance or just too stupid to figure out that someday they'd run into somebody like me, and besides, you pull a weapon and hold it like that bozo did?"

"You sound offended, Rick."

"As a professional, a former professional, for that alone that punk deserved what he got."

"That's pretty cold, Rick."

"And you worry too much."

"My yin to your yang."

"Anyway, why do you give a shit about those guys? If it

had gone down the other way, you think they'd check to see how you were doing?"

I knew he was right.

"Enough with the post mortem," Rick said. "Rack 'em up."

"Nine ball?"

"There any other game?"

Rick broke, and the one-ball disappeared into a side pocket. He stalked around the table, finally lining up a two-ball-nine-ball combination. A couple of practice strokes, then he shot—the nine-ball rattled around the corner pocket before dropping in.

We played for about an hour, Rick winning four out of five, and it wasn't that close.

"Where'd you learn to shoot like that?" I said.

"The byproduct of having a lot of down time. Another game?"

"You've got all my lunch money. Besides, I've got to run out and see my buddy, Leo."

"How's he doing?"

I put the cue back in the rack. "I'm afraid it's going to be a long, slow climb. Thinks his boss is going to kill him."

"I don't know him, but he's not the kind of guy I'd hang out with," Rick said. "Wound way too tight. I've seen guys a whole lot tougher than him crack. Not a pretty sight."

"He saved my life."

"You guys got history. I can understand that. Nothing's more valuable than loyalty, and nothing's harder to come by these days."

I wondered what he'd say if he knew my affair was with my buddy's wife.

"Rick, were you trying to kill those guys?"

Rick wiped the chalk off his hands, and then said, "Whatever the hell it takes."

"But—"

"We cool?"

"We cool," I said as we exchanged a fist bump.

ALL MY CO-WORKERS WANTED to know why the cops had questioned me. I laughed it off, told them about Eddie's murder and how the cops were talking to anybody and everybody who knew him. Assured my colleagues I wasn't a suspect.

"Too much TV, guys," was my stock closer when they eyed me with skepticism.

I waited another hour before I called Trudy, and she snatched up the receiver before I heard the phone ring.

"When they knocked on the door, I thought Leo was dead," she said.

"I'm sorry about that."

"God punishing me for what I'd done."

"Don't blame yourself. What I did was wrong, taking advantage of your vulnerability. That's not what a friend does."

"In case you didn't notice, you weren't alone," Trudy said.

"But still . . ." I trailed off, just to say something.

Ma stuck her head in the door and I held up an index finger, signaling her to give me a minute. "So what happened with the police?"

Trudy corroborated my alibi, but didn't tell the detectives about our intimate encounter.

"But they knew," she said. "That detective Stiles asked, 'How long does it take for a *friend* to pick up a bat?' He was so smug. Treated me like I was a tramp. When the kids ran in they backed off a little."

"Cops aren't happy unless they're shooting somebody," I joked.

"Why didn't you tell me you had a fight with Eddie?"

I shrugged my shoulders. "He didn't like the way I asked him about the missing five-hundred dollars."

"I told you to forget about the money, Tony. And now Eddie's dead?"

"Since I'm no longer the prime suspect, I wonder where they'll look next. I know Eddie was into some shady deal-

ings."
   "No more secrets, okay, Tony?"

22

RATHER THAN DRIVE OUT to see Leo that night, I decided to go home, have an early dinner and tell Diana about Eddie's murder, and how the cops showed up at the office and questioned me about it. I figured I'd tell her before she heard it second hand from Ma, the detectives, or God forbid, Trudy.

"Why'd they question you?"

"Background, I guess. Eddie and I had a little disagreement."

"That when you tripped over your gym bag?"

"The whole thing was silly, really. They didn't even read me my rights, so now it's over."

"What was your disagreement with Eddie about?"

Think fast. "Why don't we make love anymore?" A double-edged question—a distraction and a rationalization for my relationship with Trudy, theory being if you're not getting *it* at home, it's okay to stray off the reservation.

Diana was caught off guard—a jerk of the head, bug-eyed, then a quick recovery. "Do you really want to talk about that right now?"

The phone rang, putting our conversation on hold. Neither of us made a move to get it. The answering machine cut in after four rings with Diana's cheery greeting.

It was Leo. "Tony, call me back."

Hearing "Leo the Louse's" message didn't help Diana's disposition. She swept the glass of red wine she'd been drinking off the table, sending it crashing to the floor.

"We have to talk about it sometime," I said, sheepishly.

"You want to talk?" she said. "I told you day one I didn't want kids. You knew that going in, and if that was a problem, you should've found some other woman to be your broodmare. But you didn't. You went right ahead and married me just the same, and you've resented me every day since. I can feel it every time you're flopping around on top of me."

And then she pushed back from the table and stormed out of the kitchen, broken glass crunching under her shoes.

I didn't try to stop her.

Yeah, she was right. I knew the score going in, but I thought she'd change. Big mistake.

With trepidation, I returned Leo's call. The only way to reach him however, was the pay phone in the hall outside the rec room, and that was a hit-or-miss proposition. So not surprisingly it took a couple of redials before I got through to Leo. On my first attempt, a man picked up, did a little heavy breathing, then hung up without saying a word. The next time, a patient answered in Spanish. "*No habla Espanol,*" I said, then he tells me to go fuck myself in perfect English, and slams the handset down.

"When you coming out to see me, man?" Leo said, the words tumbling out in a torrent.

"What's up?"

"I got some news."

Trudy had told me Leo'd been talking about running away.

"One of his old buddies called and ratted him out," Trudy had said. "Told me Leo asked for money to finance his vanishing act."

Was that the news he wanted to share?

I would be attending the funeral of an old colleague about fifteen minutes from the hospital, so I said, "I'll see you day after tomorrow," in essence, paying my respects to a guy who'd been desperate to live, then visiting my buddy who was ambivalent about living.

WHAT SHOULD HAVE BEEN a fifteen-minute drive took forty-five, and I arrived only twenty minutes before visiting hours were over. The heavy traffic only served to fuel my resentment. My friendship with Leo had been strained to the breaking point.

Trudy and the kids were walking out of the elevator as I passed through security.

"I didn't know you were coming out today," I said, pecking her on the cheek.

"Say hello to Uncle Tony, kids."

They responded in unison.

I ruffled Hallee's hair, then took a playful jab at Cody. "You kids staying out of trouble?"

"Yeah, Uncle Tony," they droned, then ran off and started playing with the levers on a nearby vending machine.

"How's Leo?"

"He didn't say anything, but I can tell he's about to bail on us. To be honest, I don't want him back home. I can't leave him alone with the kids. Hell, I can't leave him alone, period. He just might burn the house down. This damn divorce can't come through fast enough to suit me."

"It's tough."

Trudy nodded, then smiled. "Am I seeing you tomorrow?"

"Believe it. I better run inside before they lock the place down."

We embraced, and I headed for the security office.

LEO WAS SITTING AT A TABLE with a man, obviously not a patient, who was writing furiously on a clipboard. Wearing a colorful Hawaiian shirt, cargo shorts, and sandals, and a full, graying beard, he looked like an aging hippie lost in a time warp while on the way to Woodstock. Leo ignored him, instead focusing on the TV on the other side of the room. I watched the employee hand a pill to Leo, who in turn chased it down with a glass of water. After the guy left I walked over and sat in his seat.

"See you're making friends," I said.

"Nah, that's my shrink."

"And I guess that pill was a little party favor?"

"Something like that. I have no idea what he's giving me, but it sure makes me feel good."

"Modern psychiatry."

"If you want to call it that. What you just saw is what I get, once a week, maybe five minutes on his slow day."

"So where'd they hide the couch?"

"Yeah—hey, look-it. I need for you to do me a favor. I'm getting out of here real soon."

I laughed and slapped him on the shoulder. "Uh-huh, and how're you going to manage that?"

"I can pretty much call the shots. Look at who's around me."

Leo was right. In the land of the blind, the one-eyed man was king.

"I've been playing their game, giving them what they want," he said. "Go to all the group meetings, telling them exactly what they want to hear. Don't stay in my room. I sit out here, watch TV, bullshit with the other wackos. The staff likes that. Shows 'em I'm adjusting."

He gave me a toothy grin. Been awhile since I'd seen that. He'd even shaved, had on a nice pair of jeans and T-shirt.

"That's what the doctor said? You can check out anytime?"

"Yep, so I need your help when I get out."

I hadn't seen Leo this upbeat since he'd told me he was porking Irena. But something still didn't sit right.

"What ya need?" I said.

"Drive me to Philly."

"Philadelphia? Why?"

"Because from there I can go anyplace. Just disappear off the face of the earth."

"Why not Penn Station or Grand Central . . . one of the local airports?"

"They'll be expecting that."

"They? You've got to be shitting me."

"You owe me, Tony, and I'm calling in my marker."

I started to object, but a guy saving your life's a mighty big marker. Leo was going "all in."

"What about Trudy and the kids? You're just going to disappear? Hang her up and leave her to carry the mess you leave behind? That what you want?"

"I want to live, and the only way I can see doing that is to disappear. Besides, it's the best thing for Trudy and the kids."

"What about the madman that's after you? Won't he go after her?"

"Trudy won't know where I am. Besides, he won't bother my family."

"You really believe that after all the shit you've told me about this Muertens character? When is he going to figure out she doesn't know anything? After he's beat the crap out of her?"

Leo punctuated his indifference with a shrug.

"You obviously haven't thought this out," I said, my anger barely in check.

"It's all I've been thinking about, man."

"Well think some more."

As I stood to leave, Leo said, "You're being followed, you know. They're watching you."

"What?"

"You were at the Queens County Clerk's office yesterday, right?"

His words exploded like an IED on some crater-filled road in Iraq. "How the fuck you know where I was yesterday?"

Before he could answer, the bell signaling the end of visiting hours rang. The orderlies started herding everyone out.

"How the fuck do you know that?" I repeated louder this time, the urgency in my voice turning heads.

An orderly approached, his hands raised as if I was one of the crazies about to throw a tantrum. "Come on, mister, let's move along. Visiting hours are over."

The orderly nudged me halfway across the room. I could smell mint on his breath; he was that close.

Leo said, "Better watch your back, Tony."

The orderly blocked me for an instant, and I lost sight of Leo. When I saw him again, he was saying something, but I was too far away to hear. I'm no lip reader, but I could swear he said, "He killed Eddie."

"Who?" I yelled. How did he know Eddie was dead? "Muertens?"

No answer, just Leo's blank stare. That and the metallic click as the doors locked behind me.

I LURCHED OUT OF THE HOSPITAL, sweating and breathing heavily, my head spinning. Although it was a beautiful, sunny day, I felt everything pressing in on me. I loosened my collar.

I *had* gone to the County Clerk's office yesterday to research a zoning issue. A rare trip for me. Leo wasn't clairvoyant, so how could he know I was there? Was I being followed?

I ran to my car, my head on a swivel—so paranoid and disconnected that I lost my balance and fell to the pavement, ripping my pants at the knee, and drawing blood. Leo had said Eddie was spying on him. But who was spying on me? Couldn't have been Eddie—hell, he was already dead.

"Is this crazy fucker's story true?" I mumbled, sounding as delusional as Leo. Nonetheless, I had to see him again—get some solid answers. But evening visiting hours weren't for another few hours. So, I drove around trying to gather my thoughts, eyes glued to the rearview, watching my back. All the while, turning over the events of the last few days in my mind. Had anything or anyone been suspicious?

One thing came to mind. A couple of nights before, I'd noticed Diana peeking out the blinds in the living room. When I'd asked if anything was wrong, she said, "There's a man and a woman sitting in that black car parked across the street. They've been there for a while. Looks like the guy's on a cell phone. I don't know, it's probably nothing."

Diana had started to feel more secure since we'd installed a new alarm system, plus decorative wrought iron bars over the street-level windows—ostensibly making us prisoners in our own home. My immediate thought was they were the mysterious "stalkers" Leo had talked about. But by the time I stepped to the window to see for myself, the car was gone.

Figuring a bike ride might clear my head, and to kill some time, I drove to Trudy's. But she wasn't home. Back on the Long Island Expressway, my paranoia ramped up, I took evasive maneuvers, exiting the LIE and hopping back on; a few quick U-turns, driving on the wrong side of a street-divide in the neighborhood adjacent to the hospital.

Convinced I wasn't being followed, I drove back to Pilgrim State. Leo was in the day room, watching a game show with some of the other patients. When he jumped up to greet me, I pulled him aside, and asked, "How'd you know I was at the County Clerk's office?"

"They call and tell me shit." He waved his arms, indicating it was no big deal, as if the calls were an everyday occurrence.

"Who calls and tells you *what* shit?"

"Muertens or one of his guys'll call once, maybe twice a week, reminding me my time's almost up, stuff like that. Last time they called, they told me where you were."

And then he paused as if there was something else he wanted to say, but was hesitant to spill it. Finally, he blurted out, "And they told me you were screwing Trudy."

POW—a wild roundhouse punch, thrown from the canvas. I wasn't expecting that, and it had to have shown all over my very red face. "How would—what the fuck, man?" I said, just catching myself before I sputtered my half-assed denial all over Leo's T-shirt. "That's . . . that's crazy."

Leo smiled. "If the dick fits . . . but hey, it's okay. I can't do anything for her anymore, and you're my friend. I'd rather her be with you than some of the other assholes I know."

I let his reference to *other assholes* slide. What could I say? After all, I was screwing his wife. "I won't even justify that bullshit accusation with a denial. Come on, Leo, how long we know each other? I wouldn't do *that* to a friend."

Deny, deny, deny. But I could tell Leo wasn't buying it. "Whoever *they* are, they're messing with you. Trying to drive a wedge between us. What the fuck's Muertens—that his first or last name?"

"It's Hike Muertens."

"Well, he can go take a hike, for all I care."

"Look, Tony, I know you're having a hard time taking all this in. I know I did before I realized all this shit was real. Ain't no joke, man. Let me prove it before it's too late for you, too."

"How?"

"You remember what I told you about the lawyer? How Muertens told me I'd know he'd got to him?"

"The *code*, right?"

"Yeah, that when I called the scumbag, the only thing he'd say to me was—'I don't do divorces.' Even though I'd already sat down with him a while back when I was exploring the possibility of dumping Trudy, so I know he does divorce work."

"You were going to divorce Trudy?"

He waved me off. "Anyway, that's the sign to let me know Muertens got to Schoolkraft."

"Dave Schoolkraft from Horror View?"

"How many Dave Schoolkrafts from Horror View you know? Come on, Tony, don't be dense. I need you with me on this, man."

"Okay, take it easy."

"So here's what we do. You call Schoolkraft on Monday, say you're looking into getting a divorce, that you'd like to know what he charges, what the procedure is, that kind of thing. You're good at deception."

I let the jab slide.

"Anyway, when he gives you the info, tell him you'll think it over. Then come back here in the afternoon. I'll call him and let's see what he says."

"Sounds like a plan."

Leo's laser sharp focus was unnerving. Almost made me think he was sane, ready to go on with his life.

"Don't use your home or cell phone. Lawyers log calls," he said, writing Schoolkraft's number on a pad he'd taken from the orderly's station. "And don't give him your real name. Try something clever like, Benedict Arnold."

23

THINGS WERE STILL FROSTY between Diana and me, and the chill was further exacerbated by her growing irritation with my frequent trips to see "Leo the Louse," as she began calling him. All I needed to add more ice to the *freeze* was to walk in with torn pants and a bloody knee.

While Leo had been too self-absorbed to notice my disheveled appearance, undoubtedly Diana would. So I stopped at a mall, bought a pair of no-name jeans and wore them home.

"I've never seen *those* before," she said, when I tried to slip in past her.

"Spilled coffee this morning, and I had one of the guys pick me up something. Made today casual Friday."

"Good to be the boss, huh?"

I laughed, then hugged her close to me.

She pulled away and said, "By the way—"

Nothing good ever followed that three-word preamble.

"—how's Trudy doing? I haven't heard from her in a while."

The question gave me pause. But Diana's eyes weren't threatening, so I stifled a sigh of relief and said, "She's doing about as well as can be expected, I guess. Bumped into her a few times visiting Leo. That's about it."

I CALLED TRUDY THAT NIGHT, telling her I wouldn't make it out Sunday. Some family function I had to attend.

"Oh," she said, disappointment in her voice. She'd obviously come to rely on our little trysts as much as I had. "Leo say anything to you about running away the other day?"

"Just that you and the kids would be better off without him."

"Well, he got that right."

Sunday was uneventful, but I was anxious just the same. Monday couldn't roll around fast enough for me. Things had slowed down in the office and it was going to be easy to get Leo down to Philly. I *had* to get Leo to Philly.

24

I FOLLOWED LEO'S ADVICE, and left the house early Monday morning to find a payphone. With the advent of cell phones, finding a payphone wasn't a simple task. Because johns and whores needed to maintain their anonymity, I figured the Jetz Motel—a rent-a-room-by-the-hour dive not too far from the County Clerk's office—might have a phone in the lobby. So I headed there to make the call. If Schoolkraft had caller ID, he'd think some poor, pathetic bastard staying at a dive like the Jetz was in desperate need of a lawyer.

There was a "No Soliciting" sign tacked to the wall near the entrance. I got a chuckle out of that. My first laugh in a few days.

Although the Housing Department had started moving homeless families into dumps like the Jetz over the past few months, the prime trade remained low-rent prostitution.

I walked into the small, dimly lit lobby. An overhead light fixture rhythmically flickered off and on, hiding and then revealing the motel's shabbiness. A prostitute lounged across a love seat, tits spilling out of her yellow halter-top. Her white skirt rode up so high on her thighs I swear I could see her snatch playing peek-a-boo in the flickering light—now you see it, now you don't.

A pimply-faced clerk thumbing a video game sat on a high stool behind a counter directly across from the door. A soda machine and condom dispenser was on the opposite wall, next to French doors that led to the action upstairs. The floor was covered with a sticky rug, threadbare from all the traffic. It sounded like I was treading on candy wrappers as I walked over to the clerk. The only other sound was the ticking of a clock behind the counter. What a dump. *The indig-*

nities guys will suffer to get laid.

"Telephone?" I said.

The clerk pointed towards the French doors, then looked up for the first time and quickly added, "Customers only, dude."

"Gotchya." I headed for the phone. Knew the kid didn't have the balls to come after me. Whatever minimum wage was, fucking with me wasn't part of his job description.

I dropped some coins into the phone, dialed the number Leo gave me. After three rings a woman cheerfully answered, "Good morning, Smith and Levine. How may I direct your call?"

I asked for Dave Schoolkraft.

"Who may I say is calling?"

I pulled my name from the Trudy sexcapades. "Arnold," I said.

"Is that your first or last name?"

"Ben Arnold."

"Oh, like that funny guy that used to be married to Roseanne Barr."

No. That was Tom. And no, he wasn't funny.

"One and the same," I said.

"Mr. Arnold, may I ask what this is in reference to?"

I told her I wanted information about getting a divorce. That Dave had been recommended by a mutual friend.

"Hold, please," she said.

Music on hold. An oldies FM station. After hearing Neil Diamond warble, "You Don't Bring Me Flowers," Schoolkraft picked up, and not a second too soon.

"Dave Schoolkraft speaking, Mr. Arnold. How may I help you?"

"Yeah, Mr. Schoolkraft—"

"Please, call me Dave."

"—Dave. I'm thinking about filing for a divorce and would like to get an idea about how much something like that might—"

"My secretary tells me a mutual friend recommended

me," Schoolkraft cut in.

"Not exactly. I had your name and number in my Blackberry. Don't recall who gave it to me, but obviously I was impressed enough to take it. Didn't want to go thumbing through the Yellow Pages. Never know what you'll get that way. This is too important."

A man walked towards me, his face turned to the wall.

"Okay, you're looking at a divorce. Contested or uncontested?"

"Well, I don't know. I haven't clued my wife in yet. Marriage's been on the rocks for a while now and I was thinking it's time to move on, get a new start while I'm still young."

I laughed, trying to draw him in. Just two guys talking.

"What about assets, kids?" Schoolkraft said.

"House, couple of cars, two kids. We've been married fifteen years. I want joint custody. An every-other-weekend arrangement won't fly. Is that enough information for you to give me a ballpark figure? You know, a range between contested and uncontested?"

"Well, let's see. I charge three-fifty an hour. Four hundred if we have to go to court."

"Whew!" I wound the telephone cord around my index finger.

"The best thing, Mr. Arnold, is to work out an amicable agreement with your spouse. That's the least-costly and best option."

"I don't know if that's possible. She's been busting my chops for—"

I was suddenly overwhelmed by the smell of cheap perfume. The whore I'd seen lounging in the lobby, slinked up alongside me and said, "Hey, baby. You don't have to call nobody for no date. I got everything you need right here, sugar." She cupped her ass in both hands, then reached out and grabbed for my crotch.

"What the hell?" I dropped the phone and shoved her away.

"What's going on?" I could hear Schoolkraft shout from the dangling receiver.

"Fuckin' homo," the whore yelled, then flipped me a double bird.

I picked up the swinging phone, and said, "Sorry 'bout that, Dave."

"Where the hell *are* you, Mr. Arnold?"

"It's okay. You were saying?"

"Sky's the limit if it's contested."

"Damn, maybe it's cheaper to keep her. You've given me a whole lot to think about. Thanks for your time, Dave."

"No problem, Mr. Arnold. Did my secretary get your contact information?"

"She did, and again, thanks for your time. I'll get back to you."

Phase one completed. Had to wait a few hours before I could get back with Leo and bring him up to date.

There was a tea and java shop up the street. A stomach ulcer had killed my coffee drinking days a few years back, but with the stress I was feeling I definitely needed a nice cup of strong black coffee to take off the edge. There was something about the ritual of holding a hot paper cup, sipping the dark liquid while trying not to burn your lips that I found relaxing.

But I didn't need an additional problem now, so I settled for tea.

I tried working through an alternate plan, but finally came to the conclusion that I had to take Leo to Philly. With him out of the way, I just might be able to cut off the disturbing tentacles Leo's mysterious Mr. Muertens had attached to me. He obviously was monitoring my movements. But why? I couldn't put my finger on it, but something didn't feel right. Paranoia was creeping in big time.

I finished the drink, then stopped at an ATM and withdrew five-hundred dollars. I didn't know when Pilgrim was going to release Leo, but when they did I wanted to be ready. And if I was lucky, Leo could be a long way from New York

by Tuesday evening.
 Out of my life, taking his troubles with him.

25

I STOOD OUTSIDE THE WARD waiting for visiting hours to begin. A handful of people were already milling around. I couldn't help but wonder what they were dealing with. Once the doors were unlocked, I headed directly for the day room. Leo strolled in a few minutes later, looking very much like a man about to take flight.

"You do it?" he asked.

"Yeah."

"Don't keep me in suspense. How'd it go?"

Leo pulled up a chair, turned it backwards and sat down, resting his forearms across the back.

"Schoolkraft handles divorces," I said.

"Now that's what I'm talking about. Okay, let's call the prick. I'm telling you, he's going to change his story the second he hears it's me calling. Just watch."

Leo sprang off the chair and we headed for the only payphone available to the inmates. A guy already had the receiver screwed to his ear, and another patient, wearing a tattered white bathrobe held together with a piece of string, stood a few feet behind him. Both of them had the pallid, far-away look of residents who'd been inside for a while.

"So, when are they letting you out?" I asked.

"Tomorrow."

"That's good, but you'll tell Trudy you're getting out any day except tomorrow, okay? That way you get a few days' head start before she's the wiser."

"Why don't you just tell her the next time you're out at my house screwing her brains out in my bed."

"I don't screw her during the week. Only on Sundays. And by then, it would be too late."

Leo tensed, his face lit up like a jack-o-lantern. Looked as if he might do something stupid, like take a swing at me.

"Listen, Leo. You accuse me of something like that, what do you expect me to say? I told you nothing's going on between me and Trudy. Come on, we're about to embark on a great adventure. Let's not start it off on the wrong foot."

"Fuck you."

"Is that any way to talk to the guy who's going to drive you off to a brand-spanking-new life?"

I swatted him on the shoulder, but he shrugged me off, still giving me attitude. So I said, "Hey, you're the one got us mixed up in this jackpot," a little too loudly, prompting Bathrobe and the guy on the telephone to turn around. Bathrobe even asked us to keep it down.

Finally, the guy hung up and Bathrobe got on the phone. We leaned against the wall a few feet behind him, anxious to play the thing out with Schoolkraft. I could just make out bits and pieces of what he was saying, which was a whole lot of nothing.

"But I don't belong in here," he whimpered.

He went on like that for a few more minutes, agitating Leo, who started banging out a steady beat on the wall with his fist.

"Hey, pal, can you hurry it up?" Leo said.

When he kept on yapping, Leo said, "Can't you see the fucking sign? Says limit calls to ten minutes. You've been running your mouth at least fifteen."

Bathrobe turned around and shook his middle finger in Leo's face. "Back off!" he said.

Leo's impatience boiled over. He took a step forward, yanked the phone away from Bathrobe and hissed, "Say goodbye, asshole," then slammed the phone back in the cradle.

Surprised, Bathrobe blurted out, "What the—?"

"What the *what*, motherfucker?" Leo growled.

I restrained Leo as Bathrobe backed away, then hurried off towards the day room, undoubtedly to fetch an orderly.

"Take it easy, Leo," I said, handing him the phone. "Let's do this."

He deposited some coins, and dialed Schoolkraft, holding the receiver between us so I could hear both sides of the conversation.

"Good morning, Smith and Levine." It was the same secretary I'd spoken with earlier. "How may I direct your call?"

Leo asked for Schoolkraft.

"Who may I say is calling?"

"Leo Radigan. I'm a client."

"May I ask what matter this is in reference to, Mr. Radigan?"

"It's personal."

Music on hold. The same oldies station. This time it was a Motown song. I knew it, but the name and the artist escaped me. *Double Jeopardy. Oldies but goodies for a thousand, Alex.* The stress of our little plan to verify Leo's code-theory was definitely starting to get to me.

From behind us someone said, "Whaddaya you guys doing?"

Leo and I were so intent on getting to Schoolkraft we hadn't noticed that another patient had joined the line. I'd seen the guy around before, always squeezing a dirty yellow tennis ball, and mumbling match scores to an invisible crowd.

"What does it look like we're doing?" Leo said.

"I don't know, that's why I asked," Tennis Nut said, then got back in his imaginary judge's chair and announced, "Game, set, match, Miss Sharapova."

I smiled and applauded. Even this head case liked hot Russian babes.

Schoolkraft's secretary cut off the music, triggering my memory. The song was Mary Wells' early 60s hit, "What's Easy For Two Is Hard For One." Hopefully, a harbinger of Leo and me cleaning up this Muertens mess.

The secretary came back on the line and said, "I'm sorry, Mr. Radigan, Mr. Schoolkraft's busy with another client right now, but he wanted me to tell you that he'll handle your divorce, and to please inform your friend, Mr. Benson, that he should weigh all of his options very carefully before he makes any decisions. Have a nice day," she said cheerfully, then hung up.

"Fuck!" Leo jammed the telephone back into the cradle.

I grabbed his arm before he could do any real damage.

This is not a test, this is an actual emergency.

"How did Schoolkraft tie me in with you?" I said.

"You guys done?" Tennis Nut said.

"Yeah, we're done," I said, but Leo told him to fuck off then slapped the ball out of the guy's hands, sending it bouncing down the hall.

"Hey—" Tennis Nut said, but Leo's murderous expression sent him running after the ball.

In pugilistic parlance, Schoolkraft had just delivered a perfect one-two combination to Leo's crazy code theory and my anonymity.

"That fucker just threatened me," Leo said. "What kinda game?"

"Take it easy," I said, trying to make light of a screwed-up situation. "The shyster's just toying with us. We'll figure it out on the way to Philly."

"You told him who you were?"

"No. I used an alias, like you said."

"Then how'd he know." Leo paused, shook his head, then said, "You're fucked, Tony."

I saw Bathrobe dragging an orderly towards us, and by his determined gait, he was looking to jam us up. I pulled Leo into a room further down the hall, and said. "What time are they releasing you tomorrow morning?"

"Ten."

"Okay, here's what we're going to do. Have all your stuff ready. I'll get here a little before ten to pick you up." I handed him one of my business cards. "Call my cell if there's a snag on your end. Then we'll head straight for Philly. Remember, tell Trudy there're releasing you next week sometime, but you're not sure when. She'll be pissed, but what the hell, you're running for your life. We straight?"

"Yeah," Leo said, still jittery.

"Don't I know you?" The same idiot who'd accosted me before was standing in the doorway. He smelled like wet newspapers.

"Like I told you last time, I don't know you," I said. "Now, please, we're talking here."

Suddenly he lunged, bowled me over a chair, and we went sprawling onto the floor. I was pinned beneath him, yet managed to grab him in a headlock, and tried my damnedest to wrench his head off.

"Get him off me," I yelled to Leo, just as three orderlies came to my rescue. Nonetheless it took all of them to pull the guy off me; one orderly on each arm, the other holding him around his ample gut, all the while, the freak straining to free himself from their grasp.

"That's him," Bathrobe yelled, jumping up and down and pointing at me.

"You're going to have to leave, sir," scowled the orderly who appeared to be the supervisor.

"Remember the plan, Leo," I yelled over my shoulder as he forced me towards the exit doors.

"TRIP OVER YOUR gym bag again?"

Diana greeted me in her usual bitchy fashion when I dropped into my easy chair later on that day.

"What?"

"You've got blood on your cheek."

"Oh. Went out to see Leo, and this," I said, touching my lip, "is compliments of a frisky patient."

Diana handed me a tissue, and I dabbed at my face.

"You okay?" Diana said, more sympathetic now.

I nodded.

"You've been seeing that louse quite a bit, lately."

"Can't you cut him some slack? He's having a hard time dealing with this divorce thing."

"What'd he expect? Lousy piece of crap."

That was about as close as Diana ever came to cursing, although I imagine she had a few choice words to say about me to her girlfriends after our little *sex therapy* session. Afterwards, I'd tried to make amends by reassuring her that children weren't an issue for me, and I didn't resent her because she didn't want to have any; that if anything, it was all my fault, and I'd try my damnedest to be a better husband. I followed up with a dozen red roses, and that seemed to settle things down between us—for the moment. But if Diana ever found out about Trudy, I couldn't muster up enough flowery prose, or give her enough roses to save our marriage.

26

THE NEXT MORNING I arrived at the hospital a few minutes before ten. Security must have had my name on some kind of terrorist watch list, because the officer on duty wouldn't let me up to the ward. So I hung outside near the entrance, waiting for Leo to show.

He came strolling out a half-hour later, threw an overnight bag onto the back seat, and climbed into the car. He was dressed in black. Looked thin, his face drawn. I hadn't noticed his frail appearance before.

"That all you got?" I said.

"Yep, the sum total of my miserable life."

After he slammed the door shut—I guessed to punctuate his assessment of his sorry state of affairs—I handed him the five-hundred bucks with the throwaway line, "This ought to help you get started with your new life."

He took the money, folded the bills and slipped the wad into his pocket, not acknowledging my charity.

"Didn't your mama teach you how to say, *thank you*?" I said.

"Thanks," he said, with little gratitude.

Yeah, I was going to be one very happy camper after I'd dropped Leo off the face of my life.

"Why'd Muertens kill Eddie?" I said.

"Eddie's dead?"

"Yeah, and you said Muertens did it."

"Not me. Eddie was into some real shady shit. He was the go-to guy for a lot of the juicers, and I heard he was cooking meth on the side. You meet some pretty nasty characters in that business."

"Did you know Eddie stole some of the money the guys

collected for Trudy?"

"Don't know nothing about that."

"You said Eddie was in Muertens' pocket, so maybe it was payback?"

"Like I said, don't know nothing about that."

Then I told Leo my six-degrees-of-separation theory—how all roads seemed to lead to Muertens.

"Maybe Eddie stole from the wrong guys this time," Leo said.

I programmed the car's GPS for the 30th Street Station in Philadelphia.

The city is only about a hundred miles down the Jersey Turnpike from New York, and depending on the traffic, it could take as few as a couple of hours, or an eternity. Fortunately, it was relatively easy getting across Midtown Manhattan to the Lincoln Tunnel, normally the slowest part of the trip. Even so, it seemed to take longer, because there wasn't a whole lot of chit-chat going on between Leo and me.

"What're you going to do after you get to Philly?" I said.

"Can't tell you in case . . . you know, in case you get compromised."

"Compromised? You think Muertens'll come after me and my family?"

"I don't know."

"You said you didn't talk to Muertens about me. Was that bullshit?"

"I didn't, but he knows who you are. Remember what I told you about being followed?"

"I swear I'll hunt you down myself if anything happens to Diana."

"It's not Diana you should be worrying about."

"What's that supposed to mean?"

"Be careful, that's all. I started out exactly where you are right now."

"I didn't steal anything."

We emerged from the Lincoln Tunnel, and entered New Jersey.

I said, "Aren't you going to miss Trudy and the kids?"

He didn't answer right away, just stared back at the New York City skyline. Finally, he said, "The kids, yeah, it's going to be tough. On them, too, growing up without a father. But they're young, they'll adjust. Trudy? I don't give a shit about that bitch."

He turned and looked at me, hard. I returned the stare, matching him steely-eye for steely-eye, until a truck's blaring horn brought my attention back to the road.

"Okay, how do I get in touch with you if, God forbid, something happens to the kids?"

He laughed, then said, "If I tell you, I'll have to kill you."

After another long interval of silence, I tuned in the car's satellite radio to the classical station. A couple of Mahler's hour-long symphonies and we'd be in Philadelphia. Leo didn't have to say another word, and that was fine by me.

We stopped and ate at a rest stop along the Jersey Turnpike about halfway between New York and Philly, Leo ordering for both of us out of the money I gave him. We were a forlorn pair—one hopeful that a new life awaited him somewhere west of Philadelphia, the other soon to be returning home to an uncertain future.

Leo insisted we sit by the windows, so he could keep an eye out for bad guys. Happy to be almost rid of him, I didn't bother to mock his paranoia.

Leo stopped chewing on a French fry long enough to say, "Lookit, Tony, tell me. You fuck her?"

He cocked his head, waiting for my answer.

"Why do you keep tripping on this? If I've told you once, I've told you a thousand times. No! I wouldn't do something like that to a friend, not even a crazy one like you. Muertens just fed you a line of shit, trying to get into your head and make you more paranoid than you already are, and looks like he succeeded, big time."

"Will you just answer the fucking question, and stop jerking me around."

"Nobody's screwing anybody. You're giving me a

migraine."

He wasn't satisfied with my answer, so I said, "If I tell you I did, will you leave me alone with this?"

"Yeah."

"She's the best lay I ever had. Satisfied?"

"I knew it, you cocksucker."

He stood and came around the table, ready to take a swing at me.

"You better chill out real quick, Leo, if you want to get to Philly. I'll leave your sorry ass right here if you don't sit back down."

He thought about it a second, then dropped back into the seat.

"Look at yourself," I said. "Getting all worked up over nothing. I told you we didn't do anything. I just can't win with you. Damned if I did, damned if I didn't. If I knew I was going to get all this grief for something I *didn't* do, I should've done it. Theoretically, of course."

"She'd never touch you," Leo said, chastised as if he were a child.

"There, you just said it. Now are we finished with this melodrama?"

"Yeah."

"Good. Philly here we come."

WHEN WE APPROACHED the exit for Six Flags, I pointed to the sign and said, "Remember the time when you, me, and the girls were here? What was it, ten years ago? Boy that was a whole lot of fun. Whatever happened to those days?"

"That was before the kids."

"What, you just get tired?"

"I don't know. Everything changed. It sorta sneaked up on me. One day I woke up and couldn't stand where I was. When those motherly instincts kick in, you go from being king of the hill to an afterthought real quick. Don't get me wrong, I love those kids, but—"

"Remember how you chickened out on the Batman ride?"

"I don't need to be walking down memory lane, okay, Tony? Not now."

I let Leo sulk about losing his king-of-the-hill perch during the mournful First Movement of Mahler's Fifth Symphony. I wondered if it would have come to that for me if Diana and I had started a family.

Leo leaned his head against the window and said, "When I was a kid, my friend Woody had a dog named Pete. Mangy black-and-white mutt, a milky white eye, a snout like fucking Porky Pig. I think Pete was a rescue. Woody told me Pete had been abused, and he needed a lot a love, and damn, Woody sure gave that dog a whole lot a love. There was hardly a time when you'd see one without the other. We used to kid Woody a lot. 'Where's your little girlfriend?' we'd say, stuff like that. But he wouldn't pay us no mind, because he knew Pete was a better friend than any of us had. I remember when Pete died; you would've thought Woody'd lost his parents in a car crash or something. That's how hard he took it."

I watched a state trooper pull over a red Corvette on the northbound side of the Turnpike.

After a long pause, Leo said, "I just wish I loved someone as much as Woody loved that dog. Who knows, things might've been different between me and Trudy. I guess I was always looking for something else in my life. What that was, I don't know, but I looked for it all the same."

Then Leo lapsed back into a long mournful silence.

Mahler's contrapuntally-active Third Movement seemed to perk him up. "Maybe I'll start a new family," he said. "Get it right this time."

"They call that bigamy," I said, jokingly.

There were no new revelations during the rest of the drive. We crossed the Ben Franklin Bridge and drove into downtown Philly. I dropped Leo off in front of the train station and wished him good luck. We shook hands, then he drew me into a hug, clutching me tight around the shoulders. Without a doubt, he was a drowning man trying to keep his head above water. But I couldn't throw him the life line he needed.

"You sign the divorce papers?" I said, not knowing when to leave well enough alone.

"Yeah. How'd you know about that?"

"It's not exactly top secret."

"With me gone, that kinda clears the field for you, huh?"

I didn't respond. What was the point? The field was already wide open, and I wasn't going to be seeing him again.

Leo sighed, then said, "Sorry, man—about everything. You've been a real good friend."

"I hope you find whatever it is you're looking for."

"You won't tell Trudy, will you?" He closed the door, then stuck his head inside the window.

"No." *Hell, no.*

"You know the bitch's in on it, too."

"What time's your train leave?"

"The first train outta here, points unknown."

"Nothing like a well thought-out plan."

I was a speed hump that didn't slow him down.

"You think it was her bright idea to dump me? What kind of woman does that to a husband locked up in a fucking mental hospital? I hate to say this, partner, but you're in for a bumpy ride."

I just shrugged, closed the passenger window, and then pulled away from the curb before Leo implicated the Pope in his conspiracy.

Bye, Leo. Here's hoping I never see you again.

27

AS I WATCHED LEO DISAPPEAR inside the terminal through the rearview mirror, the tension that had morphed into a raging migraine on the ride down began to melt away. I plugged in my MP3 player, set it to random mix, and headed for home. I sang along with the music, improvising my own lyrics over the melodies.

My troubles were over. Fuck Muertens. Fuck that clown Schoolkraft. Anxiety drained away with each passing mile. I wanted the good Tony back. The one that saw a friend in trouble and tried to help him out—not the sleazebag I'd become. Oh yeah.

On the approach ramp to the Lincoln Tunnel exit, I received a text message from Leo: *thanx for ur help. = now. c after the kids. c u on the other side. leo.*

What the hell did "c u on the other side" mean? See you on the other side of what? Was everybody speaking in codes? Codes. Leo said that's how he knew Muertens had gotten to someone.

I started to respond to the message when it dawned on me that Leo and I had never exchanged text messages before. So, where'd this message come from? I could feel the blood start pounding at my temples. The mellow mood I'd been in vanished.

I exited the Turnpike at 16E to 495E, and spiraled down the helix towards the Lincoln Tunnel. Watched the city's steel-and-glass skyline rise up in front of me, then passed through the toll and into the mouth of the tunnel. Twelve bucks to get into New York City, nothing to get out.

Give me your tired, your poor, your huddled masses my ass. They couldn't afford it.

Beneath the middle of the Hudson River, I passed a marker on the mile-and-a-half-long tunnel's wall, indicating I'd crossed from New Jersey into New York.

My cell phone rang. Ma calling. The Port Authority of New York and New Jersey, the bi-state organization that managed the Hudson River crossings, had installed an antenna so busy suburbanites wouldn't miss the call to stop and pick up a loaf of bread on the way home.

"Anything going on?" I said.

"Just the usual, but that Detective Riley dropped by looking for you."

"He say what he wanted?"

"No, just that he'd try you again later. I gave him your cell."

"I didn't get a call. Anyway, I'm heading home now."

"Did you have a productive day, Tony?"

"Extremely. See you in the morning, Ma."

28

LEO'S OLD GIRLFRIEND, DEMI SHADOW, a/k/a Irena, had told me back when we met that Leo was dead. Of course I'd assumed she was speaking metaphorically. But, why'd she look me up and drop a cryptic "shit happens" advisory? Just another mystery in the saga that was Leo.

Shadow worked at the Pink Pussycat, and since Diana was hanging out with a friend, I decided to drive out there in the hope of finding Irena, her alter ego, hanging from a pole, and ask her just that question.

I hadn't been to the Pussycat in quite a while. Even then, only a few times with Leo. Found the whole scene boring. Titillation only takes you so far. A copy of *Playboy* could fit the bill just as well, and it's a whole lot cheaper. At some point, the rubber had to meet the road.

The Pussycat was in a converted warehouse, tucked away in an industrial park wasteland tight up against the Long Island Railroad tracks, near the Westbury train station. Most of the other buildings in the complex were abandoned.

Even though it was early, the parking lot was filled with a hodgepodge of SUVs, pickup trucks, the occasional luxury car. Eschewing valet service, I drove around the lot until I found a spot.

Attractive young couples and businessmen wearing Polo Ralph Lauren were lounging at the bar and around the stage. The notion that only dirty old men and perverts frequented strip clubs was definitely outdated. Not a single nerdy, bulging-eyed weenie-wagger in sight. Still, calling the Pussycat a gentleman's club was a stretch.

Three brass poles were featured prominently at the front

of the large open area. Dancers, nude except for high, spiky heels, caressed their poles as if they were long-lost lovers. A floor-to-ceiling mirror covered the wall behind the women, reflecting an endless kaleidoscope of tits and ass off the mirrored-wall facing it.

Irena was wrapped around the center pole. A group of young business types sat at a table in front of her, shouting enthusiastically, all of them fanning folded greenbacks, in search of an orifice to make their deposits.

I took a table next to the dressing room and ordered a five-dollar club soda from a scantily-clad hostess. A man the size of a side-by-side refrigerator stood nearby, his presence discouraging anyone from trying to sneak a peek inside.

Loud techno music pounded from huge wall-mounted speakers. The pungent smell of cigars seeped into the room from the smoking lounge, leaving a grayish-yellow haze around the dancers.

Demi dismounted her pole, dropped into a full split, then sprang to her feet, and shimmied towards the suits, fondling her breasts and thrusting her smartly-coiffed crotch in their faces. The suits shouted their appreciation.

"You wanna dance, honey?"

A buxom, bleached-blonde in a frilly yellow-and-white, two-piece costume straddled the table's other chair, leaned forward and rested her tits on my table. "Buy a working gal a drink?" She was probably in her early twenties yet was showing mileage, especially around her sunken eyes.

"I'd love to, but I'm waiting for Irena."

"We've got a few around here, so which one you looking for, Hon?" Before I could answer, she said, "No matter, I can be whichever one you want me to be."

I pointed to Demi and said, "How about that one?"

"Join the line, pal." All the sweetness was gone. She got off the chair and moved on to the next table.

I ordered another club soda, and nursed it until Irena finished her routine. The suits immediately pounced on her. After she'd finished lap dances with three of them, I got her attention and she walked over to the table.

"Do you mind covering up?" I said, playing the prude.

"I'm sure there's nothing here you haven't seen before, but I'll bet not quite the same quality." She giggled like a shy school girl.

"Or, quantity," I kidded.

But I had to agree with her. She was the perfect embodiment of a healthy male's wet dream. Firm breasts, full round hips, a signature apple bottom.

"What did you mean when you told me Leo was dead?" I asked.

"As much as I'd love to just sit around and chat, I'm on the clock, and the man upstairs wouldn't like that."

I wasn't confused by her reference. I was sure the man upstairs wore a big fat pinky ring and smoked a long black cigar. One nod from him and the three bouncers walking the floor, would pounce on me in a heartbeat.

"What's the going rate these days?" I said.

"Standard's a hundred bucks, plus a generous tip, of course.

"I just want to talk."

"Sure you do, but it doesn't matter. It's all the same to me."

"How much conversation can I get?"

"You can talk all you want. Or you can just sit back and relax and let me do all the work."

"Just talk," I said, then rested my hand on her leg.

"No touching the merchandise. House rules."

I dug the money out of my wallet and handed it to her. With no place to put it, she clutched it tight in her right hand, then sat side-saddle on my lap and threw her arms around my shoulders. I could feel myself becoming aroused against her hard body as she began rotating her hips in a slow circular grind.

"Comfy?" she said.

Before I could begin to throw questions at Irena, I heard, "Boss, that you? What're you doing here?"

Shit. It was Ted Barr, the annoying junior attorney from the office, doing what he did best—annoy.

Irena cut short her dialogue with my dick.

I said, "Studying flora and fauna. How 'bout you, Ted? I thought you were gay."

"You kidding? Not me," then to Irena, "Tony's always joking around like that. I'm hanging out with some of my old law school buddies." He pointed the beer bottle he held towards the suits' table. "Guys night out."

I introduced Ted to Irena, then said, "But I assume you already know her."

"Oh, yeah," Irena cut in. "I've seen this one around a lot."

That wasn't what Ted wanted to hear.

"See you in the morning," Ted said like we were best of pals, spilling beer as he blended into the crowd.

I didn't like bumping into Ted. He had a big mouth. I figured by tomorrow morning's coffee break, just about everyone in Telecom Structures four domestic and five international offices would know I'd been in a strip joint getting a lap dance. And knowing Ted, he'd somehow try to use it against me.

"That guy's a rodent," Irena said.

"Yeah, he works for me and he wants my job."

I watched Ted rejoin his law school buddies. They all swiveled around towards me and laughed. I could only imagine what the little prick was telling them.

"Did him once," Irena said. "Like sitting on a pebble."

We both laughed, then she started up her slow grind again, flexing and relaxing her butt cheeks, teasing me.

"So, why'd you tell me Leo was dead?" I said.

"I liked Leo. He was funny, down to earth, not on the make like Ted and his buddies. We never did anything by the way. Don't look so skeptical."

"I'm not in the judging business."

"Whatever. Leo told me about his boss wanting to kill him. It all sounded crazy to me, secret codes, sneaking around. But it wasn't about what I thought. It was what Leo believed, and he believed you were spying on him."

"You're shitting me?"

It had never entered my mind that Leo would cast me as a villain in his paranoid fantasy.

"You were the only friend who stood by him. He wondered why, and wanted me to take a look at you. Leo's a good guy, so I did. I figured I'd come at you weird and see how you'd react."

"And?"

"I told Leo I thought you were okay."

"I drove him to Philadelphia this morning."

"He's gone?"

One of the bouncers glared at us, and twirled his hand above his head, as if he was going to lasso Irena. Time to wrap it up.

THAT NIGHT I TOOK DIANA to one of the local restaurants for dinner.

"You seem like your old self tonight," she said. "What's been going on?"

"Just crazy at work, but it's all good now."

Although I had high hopes of breaking my romantic drought with her, I couldn't take my mind off Leo, and the cryptic "c u on the other side" text message.

Was he really going to kill himself this time?

29

THE NEXT MORNING as I walked through the office lobby, heading for the elevators, someone called out, "Hey, Mr. Benson? Howya doing?"

Detective Riley grabbed my hand and shook it vigorously. I had to match his grip pressure to keep my hand from being crushed.

"Your secretary said you'd be back mid-afternoon yesterday. Guess you changed your plans. Mind if I tag along?"

"Ah, no. What's up, Detective?"

Riley fell in step alongside me. He was as stylishly dressed as a few days earlier. A Rolex dangled from his wrist, and it didn't look like a knockoff. He had to be the best dressed cop not on television.

"We talked to your girlfriend—"

"I told you, Detective, Ms. Radigan and I are just good friends. I'm married."

I said it like being married precluded me from having a girlfriend on the side.

"And for your sake, I'd like to keep it that way," Riley said. "Anyway, Trudy verified your story, and we have no reason to believe she was lying. But my partner? He's still wet behind the ears. Real idealistic. Little things, you know, like a guy screwing around on his old lady, bother the shit outta him."

Protesting my innocence would solve nothing. Riley was clearly enjoying my discomfort.

"He'll learn, though," Riley continued, "But for now . . . well, he wants to talk to your wife, Diana, is it? Put a cap on this puppy. Close the book on you. Me, personally? I don't see how talking to your wife'll add anything relevant to our investigation. How 'bout you, Mr. Benson? You think talking to your wife will add anything relevant to our investigation?"

I got to the elevator bank, Riley at my shoulder, and pressed the up button.

"Uh, no, Detective."

"I hear Vegas is really nice this time of year. Then again, I'll bet it's nice all year 'round. You and your wife, you ever been, Mr. Benson?"

I offered a noncommittal nod in reply.

"Can you believe me and my wife, we never been, either?" Riley said. "I'm just talking, but I bet you can have a real good time out there for a couple a grand. Cash, of course. Man, I can see it now—nice penthouse suite, a little gambling, catching one of those big-name stage shows, maybe Wayne Newton."

Riley had me going and he knew it.

"Yeah, friend a mine went out there last month, had a ball," Riley said. "Tells me you can get whatever you want, twenty-four-seven. Hell, even pussy's legal if you're so inclined. What's the world coming to?"

The elevator arrived with a ding. Once the passengers got out, I stepped inside and pressed the button for the tenth floor. Riley kept the doors open with one of his tasseled loafers. "Stiles and I'll drop by and see your wife sometime tomorrow morning. She's a teacher in Kew Gardens, right?"

"That won't be necessary, Detective."

"And why's that, Mr. Benson?"

"I hear Vegas is pretty nice this time of year, too."

The elevator shook when the closing doors hit Riley's shoe, and bounced opened again.

"Good. We'll meet up later at let's say, six, at the Fog, and we'll take care of those travel arrangements."

"How do I know you or Stiles still won't talk to my wife, or maybe you'll get the urge to take another exotic trip?"

Riley laughed, then said, "Gotta have a little faith, Tony. Trust me, I'm a cop."

He was still laughing as the elevator headed to the tenth floor.

YOU DISPOSE OF ONE PROBLEM in Philly, thinking you're free and clear, then get shackled with an even bigger one. I couldn't fully define my feelings about Trudy, but I sure as hell didn't want to lose Diana. If she was going to split, it would be on my terms—not because of an asshole like Riley.

Telecom Structures owed me about $1,600 in expense money. Accounting would cut me a check, and I'd draw the rest from an ATM without Diana being the wiser.

I buzzed Ma and asked her to come into my office. As soon as she sat down, I said, "I've got a problem, Ma," then proceeded to tell her about my transgression.

After I'd finished my tale of woe, she didn't bother to disguise her contempt. "*Transgression*? Is that what they're calling it these days?"

"Hey, I get it. I screwed up big time."

"Who is she?"

"It's not important."

"Does this *other woman* mean anything to you?"

"I don't know. I have strong feelings for her and Diana."

"Come on, Tony, give me a break."

Knowing I'd lost a little of Ma's respect, I found it difficult to look her in the eye. Massaging my temples, I said, "There's more. This other woman, she was my alibi for the night Eddie Hambrick was killed, and that cop Riley, the smooth-dressing older detective? Well, he's shaking me down, threatening to tell Diana about her if I don't send him to Vegas. I wouldn't be looking to pay off the bastard if I didn't care about Diana."

"Or you just don't want to face the problem head on."

"Thanks, Ma."

"If my husband cheated on me, I'd cut off his pee-pee."

"*Pee-pee*? Is that what they're calling it these days?"

Ma smiled, dialing back a little of the tension.

"Why don't you just report him?" Ma said.

"Because Diana would find out about the other woman and that would be that. I told you I want to save my marriage."

Ma shook her head. "So stop screwing around."

"It's not that simple."

"Then you'll get what's coming to you," Ma said. I could always count on her to cut through the bullshit. "Why are you telling me all of this, anyway?"

"I want you to take a picture of me handing over the payoff."

"What good will that do?"

"I need something on him, just in case he comes back to take another bite outta my ass. You're the only one I can trust to do it."

Ma rubbed her chin. "Gee, lucky me."

"I'm meeting him tonight. We'll get there early and set you up."

"Uh, he knows who I am," Ma said. "He'll figure something's up, especially when he sees me pointing a camera at him."

"I'll take a table where you can see me give Riley the cash, but he won't see you. Just point, click, then leave."

I handed her the digital camera I used for site surveys, showed her how to use it, then said, "See? Nothing to it."

She still looked skeptical.

"Don't forget to take the lens cap off."

"I don't know, Tony. What if he sees me?"

"He won't. But if he does, you're just out having dinner at your favorite diner. No harm in that. My treat by the way."

"The last thing I need is to get on the bad side of a crooked cop."

30

MA, DRIVING HER GRAY HONDA CR-V, turned into the Fog's parking lot and pulled up next to me. She seemed to shrink behind the steering wheel when she saw me. I waved for her to follow me inside. It was five-thirty.

"You got the camera?" I said.

She nodded, and then showed it to me.

"Okay, let's do it," I said.

We walked into the Fog and waited while the hostess led another couple to a table.

"It's going to be okay," I said. "He won't even know you're there."

The camera shook in her hands, and I wondered if she would be able to take a photo I could use.

Once the hostess returned, I said, "I'm expecting a friend, so there'll be two of us."

"Your friend's already here," she said.

"What?"

"Detective Riley. He told me to bring you over. Please follow me."

Ma let out a yelp, handed me the camera and ran out the door. I had a strong urge to follow her, but I put the camera in my pocket, fell in step behind the hostess.

Riley was sitting by the window, his arms spread across the back of the booth. He had a panoramic view of the parking lot, and he'd seen Ma and me the second we arrived. I'd been outfoxed.

"Gimme that fucking camera," Riley hissed, holding his hand out, all of the smooth sophistication gone.

I handed over the camera, and Riley smashed it on the

table, removed the flash card, then tossed the camera back to me. Looking around to see if anyone was watching, he said, "Open your shirt and empty your pockets. Turn 'em inside out."

Again, I complied—pulled out the thick roll of bills, and handed it to Riley. I'd gotten mostly small denomination bills, so the payoff would look a whole lot larger than it actually was, thinking it'd be the better for the photograph. But there would be no photograph because the camera lens was broken, Riley was holding the flash card, and my photographer was speeding out of the parking lot.

"Now sit your ass down," Riley said. He patted the space next to him. After I'd settled in, he ran his hands over my clothing. "You trying to get me on tape, too, asshole?"

"No, Detective."

A waitress came over to take our order, but Riley waved her away.

"Who the hell you think you're fucking with? Some wet-nosed rookie just out of the academy? This little stunt's going to cost you double, asshole. As a matter of fact, let's round it up to an even five grand."

"I don't have that kind of money."

"That's your fucking problem. You'd better be here tomorrow, same time, with cash. And no games or you'd better start looking for a real good divorce lawyer. Oh yeah, and tell that old bitch that was with you to keep her yap shut, or else. Now get the hell outta here before I start taking this personally."

WHERE WAS I going to get another three thousand dollars without alarms going off all over my world? I had no choice but to tell Diana about Trudy and face the consequences. At least give our marriage a fighting chance to survive, even though I had a pretty good idea of how it was going to end—with me finding a good attorney.

I checked the office to find out if Ma had called in, to see if she was okay.

Ted Barr covered the phones after hours, primarily for our West Coast clients, and he told me he'd talked to Ma about fifteen minutes before I called.

"Said she had an emergency and wouldn't be in the office for a while," Ted said.

"She say anything else?"

"No, that was it, but she sounded pretty frazzled."

I'll bet she did. Sorry, Ma.

"Oh, she left the name of a temp to cover for her until she got back. Said you'd used him before."

"Why don't you call and make the arrangements for me, okay, Ted?"

"No problem, Tony. Been back out to the Pussycat?"

"Bye, Ted."

I tried Ma's cell phone and got her outgoing message. I asked her to call me. Next I tried her at home. Her husband, Bill, answered, presumably with his pee-pee still attached.

"Jill told me what you did," Bill said, "and you'd better cover for her if you don't want any more trouble."

"She say that?"

"No, I'm saying it."

He hung up before I could respond.

31

WHEN I GOT HOME, Diana and Janet were sitting at the kitchen table, having tea. They must have been celebrating a special occasion, because Diana was using her grandmother's antique china, set on the bamboo placemats we'd bought on a trip to the Far East.

Diana greeted me with a big hug, and said, "Janet's getting married."

She released me, started clapping her hands and bouncing around on her toes.

Janet held out her left hand, fingers spread, showing off a large engagement ring. "It's platinum with twenty diamonds, almost half a carat."

"Congratulations. Who's the lucky guy?"

"My old high school crush. We met up again at our fifteenth reunion and we just hit it off. I've been out to California a few times since, and he's here, now. He popped the question last night and of course I said, yes."

Janet let out what sounded like an Indian war cry, then squeezed out a little-girl's giggle. "He's a lawyer, you know. Just like you, Tony."

Big fucking whoop.

"Janet's going to move back to California when the school year's over," Diana said. "I'm really going to miss her terribly."

Diana and Janet hugged each other, their moistening eyes glistening in the harsh kitchen light.

"By the end of the summer I'll be Mrs. Janet Smith-Tiller."

"Boy, that was really fast," I said.

"You know when you know," Janet said.

"Tony, come on and join us. Have some tea."

"Tea? This calls for a bottle of the bubbly. There's champagne in the fridge."

I went into the kitchen and found the bottle behind the club soda. I'd been saving it for a special occasion, and Janet's pending nuptials would likely be the last happy event I'd be a party to in the foreseeable future. I handed each of them a slender flute, and took a crystal-cut tumbler for myself.

"We haven't used these glasses since we got married," Diana said.

I poured the sparkling wine for them, sparkling water for me, and Diana proposed a toast. "Janet, I hope you'll be as happy as Tony and I've been."

Whew! Telling her about Trudy just got a whole lot harder.

We clinked glasses, ringing out a joyful, happy sound. After we'd drained our glasses, we shared a group hug. I wished Janet luck, while Diana laughed at the silliness of it all.

But every relationship begins that way, or should. Yet, somewhere along the line it all goes awry—at least fifty-percent of the time.

I couldn't tell Diana about Trudy. Not then. Not ever. I didn't have the guts to get out in front of the affair, for fear it would steamroll me. Maybe I'd wake up in the morning, and realize all of it—the affair with Trudy, Riley's blackmail—was all just a bad dream. Uh huh, that same sort of vision I'd experienced during my junior year in high school. I'd crammed all night for a French final. I knew there was no way I was going to pass, but I had this crazy feeling that somehow when I walked into that classroom the next day I'd be prattling like a native speaker.

Reality had a different scenario in mind. The bad dream was being awake.

After Janet left, Diana said, "Trudy left a message on the machine for you, Tony. She wants you to get back to her."

"She say what she wants?"

"No, but she didn't sound so good."

"What do you mean?"

Diana refilled her glass, then said, "Wasn't anything she said. I just got the sense there was something wrong."

So I called. After eight rings, one ring away from hanging up, Trudy answered with a dull, "Hello?" When I told her it was me, she blurted out, "Leo's dead."

She said it just like that—no buildup, no preamble, no inflection. Just, "Leo's dead." She could just as easily told me Leo had gone out to get a loaf of bread.

"What?" I said, trying to catch my breath. "I just took . . . I just saw him the other day. He told me he was getting out of the hospital, uh soon."

Trudy's revelation had caught me off guard, and I almost blurted out that I'd driven him to Philadelphia. How could he be dead? He should be halfway to somewhere by now.

"Where? How?" I stammered.

"He killed himself in his boss's office."

"No way."

"I don't have all the details, but I'll fill you in when I get them."

"Ah, anything we can do to help? Diana and me?"

"I'm okay. I half expected something like this to happen anyway. My mother's here now. We're going down to the morgue later to identify the body."

After I hung up, Diana asked, "What's the matter? You're as pale as a ghost."

"Leo's dead. Suicide."

In a daze, I yanked a jacket out of the closet.

"You're kidding?"

"I gotta go."

"Where?"

"Trudy wants me to check out a few things for her. I told her I'd help."

"What things? When're you coming back?"

"I'll call you later," I hollered over my shoulder.

32

I HEADED FOR THE NEIGHBORHOOD BAR on Union Turnpike, a few blocks from the house. Back in my drinking days, it was usually the first place I'd stop after work. I grabbed a stool at the far end of the dark mahogany bar, away from all of the revelers watching a baseball game on television.

I had a lot to think about, so I jumped right off the wagon and ordered a double vodka martini from the petite redhead bartender to help the thinking process along. Just like that, a year and a half of sobriety gone.

Leo didn't kill himself. Muertens and Schoolkraft were somehow involved. Although I didn't have a shred of proof, in my gut I knew they'd killed him.

An hour and three martinis later, I was no closer to understanding any of it and paid little attention to the television. I couldn't hear the broadcast, but I knew the game had gone into extra innings.

"Slow down there, sweetheart," the pretty bartender said when I ordered another drink.

Not likely. Just like riding a bike.

Two guys walked in, and took up stools near me, invading my space. They were an odd couple. Mutt and Jeff. Mutt couldn't have been a millimeter over five feet. He carried some weight, most of it packed tight in his chest and shoulders. The dome light over the bar reflected off of his bald head. Jeff was more than a foot taller. He also appeared to be in good shape. A heavy dark mustache, turned down at his chin, gave him a malevolent look.

After they'd settled in and ordered drinks, Jeff said, in a high, squeaky voice, "Wonder what this scumbag's old lady'd say if she got a look at these?"

Something in his voice made me look up and turn towards him. All right, it was *scumbag* that got my attention. Mutt, sitting on the stool nearest to me, was eyeballing an eight-by-ten glossy lying on the bar in front of him. I glanced at the photo and . . . shit. The scumbag was me. Specifically, Trudy and me in the throes of one of our lovemaking bouts.

Mutt met my slack-jawed surprise with a shit-eating grin.

"So whadaya think?" he said to me.

"Where the hell did you get those?" I said.

"There's a man we know who wants to meet you to discuss a business proposition," Mutt said. "So why don't you come along with us and we'll introduce you to him."

"You're not going to give us any trouble are you?" Jeff said.

I knew their game—blackmail. Friends of Riley who also wanted an all-expenses-paid trip to Vegas. "Tell Riley to go to hell. It's not tomorrow yet."

How the hell did Riley get pictures? I studied the photo and tried to figure out when it was taken. I couldn't. Being naked, there wasn't much to distinguish one sexcapade from another. Place was simple—Trudy's bedroom—but I hadn't been there in almost a week.

The two leg-breakers exchanged a quick glance, then Jeff said, "You live near here, don't you?"

No way did I want these two assholes going to my house, throwing Diana into the mix. It dawned on me I was way out of my league with Riley. Too many resources—like these two clowns—for me to do anything but go along.

Resigned to the obvious, I said, "Let's go," paid for my drinks, and followed them outside.

When I headed towards my car, Jeff said, "Leave it. You're coming along with us." When I hesitated, he said, "Don't worry, we'll bring you back."

Comforting. At least there would be a later. But will I be able to drive? How far was Riley willing to go to collect a lousy five grand?

They led me to an old four-door Crown Vic parked on the street. Mutt held open the front passenger door and I slid in. Mutt slammed the door, shuttled around the front and climbed behind the wheel, his head barely clearing the dash.

The seat directly behind me groaned when Jeff got in. "Buckle up," he said. "This heap doesn't have a passenger-side air bag. Can't have you going through the windshield, now can we?"

"Let me call my wife and tell her I'll be late."

"No need for that. This won't take too long," Mutt said.

"Yeah, we'll have you home in a jiff," Jeff said.

"Where's Riley?" I asked.

No response.

Mutt turned on the radio, couldn't pull in a station, so we listened to white noise—random fragments of some DJ's rapid fire chatter occasionally breaking through.

Mutt got on the Grand Central, headed towards the city, then exited at Roosevelt Avenue. Citi Field, the New York Mets new baseball stadium, was still lit up, and I heard the buzz of fan noise over the rumble of a city-bound Flushing train passing by on the elevated tracks.

We drove east, past the stadium, through the area populated with junkyards.

"Where're you taking me?"

"Don't worry, we're almost there," Mutt said.

As if on cue, he pulled into a parking lot fronting a low cinderblock building and skidded to an abrupt stop, gravel kicking up and pelting the underside of the car. The sign across the front of the building's façade read, HM SECURITY SYSTEMS, INC. There was a lone car, an old Caddy Seville, parked in a handicapped space.

Mutt got out first and opened the door for me. I stepped out onto the lot, then froze.

"Let's go," Jeff barked, pushing me towards the building's front door, the gravel crunching under my foot.

The door was unlocked. We entered an area that looked like it might have been the customer service department.

Computer terminals were on each desk, monitor screensavers displaying shifting patterns of colorful geometric shapes in the dimly lit room.

A light shone from beneath a door at the far end of a long hallway, and with me sandwiched between Mutt and Jeff, we headed towards it, past bookkeeping and the operator's room. At the end of the hall, Jeff moved around me and tapped on the door. A voice yelled for us to enter.

Shoved into the office, I almost stumbled headlong into a desk. I found myself standing inside the chalk outline of a body, broken in spots by dried blood. Took two quick steps backwards and yelled out, "What the hell?"

The mystery man sat at the desk, hidden behind a copy of the *Wall Street Journal*. His response, "A-ha."

The desk was clear except for a nameplate with HIKE MUERTENS, THE PRESIDENT engraved in the plastic. I was bewildered. *Riley and Muertens working together?*

Pictures were haphazardly hung on the walls. Muertens with a Little League team sponsored by HM Securities. A bowling team. Lots of photo ops with prominent city and state officials. A real solid citizen.

There was a row of gray metal four-drawer file cabinets against the wall behind him, and a trophy with a professional bowler on a plastic pedestal rested atop one of them. A couple of equally worn chairs were in front of the desk. No one invited me to sit down, so I just stood there, hands at my sides.

"Boy, this stock market is killing me," Muertens said. "I'm telling you, if these thieving bloodsuckers don't stop stealing my money, I'll have to take somebody out."

I broke in and said, "Where's your pal, Riley? He going to pop out of Door Number Three and scare the shit out of me?"

Muertens didn't skip a beat, kept talking like I wasn't even there.

"Or maybe I should just cut my losses," Muertens said. "Wha-do-you think about that, Sport?"

My gasp was quick and involuntary. Was he referring to the word puzzle I found in my house—posse-cress-locker-butter? *What a prudent man does when the stock market turns to shit—cuts his losses?* How could he possibly know I did word puzzles?

He set the newspaper aside and said, "Don't say you weren't warned."

Meurtens was a gnome. He was swallowed up in a wheelchair, a little kid playing grown up. Ruby-red face, as if he'd just scrubbed it with a Brillo pad. Wispy strands of thin gray hair fell across his forehead. He looked sixty, but he had the fine, curved features of someone closer to fifty.

"You seem disappointed," Muertens said. He brushed the errant strands off his face, pushing them back over his Mr. Potato Head ears.

"Why am I here?"

"I needed a ship, and lo and behold, it just sailed in. The good ship, *Arnold*. How ya doing? Ah, never mind. You don't look so good."

"He was knocking 'em back when we picked him up, boss," Mutt said.

Muertens rested his elbows on the desk and dropped his chin into his palms. He smiled, but his eyes didn't. Gnome or not, he was one cold son of a bitch.

He noticed me staring down at the chalk outline.

"Your buddy Leo." Muertens said. "What a scene. You should've been here. Snatched him up in Philly, waiting to get on a train. Came along quietly almost like he was expecting us to show up. Heard he didn't say shit on the ride back here."

The dark pools of Muertens' eyes absorbed and reflected my fear. Another smile, then he said, "So we bring him back here. Keep him on ice for a while. Make sure all the paper work's in order. First, I make him write and sign a termination note I dictated."

"Suicide," I said.

"Symantics," Muertens said.

"He catches on fast, boss," Mutt said.

I sensed the leg breakers stirring behind me. I guessed nobody talked to Muertens like that. The gnome was now grinning, ear-to-ear. "So, I tell your buddy to stand in front of the desk, pretty much where you see the chalk. Slim hands him a knife he'd stolen from your buddy's house out on the Island. I say, 'You wanna kill yourself? Go ahead, do it.' All the begging, crying. He's sorry, he'll make it right, blah, blah, blah. The little cocksucker pissed all over himself. He was pitiful. But what do you expect from a guy that tries to kill himself with sleeping pills. I can still smell the piss. Fucking pussy."

I pushed up on the balls of my feet, held the position for a second, then dropped my heels back onto floor.

"The weasel started poking himself. Frankly, I started to get bored. Slim did, too. So finally I shoved the thing in myself. Blood all over the place. Musta hit the mother lode, because he bled out like a stuck pig right there where you're standing. You see, I'm a hands-on kinda guy, a regular DIY guy. You a weasel, too, Mr. Arnold?"

He opened the middle desk drawer, and dug out a duplicate set of the 8-by-10 inch glossies I'd seen in the bar and said, "The guys say they really liked that hip action of yours. Very impressive."

"Everybody's got to be good at something," I said.

"Smart ass, huh? We'll see how smart you are in a couple of weeks."

My mind was racing, my legs shook. All I could muster was an anemic, "Why are you doing this?"

"Because I can. I like it. And I'm damn good at it, too. Like you said, everybody's got to be good at something, right? But I suspect you already know how good I am."

"You're the sportsman of the year, boss," the goon Muertens called Slim said.

Muertens nodded, studied the photographs. "She's a nice little piece of ass. You haven't been out there this week, have ya? Well, too bad and too late."

"Trudy had nothing to do with this," I whined. "She's got two little kids."

"You think I give a fuck about that bitch? She's a filthy whore. Isn't there any more loyalty in this world?"

"It wasn't her fault."

"Yeah, I know. The slut tripped and fell on your dick."

Scared shitless, I blurted, "You're crazy."

"Oh, you're the good guy, right? Screwing your friend's wife. Or, were you doing him a favor?"

They all laughed at that one—atonal three-part harmony.

"Why me?"

"*Why me*," Muertens mocked. "You still don't get it, do you, you dumb shit? Couldn't just step aside like all of Leo's other so-called friends did. Bet you were just hanging around for the pussy. I tell you, pussy's the ruin of many a man."

"It wasn't like that. Leo was my friend. I tried to help. There's nothing to be gained by killing me."

"Oh, I don't know about that. The little inheritance you left me should do just fine for starters."

"I didn't leave—"

"Can't change the script too much. Gotta get the money."

Muertens took a legal-sized manila envelope from a file cabinet drawer, opened it, took out some papers, and slid them across the desk towards me.

"Pull up a chair."

I did as he ordered, and started reading the papers—a codicil to my will and a life insurance policy.

He handed me a pen and said, "No need to read the fine print. Just sign on the dotted line. I'll take care of the rest."

The envelope bore the Smith & Levine letterhead. That scumbag Schoolkraft was in on this, too. My hesitation prompted one of the goons to close in behind me. A hard blow to the back of the head pitched me onto the front of Muertens' desk.

"Gotta problem?" Muertens asked.

"No." With a trembling hand, I signed the codicil. "What

happens now?"

"Oh, I think you know. We don't vary the script too much. A little modification here and there. We like to think of ourselves as flexible. Adaptable. *Artistes*. In fact, you might want to throw in a suggestion or two. But remember, the script always ends the same way. Somebody dead and me getting paid."

I squirmed in the chair, fantasized about going across the desk and choking Muertens to death.

"In the meantime, go out, and have fun," he said. "Enjoy yourself. Live each day like it might be your last."

I heard Mutt and Jeff behind me, slapping a meaty high five.

"That strip club your buddy Leo really liked, for example. Wanna see some pictures?"

Mutt and Jeff cranked up the laughter.

"Hey, how's this for a novel idea," Muertens continued. "Why don't you go home and bang the old lady. You never know, you might enjoy it. Save you a little gas since you won't have to make that long drive out to the Island to get laid. But you might wanna hurry. I don't like to make predictions, especially about the future. That option's about to expire."

My stupidity clicked in again. "You're fucking nuts—"

One of the goons punched me in the back of the head, knocking me out of the chair and onto the floor.

"Have some respect," Jeff said. "Now get up."

I sat back down. Anticipating another blow, I wrapped my arms around my head.

"My advice to you is not to get anyone else involved in this. This is *our* little thing. Our *cosa nostra*. Your friend had a hard time understanding that. You got family out in Jersey, right? Some in Atlanta? Seem like nice folks, from what I can tell. I don't think they'd like to meet me, though. Still haven't figured out what to do 'bout the wives yet, but that's kinda up to you."

Paralyzed with fear, I nodded.

"You believe in the power of prayer?" Muertens said.

I covered my head again, and said, "What's that got to do with anything?"

"Prayer is man's wireless communications to God. You are in communications, right?"

Still covered up, I shook my head.

"Well, you might wanna try it, although I can't say it's worked so far."

"Thanks for the tip," I said.

That deathly smile of his again, then, "I'm tired. Get this piece of shit outta here."

THE GOONS DROVE ME BACK to the bar. Same seating arrangement—Mutt at the wheel, and Jeff's large shadow hulking behind me.

The Mets game was over. Cars spilled out of the Citi Field parking lot, backing up traffic on Roosevelt Avenue. What faces I could make out under the gloomy elevated tracks didn't appear to be happy, so I assumed the home team had lost.

My car, windows closed and unbroken, was still parked out front when Mutt and Jeff dropped me off. Had all the hubcaps and tires, and they were still inflated.

I couldn't figure out how Muertens was able to track me so closely. The car had to be bugged. I'd have Rick Myerson check it out in the morning.

Couldn't go to the cops. What proof did I have to accuse a prominent local businessman of murder? The codicil wouldn't show up until after I was dead, and I had no clue what insurance company underwrote the life insurance policy. Was Riley involved with Muertens? Even if he wasn't, Muertens knew too much about my family and loved ones. I had to protect them with my silence.

I didn't know Muertens' timetable, or if I'd survive at the end of it.

Neither had Leo.

33

MY LIBIDO WAS TOO LOW to take Muertens' advice. I just wanted to crawl into bed, pull the covers over my head and never come out. But that wasn't possible. Muertens wouldn't let it play out like that.

Diana was still up. She kissed me on the cheek when I walked into the kitchen.

"You've been drinking. Are you drunk?"

"No. Just a *coupla* pops."

"Why now? You've been so good."

"This Leo thing's really got me upset."

"That's no excuse, Tony. Maybe you should look into A.A. like we talked about before. I can't have you going back to where you were last year. I won't have it."

She was right, but her voice was irritating—fingernails scraping across a blackboard.

"What've you been doing all night besides drinking?"

"I really don't want to talk about it right now."

"You're upset. Okay, I understand that, but we *will* talk about this tomorrow. You can't keep your feelings bottled up inside. It's not healthy for either of us."

"I'm sorry for everything."

It was all bullshit. My nuts were being squeezed by good old fashioned down-to-the-bone fear. A psychotic dwarf was going to kill me and I had no idea how to stop him.

"I drove Leo to Philadelphia," I said in a weak attempt to justify my falling off the wagon.

"What? You helped that sleazebag run away from his responsibilities?"

"You shouldn't talk about the dead like that. Besides, Leo didn't kill himself."

"Then why'd he come back?"

"You're not listening. Leo *did not* kill himself."

"How do you know that?"

"He was happy, looking forward to starting a new life. I gave him five-hundred bucks."

"Trudy know what you did?"

"No." I told Diana how Leo'd called in his marker. "I owed him that much. He thought Trudy and the kids would be better off without him in their lives, and I agreed."

I sagged against the counter.

"Tomorrow, Tony. We'll talk about it tomorrow."

Diana skulked away, leaving me wondering if I'd told her too much.

34

THE NEXT MORNING I stayed in bed while Diana got ready for work.

"Come on, you're going to be late."

She jabbed me in the ribs.

"I think I'm getting a cold," I said, then coughed for emphasis.

"Still hung over, uh?"

She bent down to kiss me, but I shielded her away. "I don't want you getting sick, too."

"Don't think a *cold* is going to stop of us from having our little talk tonight."

Diana wore a smart sweater and skirt combination, and I said, "I like it."

"Flattery's not going to work, either."

I called the temp and told him I wouldn't be in the office until later, then spent most of the morning pacing around the house, trying to figure out my next move, but kept coming up empty. Frequently, I'd stop and peek out of the closed blinds looking for an old Crown Vic out front with two goons sitting in it. I didn't see anything suspicious. "Unless they're disguised as trees," I mumbled.

Around noon, I concluded there was no point in just hanging around the house, so I decided to go into the office, hoping the stack of applications I was sure to find on my desk would divert my roiling mind.

I was partly right. Plenty of applications, but they didn't prove to be the diversion I'd hoped for. Instead, I played *Minesweeper*, usually blowing myself up after two or three mouse clicks, while continuing to stress over my predicament.

It was clear to me that Leo wasn't Muertens' first victim. He was too self-assured, the scam far too organized and efficient. It seemed as if he had every angle covered.

Like good Kentucky bourbon, Leo had gone down nice and easy. Muertens expected me to go the same way. But what if I could do the unexpected, maybe turn the tables?

I'd caught a crazy moralistic vibe coming from Muertens—to justify his criminal behavior? Leo not only stole from him, but also cheated on Trudy. Although I didn't steal, I certainly cheated on Diana, and worse yet, with a friend's wife. Muertens had said, *isn't there any more loyalty in this world*? Was the crazy bastard playing the avenging angel for fun and profit?

I surfed the web for suicides that could be Muertens' handiwork, Googling "suicide New York City," and was surprised to find there were almost as many suicides as homicides. New York's strict gun control law made it difficult to get a firearm, so most suicides either jumped off tall buildings or bridges—the George Washington Bridge was a popular jumping-off spot—the rest either overdosed or slashed their wrists.

I refined my search, entering "suicide New York City knife," and found the headline: WALL STREET EXECUTIVE STABS HIMSELF A DOZEN TIMES. There were more than twenty hits, but I chose the story in the *Post*, which summarized the incident: Depressed over a string of market losses, the broker repeatedly stabbed himself in the gut with a 13-inch Wolfgang Puck kitchen knife. When told he would recover, the broker was reported to have said, "I should've used a Ginsu."

I remembered Muertens saying something about losing money in the market—"if these thieving bloodsuckers don't stop stealing my money, I'll have to take somebody out." Could this broker be the thieving bloodsucker Muertens was talking about? It was a long shot, but I'd have to look him up, and compare notes. The broker's name was Luke Skillman.

I called Rick Meyerson.

"I missed the dress-code-change memo," I said when he sauntered into my office.

Rick was wearing an old pair of work pants and a gray NYU sweatshirt with the sleeves cut off at the elbows.

"Got to inspect a location up in the Bronx," Rick said. "What's up?"

"I think one of our competitors might've placed a GPS tracker on my car."

"That's serious business."

"Lately, I've been bumping into the same guy at every luncheon and conference."

"This isn't a big industry. Incestuous, actually, so you'd tend to see a lot of the same people."

"How about at a strip club?"

"I heard about that. You and your 34-triple-D girlfriend."

"That story's bullshit, Rick, and you know it. I was there checking on my friend Leo."

"Sure. But FYI, I hear the bosses weren't amused."

I was going to have to kill Ted or fire him—whichever crossed my mind first the next time I saw him.

"Anyway, I'll check out your car," Rick said. "Just leave it here tonight, and take a vehicle out of the car pool. I'll get it back to you tomorrow."

"Thanks, Rick."

I threw him the keys.

"By the way, who's this guy you keep running into?" Rick said.

"Name's Hike Muertens."

"What kind of name's that?"

"Beats the shit outta me, but maybe you can do a background check on him while you're at it."

"Sure thing, Tony."

"One other favor. Take a look at Ted for me, too, will you? I got his review coming up."

"Got to run that past HR first."

"This has to be off the books, Rick."

"We can both get fired for pulling that kind of shit, not to mention being sued for invasion of privacy. I don't know about you, but I got kids to put through college. I can't do that standing in the unemployment line or, worse yet, behind bars."

"Rick, I can't tell you why, but I really need your help on this."

"Sorry, Tony. No can do."

"I understand. Just let me know what you find on the other thing, okay?"

Rick smiled, casually flipped me a single-digit salute and left. I went back to the computer.

I didn't know if Skillman was one of Muertens' victims, but his bio seemed right—broker, either a thief or incompetent, and the attempted suicide. Not to mention Muertens' threat to take out the bloodsuckers.

With a little more research, I discovered Skillman was staying at Breezeway Terrace, a private sanatorium on Long Island's North Shore. Their website described Breezeway as a "commodious country residence." Going by the photographs, it looked like a country club, with a spacious lawn and gardens, Long Island Sound sparkling in the distance.

Brokerage houses try to keep employee scandals—especially those involving mismanagement of client funds—hidden from the public. If that was the case, Skillman would be stuck away someplace private and exclusive like the Breezeway. And, unlike the institutions Leo had been warehoused in, I was sure Skillman had a private room with a phone. I dialed the main number, got an upbeat operator and she put me through to Skillman's room when I identified myself as Jeff Fischer from accounting.

Skillman picked up after two rings, then dropped the phone. I heard him fumbling with the receiver, trying to pick it up before he finally said, "Hello?"

He sounded shaky, not unlike Leo in those early days, and my mind raced back to that crazy card game.

"You from accounting?" Skillman asked.

The operator had screened the call.

"My name's Mr. Fischer."

"I don't know you. Where's Susan?"

I assumed Susan was Skillman's usual contact when he or the sanitarium needed money.

"Don't hang up. We have a common enemy. Muertens."

"I—I don't know no Hike Muertens."

Bingo.

"You can't hide from him, Mr. Skillman," I said. "I know what Muertens did to you. I'm on his dance card, too, and I need your help."

"Then you know I can't help you."

"Why's he after you?"

He hesitated.

"If you think I'm helping him, forget it, because there's nothing you can say he doesn't already know."

He remained quiet for another beat, then said, "You're right. He thinks I stole from him. But all I did was make a few bad investment decisions."

"How much did he lose?"

"A lot. How about you?"

"My buddy stole from Muertens. Peanuts, really. Me? All I did was have an affair with my buddy's wife."

"Where's your buddy now?"

"Dead. They say it was suicide, but I think you and I both know that's bullshit. Anything you can tell me that might help?"

"If I had that kind of information, you think I'd be hiding in here?"

A knock on the door, and I asked Skillman to please hold on, then looked up to see Ted at the door. He smiled and said, "Guess who I found wandering through the halls?" Detective Riley pushed past him and entered my office. Ted beat a hasty retreat before I could fire him.

I said to Skillman, "I gotta go. Good luck," then dropped the call.

The usually dapper Riley looked out of sorts in a blue

workout suit. He took a seat, picked up one of the elephants off my desk, and said, "Where's my money?"

"I didn't know you were here."

"Got a new secretary, uh? Boy, that old bitch sure could motor."

"What do you want, Detective?"

"Don't be dense, Benson. My money."

"It's not six o'clock yet."

"After that little stunt you tried to pull last time, I don't trust you, asswipe."

"Well, you know what, Detective Riley? Screw you. I'm not giving you another dime."

"You decide you don't want to be married no more?"

"You're too late. Your buddy Muertens already made that decision for me."

"You fucking with me, Benson? Where's my money?"

I took a legal pad from a desk drawer and started writing.

"Here's my home phone, and my wife's school and cell phone number. So, you go right ahead, Detective. Call her and complete your *investigation*."

I tore off the sheet of paper and stuck it under Riley's nose. He knocked it out of my hand, sending it feathering to the floor.

"You better keep your fucking mouth shut, you hear?" Riley said, then swept my herd of ceramic elephants off the desk, sending them flying against the wall.

"Oops," and then he was gone.

Ted, hearing the racket, ran to the door.

"What was that about?"

"Fuck off, Ted."

DIANA GOT HOME about five minutes after I did.

"Whose car's that in the driveway?" she said.

"Company car. I'm having some work done on mine. I'm joining AA. Found a location in Forest Hills. I'll stop by tomorrow."

"That's great, Tony. We'll get through this, you'll see."

"I know." I was so full of shit, it hurt.

"I guess you're feeling better?"

"A little. I went into the office this afternoon. Needed to catch up on some paperwork. Drank a lot of liquids. The nonalcoholic kind, in case you're wondering," I said, laughing, trying to keep her at ease. "Starve a cold, feed a fever. Isn't that what they say?"

"It's the other way around, dopey," she said, buying into my false merriment. "I brought you an antihistamine, and the best medicine of all, chicken soup from the deli."

"Thanks."

Diana started putting things away, then set the plates and utensils on the table. The wall phone near the refrigerator rang and she answered, "Hello? Oh, hi." She mouthed to me, "Trudy." Then to Trudy, "How're you holding up?"

She paused as I supposed Trudy gave her a rundown, then, "I'm getting dinner ready, so let me put Tony on. He's a little under the weather. Take care of yourself. We love you."

She handed me the phone.

Trudy inquired about my health, which I quickly dismissed, then said, "I just got back from the Queens County morgue, identifying Leo's body."

"That sucks. I thought you went last night?"

"Couldn't muster up the energy. I'm so angry."

"You've got a right to be. Anything from the police?"

"Preliminarily, they're ruling his death a suicide. Something about forensics and Muertens' story being consistent with the evidence they found at the scene."

"And I'm sure Leo's mental history made it a whole lot easier for them to come up with that conclusion," I chimed in.

"Yeah. They said they'd make a final determination after the coroner delivers his report. But it pretty much sounds like a done deal."

"You make funeral arrangements yet?"

"No. I can't do anything until his body's released, and I

don't know when that'll be."

"Well, let me know if we can help."

I heard Trudy's mother yell for the kids' clothes. Trudy answered, "Mom, hold on a sec," then to me, "I gotta go. When can you come out? I really need you here with me, Tony."

"Diana's pretty upset, so why don't I try to get out tomorrow, okay?"

I could tell Trudy wasn't pleased with my noncommittal answer.

35

ON FRIDAY MORNING, TRUDY reached me at the office. She'd received the police report, and it was official. Leo's death was a suicide. His body had been taken to a funeral home in Plainview near her house. The viewing was set for Sunday night, burial Monday afternoon.

As much as I wanted to, I couldn't just hang around the house, waiting for the other shoe to drop. Leo'd said Muertens passed around photos of his peep show handiwork to his neighbors, and I figured it was just a matter of time before he started circulating the photos of me and Trudy.

My wrath was now diverted to Schoolkraft. I had to take him out. He'd be easier to get to than Muertens. Shakespeare's *Dick the Butcher* sounded my new battle cry: "The first thing we do, let's kill all the lawyers."

Leo had sought out Schoolkraft's advice and counsel when he was thinking about divorcing Trudy, but ultimately Schoolkraft not only had betrayed him, but also the lawyers' code of professional responsibility. Big time.

My plan was simple. I'd confront Schoolkraft in his office, introduce him to my SIG, persuade him to confess his role in Leo's murder, implicate Muertens, and get the whole thing on tape. Then I'd splatter his brains all over his big desk.

"Hey, Tony. Got a minute?"

I looked up. Rick Meyerson was standing in the doorway.

"Yeah, come on in. Pull up a chair."

As he went to sit down, he stepped on a ceramic tusk I'd somehow missed during my cleanup.

"Where're your elephants?" he said.

"Clumsy me . . . accidently knocked them off the desk. Anyway, whatcha got?"

"She's clean as a whistle."

"Nothing?"

Rick twisted the end of his bushy red mustache. "Don't sound so disappointed."

"Just surprised, that's all."

"Got under the hood myself." He laughed, then added, "Even changed the oil."

"I guess, like you said, this business is incestuous. You were probably right. Just a coincidence."

"Generally, I don't believe in coincidences, but in this case I think that's all it is."

"Appreciate you getting on this right away, Rick."

"No problem. Muertens, that's the guy you said you seen around, right?"

I nodded.

"He doesn't seem like a strip-club-kinda-guy."

"You saying I do?" I said, half mocking, half chiding, thinking, *that fucking Ted*.

"Just saying that Muertens is a big-time businessman. Real active in the community. Sponsors various charities, mostly for kids. A big-time political contributor."

"Doesn't mean he can't have an alter ego, like John Wayne Gacy."

"True, but Muertens seems like a solid citizen. What're you looking for, actually?"

I shrugged. "You said he's a businessman, so what does he do, *actually*?"

"He definitely casts a wide net. He's got a security company, car service, real estate, apartment buildings in the outer boroughs—"

"Apartment buildings? Maybe that's why I've seen him around so much, looking to get antennas installed on some of his buildings. I'll check and see if he's submitted any applications. Anything else?"

"Yeah, he runs an insurance brokerage operation out of

his real estate office. You know, car, homeowners and life insurance. Far as I know, that's it."

If I'd been a dog, the hackles along the back of my neck would have stood up. Damn. Muertens was the front end of the money-grab. This was too easy. Different policies with different beneficiaries, underwritten by different companies so the actuaries wouldn't catch the pattern, wouldn't get suspicious, as Muertens collected hundreds of thousands, perhaps millions of dollars in death benefits—deaths that greedy, twisted psychopath caused himself.

Muertens had everybody fooled. Everybody except the dead.

And the soon-to-be-dead.

36

IT WAS ALMOST 11 O'CLOCK Saturday night when the phone rang. Diana answered. From what little I could hear in the other room, I thought she might've been chatting with her friend, Janet, about the impending nuptials.

But then I heard her say, "Nice talking to you, too. Hold on, Mr. Muertens . . . okay, Hike," and finally, "Tony, it's for you."

I hesitatingly picked up the cordless phone and retreated into the kitchen.

"Hey, Tony," Muertens said, all bright and cheerful.

I turned the faucet on so Diana couldn't overhear, then whispered, "What do you want?"

"Just checking in, see how you're making out. By the way, your wife, Diana? She sounds like an absolutely delightful woman. Boy, I'd bet the ranch you'd hate to lose a fine woman like her."

"Keep her out of this," I snapped.

"That's kinda up to you."

"Don't call here again."

"Or what?"

"I'll hang up." And I did.

Barely ten seconds passed before he called back. I snatched up the phone before Diana got to it.

"Don't do that again," Muertens said, the slick politician persona gone.

"Or what?" then I dropped him a second time.

Diana entered the kitchen, and said "You left the water running."

I turned the tap off.

"I never heard you mention Hike before."

"That's because he's nobody."

"Says you two are buddies."

"He owns a few apartment buildings. He's been calling me at the office a lot, and now at home? Some buddy. More like a royal pain in the ass. He's just looking to cash in."

"Well, he sounds charming. Says he's going to talk to you about us getting together."

A double date? Are you shitting me! He's a murdering psychopath. But I kept my cool and said, "We'll see. What did you two talk about?"

"Nothing really. He was telling me about this new restaurant that opened in Long Island City. You know, just small talk. Oh, and he said you were out at his office this week."

"That all he say?"

"Pretty much."

"He calls again, watch what you say to him. The guy's a venomous snake."

"Guess that means we won't be going out to dinner with the Muertens, huh?"

37

LEO'S WAKE WAS LIKE all of the others I'd attended over the years, except for one major difference. The deceased was a good friend.

Diana and I drove out to the funeral home Sunday night, signed the guest book, then entered the small chapel. It was preternaturally bright, as if the gates to heaven were standing wide open, waiting for Leo to enter.

Trudy and the kids were already there, sitting in the front row along with who I imagined were her relatives. Diana and I walked over, offered our condolences, and then took a seat a couple of rows behind them.

Trudy was distant, not maintaining eye contact with either Diana or me. Although she could have been caught up in the moment, more than likely, she was pissed that I hadn't gone out to see her.

Leo's highly-polished closed casket was at the front of the chapel. Floral reefs, and Leo's life displayed in black-and-white and color photographs flanked the casket. An American flag draped behind the photographs.

Knowing Leo was inside that coffin unnerved me. I began to sweat and my legs twitched. Odds were I'd be joining him soon, laid out in a similar pine box at some other funeral home.

What secrets did Leo take to the grave? He'd made no secret of his boss's intention to kill him, but no one believed him, including me. He was just another nutcase who should have been kept off the streets. Now he was dead. Worse yet, I was next on his killer's list and sure as hell, no one was going to believe me, either.

"I'm going to take a look at the photos," I said to Diana.

As I walked past Trudy, I touched her lightly on the shoulder. She stared up at me with the same indifference she'd shown before.

I scanned the pictures. A young Leo in a soccer uniform he'd eventually grow into. The proud high school graduate. Leo beaming at his wedding. In the delivery room holding Cody. No way he could've imagined it would all end like this.

Heading to the casket, I should have been pondering things spiritual—maybe redemption, or the nature of heaven and hell—but all I could think about was Muertens. I imagined myself floating high above my casket looking down on the somber scene, while trying to hear what people were saying about me. There would be Ted Barr, barely able to control his glee; Diana trying to hold it all together while loathing my cheating ass. Would anyone speak up for me and say, *"You know, he really wasn't a bad guy."*

My reverie was interrupted by a light brush against my shoulder. It was Trudy who whispered, "Where have you been?" An accusation, not a question.

"Sorry, couldn't get away. But I've been thinking about you. You okay?"

Without answering, she turned and returned to her seat. That's when I saw Demi Shadow sitting in the back row near the exit.

Diana eyed me as I nervously made my way towards Demi. Standing over her, I said, "What are you doing here?" I glanced back to see if Trudy was watching me. "How'd you know Leo was dead?"

"Got a phone call."

Shadow was dressed in black, but she didn't look as if she was in mourning. Too tight, too short, too much skin. Appropriateness aside, she looked sumptuous.

"A call from whom?" I asked.

"He didn't give me his name. Just said he was a friend of Leo's."

"He tell you how Leo died?"

She shook her head.

"Leo committed suicide."

"Wow. Didn't see that one coming. I thought you told me you drove him to Philly?"

I let her question linger, then said, "I wouldn't hang around if I were you. There's bound to be questions." I looked at Trudy. "I can hear the whispering already."

Demi Shadow nodded, got up, and headed for the exit.

"Sorry about your friend, Demi," I said to her retreating figure.

When I returned to my seat, Diana said, "That was her, wasn't it?" When I hesitated she said, "She's got some nerve."

"Leo's dead. Let it go."

Trudy's brother, Stuart, came over and said hello. I'd met him once at one of Leo's kids' birthday parties, and we'd exchanged small talk.

I asked him, "How's Trudy holding up?"

"Not bad, considering. But it's not going to hit her hard until after this is all over, once everybody's left and she has to get on with her life."

"How're the kids doing?" Diana said.

"Thank God, they're young, and won't remember much. But what a great guy, father, husband, and brother-in-law Leo was. He'll be missed," Stuart droned on.

Someone started coughing. Bullshit has a way of making you do that.

"Well, I guess that just about covers it," I said.

Diana nudged me in the ribs, but I knew Leo didn't like Trudy's family. Manipulating phonies, he'd called them.

"Where are all his friends?" Stuart said.

I shrugged. *There were no friends. Muertens had taken care of that.*

There was more innocuous small talk before I excused myself to find the men's room.

As I stepped into the vestibule, I saw Muertens' goon, Jeff, hurrying out the front door. I ran after him, but lost him in the dark parking lot. I stood on the steps for a moment, allowing my eyes to adjust. After a few seconds, the taillights of a Crown Vic flashed as it exited the parking lot.

Shit, Muertens is on my ass already.

But Rick Meyerson had checked my car for bugs. Said it was clean.

I spent the ride home questioning why Rick had betrayed me.

38

THE LOT IN FRONT OF Max's Auto Repair was a graveyard of cannibalized cars. I pulled into an empty bay inside the garage, where grease-covered mechanics worked underneath cars jacked up on racks.

I had to know why Rick didn't find the tracker.

"You got an appointment?" a large black mechanic in blue work clothes yelled above the din.

"No, but Max is expecting me, Mel," I yelled back.

He looked surprised at me calling him by name, apparently oblivious to the big yellow "MEL" embroidered above his shirt's left breast pocket.

"In there," he said, pointing to the customer waiting area.

Max was leaning against a vending machine, sipping a can of soda while going over an invoice with a customer who, judging by his anguished expression, was none too happy.

A young woman holding a toddler sat nearby, watching a cartoon, seemingly oblivious to the furor right next to her.

"You back already?" Max said to me after the customer stalked off.

"I want you to take a look at my car."

"Okay, but what's the problem now? You just had it in here, what, three weeks ago? Told you those German cars were overrated. Next time, buy American."

Max was rail-thin, and might have been considered handsome were it not for the acne scars left over from childhood. I'd met him when he was the head mechanic at the Mercedes dealership that serviced my car. I liked the work he did and when he opened his own shop I'd loaned him the seed money he needed to get started. He'd repaid me and servicing my cars was the interest.

"I'll remember that, but right now I need you to check for anything that's not supposed to be there."

"Like what?"

"You're the mechanic, you tell me."

He gawked with an uncomprehending grimace.

"An IED," I said.

"What's that?"

"A bomb."

"You're kidding, right?"

"Good. I got your attention." I pointed to the car. "There's a GPS tracker hidden in there somewhere, and I need you to find it."

"Come on, Mr. Tony, stop yanking my chain, will ya. I'm busy here." Max laughed, then directed my attention to the five cars on hydraulic lifts and the half-dozen lined up outside waiting to be worked on. "I got no time for jokes."

"Do I look like I'm joking, Max?"

He sat down, laced his fingers behind his head and said, "You *are* serious."

He waited for me to say something. When I didn't, he said, "You know, those trackers can be as small as a matchstick and they can be hidden almost anywhere."

"Then go through the whole damn car," I said, startling the woman and the kid. "Tear it apart if you have to, but find it."

Resigned, Max said, "Okay, okay, but do me a favor. Bring it back tomorrow morning, early when I'm not so busy."

"And have this fucking—sorry, miss—have this mystery man up my ass for another twenty-four hours? I'll be back in an hour."

"I got a few cars ahead of you, Mr. Tony. Besides, I don't know if a hour's enough time to, you know, break down the car. I don't do this kind of thing every day, like never."

I threw him the keys, then said, "One hour."

"Mr. Tony—"
As I left, he cursed me in Romanian.

39

I HOPPED OUT OF A CAB in front of Smith & Levine's office across the street from the Queens County Court House. The four-story building was occupied mostly by lawyers and bail bondsmen, which explained the steady stream of desperate-looking people cycling in and out of the main lobby. The directory told me the firm's six attorneys were located on the third floor.

But the only one I was interested in was Dave Schoolkraft.

Building security was lax. Carrying a plastic shopping bag with my lunch inside, I posed as a food deliveryman and had no trouble getting to the elevators. I was the car's only passenger. I pressed the buttons for the third and fourth floors, got off on the third floor and stepped into Smith & Levine's small office, then pressed the down button so the elevator would be there after I'd checked out the office.

The reception area was just outside the elevator bank, the offices arrayed in a horseshoe around it. I spotted Schoolkraft's nameplate on the door directly behind the young woman manning the desk.

"May I help you?" she said.

I looked at a blank piece of paper and said, "Whoops, wrong floor." I'd obtained the information I'd come for, turned and walked into the waiting elevator.

Now I had to find out Schoolkraft's routine. When he arrived at work, when he went to lunch, when he went home. But all this would have to come later.

When I got back down to the lobby, I called Ma on her cell and, much to my surprise and relief, finally reached her.

"How are you, Ma?" I said, then took a bite of the pastrami sandwich I'd picked up for my bogus delivery.

"Surviving. I'm up at my sister's place in Rhode Island. Are you eating?"

"Hold on." I rewrapped the sandwich and put it back in the bag, then said, "Believe me, Ma, I never meant to put you in harm's way."

"Blackmail's a nasty business, Tony."

"I wasn't thinking."

"You seem to be doing that a lot lately. Diana leave you yet?"

"Soon, I think."

"What about that dirty cop, Riley?"

"He's history. I've got another situation that trumped him."

"Whatever's troubling you, Tony, it's gonna hurt to get through it. But you'll be all right."

"I hope so, Ma."

"I'm praying for you, Tony."

"Believe me, I need it,"

"Bill told me you called. Said he wasn't very nice."

"Can't blame him. You protect the ones you love."

An uncomfortable silence, then Ma said, "Well, I've got to go."

"When are you coming back? I need somebody I can trust."

"You take care of yourself, Tony." And with that, she was gone.

40

I GAVE MAX AN EXTRA HOUR to finish up. When I returned he was putting the spare tire back in the trunk.

"I didn't find nothing that shouldn'ta been there," he said.

"You sure?"

He closed the trunk and patted the rear fender. "Did the job myself, seeing how important it was to you. Went through this baby with a fine-tooth comb. Checked the undercarriage, wheel wells, tires, lifted the floorboards, rocker panels. Went under the hood, engine, everything. The DEA woulda been proud."

"Damn it!"

"No. I'm telling you, if something was there, I woulda found it. Even rotated the tires. By the way, you'll be needing new wheels pretty soon. If I can ask, Mr. Tony, what's this all about?"

Maybe there was a logical explanation for Muertens' goon being at the funeral home. Muertens knew Leo was dead—hell, he killed him—and it wouldn't be hard for him to find out the funeral arrangements. You didn't have to be a *brainiac* to figure out I'd show up at some point.

At least Rick Meyerson isn't involved in Muertens' plans. What's wrong with me? Even thinking Rick would betray me is . . . shit, now I'm sliding down the same paranoia wormhole Leo had fallen into. Then again, Leo had a right to be paranoid. Still . . .

Ignoring Max's question, I said, "How much I owe you?"

He gave me one of those patronizing smiles reserved for senile old grandparents and waved me off, saying, "It's okay.

You're a good customer, Mr. Tony. Just glad I could put your mind at ease."

41

ONLY THE SMALL CAST from the funeral home Sunday night attended Leo's funeral service the next afternoon.

It was obvious Reverend Peach, who conducted the service, didn't know squat about Leo. The good reverend continually got names mixed up, confusing brother for brother-in-law, and the kids for God-knows-who. Thankfully, he didn't introduce anyone as Leo's dead father.

No one gave a eulogy.

Afterwards, all of the relatives piled into two black limousines parked behind the hearse, and we fell in at the back of the line, following the high-speed caravan out to the Catholic cemetery in Farmingdale.

"It's like Trudy can't wait to get Leo into the ground," I said after we'd run through yet another traffic light.

"That's because she probably knows about his extracurricular activities," Diana said.

"Can't be sure about that."

"Why do *you* think Leo killed himself?"

"Obviously, the guy was deranged," I said.

"But paranoid delusions don't usually occur in older men."

"Diana, Leo's dead. It doesn't matter anymore."

"I'm sure it matters to his kids."

"Well, there's nothing we can do about that now."

Diana was quiet for a moment then, said, "You know, he drove a wedge between Trudy and me. We used to be really good girlfriends."

"Maybe you can start over again, now that she's—"

"A widow? We'll see. How are you doing with AA?"

The caravan slowed, then stopped at a traffic light.

The first tap on the rear bumper was barely noticeable. Not unusual in a busy suburban area. You just let stuff like that go, especially when I saw the driver hold up his hand, as if to say, *My bad*. But a second harder bump made me take notice.

"What the hell!" I said.

Muertens?

"Forget it, Tony. Just keep going," Diana said.

SIMPLE WHITE HEADSTONES stood at attention for as far as the eye could see. It was a beautiful bright sunny day and the monuments shimmered like little villas on a Greek island. The casket was suspended over the grave, a mound of dirt piled up alongside. Workmen fidgeted in the wings, anxious for the ritual to be over so they could finish up and call it a day.

Mourners, each holding a red rose, formed a semicircle around Trudy, as the reverend read scripture from a dog-eared Bible. "Ashes to ashes, dust to dust—"

As the prayer concluded, I scanned the grounds looking for Muertens' goons and the Crown Vic. Another funeral was in progress nearby.

"What's the matter?" Diana asked.

"Leo wasn't a religious guy, so I guess part of his punishment is being stuck with someone who doesn't know jack about him presiding over his final acknowledgement on earth."

Finally, the preacher said a resounding, "Amen," prompting all of us to echo the sentiment.

Once the gravediggers lowered the coffin, the reverend dropped his rose into the hole. Then Trudy stepped forward, sending a shower of pebbles plunking off the casket. She pitched her rose in, followed by Leo's mother. A line had formed behind Trudy, and each of us, in turn, followed suit.

Last respects were paid, then the gravediggers began to finish their work. And just like that, it was over.

Goodbye, Leo. It was nice knowing you. I'll probably be joining you soon, buddy.

But first I have some unfinished business to take care of.

42

I DROVE OUT TO TRUDY'S on Friday. Leo had been in the ground for less than a week, but what the hell. We were screwing while he was alive, so we weren't any more unfaithful now that he was dead.

We made love, but it was perfunctory, by the numbers, the old passion noticeably lacking and Trudy said so.

"What's the matter? You seem preoccupied, somewhere else. You getting tired of me?"

Overcome with guilt, it all just came gushing out.

"Leo didn't kill himself, he was *murdered*."

"What?"

"His boss, Muertens and a lawyer named Schoolkraft killed him. I drove Leo to Philadelphia. He was looking for a new life."

"How could you help him run out on me and the kids?"

"He thought it was the best option, and I agreed."

"Where do you get off thinking you can decide what's best for me?"

She hammered my chest with both fists, until I wrapped her in my arms. She struggled, but relented.

"I've seen things over the last few weeks to know that Leo was right all along. They brought him back and killed him. Now they're after me."

"No. No. This can't be happening again," she moaned.

"It's true. Muertens has already given me a death notice. He might want to hurt you too. He's a fucking maniac."

She tore away from me, and screamed, "I don't want to hear this. Put your clothes on and get out. Now!"

"He's got pictures. You and me—"

But she didn't hear me. I was talking to an empty room.

I showered, got dressed, and as I drove away, I had the feeling I'd never see her again.

43

DRESSED CASUALLY LIKE an office worker on a lunch break, I set up a surveillance post on a bench across from Schoolkraft's office on Queens Boulevard's wide center divide.

Behind me, remote broadcast vans were lined up in front of the County Court, their satellite antennas raised to the heavens. A crowd of reporters, microphones at the ready, were posted on the courthouse steps. Traffic in both directions had slowed to a crawl, rubber-necking drivers trying to see what the spectacle was all about.

An elderly gentleman ambled across the street, weaving through the slow-moving cars, nodded to me, then sat at the other end of the bench. He was wearing a baggy old tweed jacket. A serge cap was pulled rakishly to the side, and from the way he was dressed, I guessed he was one of the new Eastern European immigrants who'd moved into the area. He removed a sandwich from a paper bag, took a big bite, then tore off pieces of the crust and threw them to a pigeon pecking at the dirt a few feet away. Soon there were a dozen of the winged scavengers fighting over the crumbs scattered around the old man's feet.

I kept a wary eye on the old guy, while at the same time looking out for Schoolkraft and the roving Crown Vic. I didn't want to tip my hand to Muertens.

"You know what my friend *Jack the Butcher* said?" I asked the old guy.

He stopped scattering the crumbs, scratched at the gray stubble on his chin and looked at me with a quizzical cock-eyed expression that had an underlying taste of fear.

"Let's kill all the fuckin' lawyers," I muttered. "That's

my new motto."

He said something unintelligible—probably Slavic—put the half-eaten sandwich back in the bag, got up and started shuffling back across the street, the pigeons flapping behind him.

I followed his getaway, and just as he reached the sidewalk, caught a glimpse of Schoolkraft pushing through the revolving door into his building.

Almost time to start up the action.

AFTER MY RECON MISSION, I was back in the office working on the response to the Metro Tech request for proposal when Ted poked his head inside the doorway and said, "Hey, Toe-nee, my man. What's up?"

"What's going on, Ted?"

"You know, you can't always tell a book by its cover."

"What the hell're you talking about?"

"Un-huh," Ted snickered, then sauntered off.

"Idiot," I mumbled.

I'd barely gotten back to the RFP when Rick Meyerson entered the office accompanied by two of his staff who hung by the door, hands clasped behind their backs, military style. Rick grabbed a chair in front of the desk and said, "We need to talk."

"Am I in some kinda trouble?" I quipped.

Rick dropped some photos face-down on the desk.

"What're these?" I said.

"Take a look."

I turned them over.

Shit! Muertens had beaten me to the punch—the glossies he'd been so impressed with, plus a grainy shot taken at the Pink Pussycat with Demi Shadow sitting on my lap.

I handed the toxic photos back to Rick and asked, "Where'd you get these?"

"You've gone viral, my friend. Apparently everyone in your contacts list got hit with an e-mail from you with these photos attached. I'm guessing you didn't send them, so you got any ideas who might've?"

Still stunned, I wrestled with telling him about Muertens, but my embarrassment won out. After my silent response, he said, "Well?"

"Nope."

Rick leaned in closer and whispered, "You mentioned a while back that you were screwing around. Could this be your old lady's doing?"

"Why would she? It's hard collecting alimony from a guy with no job. I assume that's why you're here," I said, making it sound as if Rick had personally wronged me.

"A woman scorned—"

"So what now?"

"You violated the personal conduct clause in your employment agreement and the brass at HQ is not happy, to say the least. So, as of right now, you're on administrative leave with pay until HR gets the completed paperwork. You can appeal, but why bother?"

"This is bullshit, Rick."

He nodded, then said, "These gentlemen are going to escort you from the building, Tony."

"Look, Rick—"

"Sorry, pal, but I need your card key and company ID."

"Okay, but can you give me five minutes to gather up my personal things? Don't worry," I pleaded, "I'm not going to steal company secrets."

Now it was Rick's turn to go silent. I could tell he was struggling, trying to separate business necessities from our friendship. Finally, he said, "Frank here is going to be your guardian while I go take a leak. I'll be back in five minutes."

"Thanks, Rick," but he'd already disappeared.

A crowd of curious co-workers, smelling blood in the water, had begun to gather outside my office, so I asked Frank to close the door.

"You need to sign these papers for HR," Frank said.

"I'm not signing anything," I said. "Not without a lawyer."

Let the brass chew on that.

The phone chirped a few bars of *You Light Up My Life*. I'd programmed a special Diana-ringtone using the sappy 70s love song.

"That's my wife. Mind if I get it?"

The two guys looked at each other. Frank brushed an imaginary speck of lint off his jacket's lapel, then said, "Sure, why not."

I picked up the receiver. Got it halfway to my ear, close enough to hear Diana scream, "You lousy bastard!"

I was gone before Rick returned.

I left Diana's birthday elephant standing in the middle of the desk.

44

SURPRISED TO FIND THE LOCKS hadn't been changed, I slowly turned the doorknob, and tip-toed through the living room. The weak floor boards near the couch gave me away with a long, squeaky groan.

Without warning, Diana charged out of the kitchen, wielding an ornamental baseball bat she'd bought for protection shortly after the break-in, screaming, "You lousy piece of shit," then took a swing at my head. I ducked and stumbled backwards, yet she still managed to land a glancing blow on the meaty part of my left shoulder.

The bat was only about half the size of a Major League model, but it still packed one helluva wallop.

I reached up and grabbed her wrist as she reared back to take another swing at me. Unable to use the bat, she slapped me across the face with her free hand. I clutched her wrist before she could strike me again.

Her face was a mask of deranged madness, not unlike the countenance of some of the patients I'd seen while visiting Leo at Pilgrim State.

"Stop," I yelled. "I'm sorry. I didn't mean to hurt anyone," softer, now.

She went limp then, and dropped the bat onto the floor. I let go of her wrists, and her hands fell against her hips, all emotion, gone. "You're a coward," she whimpered.

"I'm not looking to fight, Diana. Just picking up a few things, then I'll be out of here."

"How could you? And with my *friend*?"

I waved her off, not dismissively, but simply because I didn't have a satisfactory response. The truth was too complicated to explain in a sound bite.

She started crying, gently at first, then building to a crescendo, her body wracked by spasms of all-out wailing. I moved to comfort her, but she shoved me away.

"Get the hell out," she said.

There wasn't anything to say after that.

I hastily gathered a few items of clothing, toiletries, and my SIG, and left the house.

45

MY LIFE UNRAVELED pretty quickly after that. Flyers spread throughout the neighborhood along Union Turnpike added more embarrassment, further isolating me. I thought of Trudy and wondered if she was getting a similar treatment, but at that moment, I couldn't worry about that.

I moved into the Jetz, the very same dive I'd phoned Schoolkraft from just a few short weeks ago. The pimply-faced kid I'd intimidated was still behind the front desk.

Recognizing my desperation, he seemed to take special glee giving me the shittiest room at the end of the hall, then said, "Phone's through the French doors, jerkoff."

My new home was small and cramped, a narrow space covered with a throw rug separating the single bed from the faux antique dresser. An industrial light fixture cast a jaundiced pallor over everything. I avoided looking into the mirror above the dresser, afraid to see the face of the sorry man I'd become.

A metal box at the foot of the bed had a sign scribbled on it that read, "five-minute soothing massage for twenty-five cents," so I threw back the faded rainbow comforter, dropped a quarter in the slot, and laid back on the sagging mattress. The springs squeaked as I squirmed around trying to get comfortable. The massage was more mildly annoying than soothing. You'd have to bring your own energy to get a party started on that bed.

I got up after three minutes, and moved to the battered chair next to the room's only window, peering mindlessly out at the cars lined up at the car wash across the street. The television in the adjacent room blared through the paper-thin walls.

I had a pretty good idea how Muertens liked to stretch out his little games, so I figured I had a little more time before he really dropped the hammer.

Although Leo had felt safe in hospitals, he made himself a stationary target—easy to find, easy to keep an eye on. Muertens knew where he was all the time. And later after Leo had been released, he'd remained stationary, holed up in his house.

I couldn't wait for Muertens' next move. I dialed Schoolkraft's number. He was in the office.

I put the gun and a cheap tape recorder in my pocket and went in search of redemption.

46

FROM THE UPPER LEVEL of the parking garage next to Telecom Structures, I watched Ted through a pair of high-powered binoculars prance around my old office like he was King Shit. I hadn't been gone two days, but he'd already made himself right at home—moving in his files and personal belongings.

Ted was a man of routine. He always left for lunch at the same time, and as he put on his jacket, I knew it would take him less than five minutes to get to his car. That's how long it used to take me.

I watched him stroll loosey-goosey to his car, not a care in the world. When he was only a parking space away, I stepped out of the shadows and said, "Hey, Ted. How's it going, man?"

Startled, he stopped dead in his tracks, pointed to the Sig pressed tightly against my thigh to keep my hand from shaking, and said, "Is that thing real?"

"You really want to find out, Ted?" I said, now leveling the weapon at his chest.

He cowered and whimpered, "Please don't kill me, Tony."

I lowered the gun, and he slumped back against his car.

"Tell me the truth, and this goes no further. Lie to me?" I paused, trying to lay on a cold-blooded-killer persona, then continued, "Well, I guess the same holds true for that option, too."

I moved in close, jamming the gun into his gut, shielding it from passersby.

"Whatever you want, Tony," he cried. "Whatever you want."

A car slowed, and the driver yelled out, "You guy's leaving?"

"Not yet," I said, and he drove off.

My eyes still riveted on Ted, I said, "Tell me about Muertens. When'd he first contact you?"

"Honest to God, Tony, who's Muertens? I don't—"

I pressed the SIG harder into his stomach. He grunted—clueless.

"The strip club photo. That was you, right?"

"I took it, yeah."

"Why?"

"Uh—"

"You wanted my job, no matter how the hell you got it, right?"

"Yeah. When that e-mail with you, you know, circulated around the office—"

"You decided to pile on."

Ted's tearing eyes were wild with fear.

"Nothing personal, Tony. You always … always treated me fair. I just wanted—"

Another car slowed. I waved the driver on.

I was really pissed now, but no matter how much I despised Ted, I believed him. He was exactly what he was when I hired him, nothing more, nothing less—a gutless weasel. My mistake was underestimating him. Asshole wanted my job—shouldn't every good employee want his boss' job? But by any means necessary? I didn't see that coming.

"You got what you wanted, Ted, so we'll leave it at that. You forget this, and you'll never see me again. If not—"

"No problem, Tony."

I stepped back, gesturing with the gun for him to leave. "Enjoy your lunch, Ted."

He scampered to the front of the car, unlocked the door with the remote, jumped behind the wheel and quickly backed out, almost slamming into an oncoming car.

My gun hand started shaking again.

47

THE JETZ WAS A COUPLE OF MILES FROM Schoolkraft's office. Walking was the best way to get there undetected, my reasoning being that Muertens would likely have eyes on my car. So, to avoid being spotted, I sneaked out a side exit away from the parking lot, veered onto neighborhood streets, and eventually crossed a footbridge over the Van Wyck Expressway. I got to the Boulevard near the cemetery and headed for Schoolkraft's, calling first to make sure he was there.

It took me about forty minutes to cover the distance, but when I entered the lobby I was certain I hadn't been followed. I signed in the visitor's log, took the elevator to the third floor, and walked directly into the lawyer's office. This time a different receptionist manned the front desk.

"Good morning may I help you?" she asked, all dimpled cheeks and good cheer, and just like that, all my advance preparation—gone. I'd come up with a menacing *nom de guerre*, Jack Butcher, to sign in, but suddenly overcome with performance anxiety, I could only hem and haw. "Ah . . ."

My hands were jammed deep in my pockets, one groping for the SIG, the other fumbling for the tape recorder. My fingers were as numb as my brain.

The receptionist stared at me, puzzled. "Sir, are you okay? How can I help you?"

Only then did I find my voice. "Dave Schoolkraft . . . I'm here to see Dave Schoolkraft."

She gave me a hurried glance, then flipped open a day planner.

"Do you have an appointment, Mr.—?"

"Uh, Butcher."

A frown, "I'm sorry, sir," she said. "I show nothing scheduled—"

"He's expecting me," I cut in.

"Well, he's with a client, Mr. Butcher. Why don't you have a seat and I'll let him know you're here." She eased her hand toward the desk phone to intercom Schoolkraft.

"That won't be necessary," I said, then bolted toward Schoolkraft's office, thrusting the tape recorder menacingly at the door, trying to find the RECORD button on the SIG in the other hand.

"Sir!"

Shit. Frantic, I found the RECORD button and stepped into the scumbag lawyer's office, my weapon now at the ready.

Schoolkraft was still holding the receiver when I burst through the door. The client sat in front of Schoolkraft's desk, and he jerked towards me as I made my loud entrance. He and Schoolkraft had been going over the set of floor plans spread out across the desk.

"What the hell?" Schoolkraft shouted. Real tough guy, but he dropped the act when he saw the gun, then put the phone back onto the cradle. His eyes darted between the gun and his client—hesitant, now unsure what to do or say. Not that I was any snappier. I'd practiced my gun-handling moves in front of the silver-spotted mirror before I left my fleabag motel room. Sorta like Travis Bickle, the dysfunctional cabbie in *Taxi Driver*. Instead of emulating Robert De Niro's cool toughness, I was more like a gun-control dweeb at an NRA convention.

The client, eyes wide, raised his hands like it was a stickup or something. I pointed the SIG at him, and shouted, "You, get the fuck out." And he did just that, bolting from the room, slamming the door behind him.

I had no idea how much time passed—Schoolkraft bug-eyed with fear, me figuring out what the hell to do next. But that all evaporated with the receptionist's frantic message over the intercom: "I've contacted the police, Mr. Schoolkraft. They're on their way."

Not much time. They were coming from across the street.

Before the scumbag could heave a sigh of relief, I reached across the desk and slammed the barrel of the gun across the bridge of his nose. A sharp crack, a smattering of blood and, much to my delight, a cry of terror.

"Why'd you kill Leo?" I shouted.

Schoolkraft cupped both hands over his nose and mouth, blood oozing down the front of his shirt. "I . . . I don't know what you're talking about."

I whacked him again, this time slamming the weapon against the side of his head. That produced the desired result, because when I repeated the question, he stammered, "Muertens is my client . . . he wanted to . . . Jesus, please don't hit me again."

In a reflex action, Schoolkraft threw his arms over his face to ward off an anticipated blow. This time, I caught him on his left hand, and he let out a yelp. I grabbed him by his tie, yanked him across the desk. How much more could he take? How much further was I willing to go?

Again, the voice of the receptionist bellowed from the intercom: "Mr. Schoolkraft, the police are here. Are you okay, sir? They want to know—"

"Hope they brought a body bag," I screamed. "Come through that door and this asshole's dead."

That's when the lawyer started crying—and talking. "It was all Muertens' idea; I just handled the paperwork. He had your friend killed—"

"Leo? Make it clear, dammit. Details," I said, thrusting the SIG at him. I had to feed the tape recorder now running in my pocket.

"Yeah, Leo. And his wife went along with it . . . Trudy, her name's Trudy; the bitch you're screwin'." *Does everybody know about me and Trudy?* "And you're next . . . Muertens wants you dead, so he can collect—"

Again, the intercom buzzed to life. "Mr. Butcher? This is Lieutenant Foy, hostage negotiator for the NYPD. Is everything all right in there? I'm out here in the next room, so please pick up, and talk to me."

"Stay back," I yelled.

"How can I help you get out of this, Mr. Butcher?"

My attention diverted, I heard Schoolkraft pushing away from the desk. I turned back to him, the SIG shaking in a crazy dance of nerves, and much to my surprise, the damn thing went off. Honest to God, I only wanted to scare him — instead, I blew a hole through his shoulder.

Suddenly, the door burst open, and then a blur of sharp pain and screams.

My pain, as I was tackled from behind, my head and shoulders ricocheting off Schoolkraft's desk. Viselike hands grabbed at my wrists. My head jerked backward by my hair and then slammed against the floor.

My screams, mixed in with the lawyer's screams and, of course, those of the cops.

"Don't fuckin' move," from one cop, his hand pressed against the back of my neck, his knee jammed into the small of my back. Belligerent shouts came from all directions. A sharp kick to the ribs; my arms violently jerked back, almost to the point of dislocation.

And then cold cuffs metallically snapped shut, followed by the deathless prose: "You have the right to remain—"

"Goddammit, don't move, asshole," from another cop, the toe of his boot exploding against the side of my head."

I never heard the rest of Miranda. Indeed, I remained silent—my lights suddenly extinguished.

48

TWO JOYLESS EMS TECHNICIANS checked out my head wound, and when it turned out to be superficial, the cops hauled me off to a local precinct, where I was photographed and fingerprinted. Two burly officers threw me into a dingy cage occupied by a disheveled prisoner sitting on the floor, his back against the bars, and his head buried in his hands.

When the cell door slammed shut, one of the cops said to his partner, "This fine upstanding citizen just beat the shit out of some shyster. Shot him up, too."

"So, why're we locking him up?" his partner said, then started laughing.

"Beats me," the first cop said, then turned to me and added, "Better get some sleep. You'll be taking a trip to Central Booking for arraignment in the morning, and that bus leaves real early."

"Yeah, see you in the morning, killer," the other cop said, still laughing.

After the cops left, I said to my cellmate, "Guess there's no love lost between cops and robbers."

He grunted, and that suited me just fine, because I wasn't in the mood for conversation.

The cage, with bars across the front and sides was backed against the wall in a sparsely furnished room. A table with two folding chairs took up the center of the room. A bare light bulb caught in the draft of an air vent, swayed above the table. The room could have been a place where the cops played cards on their breaks, or tuned up suspects.

I leaned back against the bars, pulled my knees into my chest, and tried to work through the jackpot I'd put myself in. Was it all because of my friendship with Leo, or the affair with Trudy? Either way, the punishment didn't fit the predicament.

My cellmate looked up and surveyed the room as if he was taking in his surroundings for the first time.

"I'm waiting for my old lady to come and bail me out," he mumbled. "You got a cigarette?"

I shrugged and just stared back at him.

The guy was a mess. His shirt was unbuttoned to his waist, and a red tie hung around his neck like a noose. Long strands of loose hair spider-webbed across his forehead. He smelled like a brewery.

"Just a couple of pops after a hard day. That too much to ask? Should be a constitutional right or sumptin'. It's them MADD bitches' fault. Fuck 'em."

The guy dropped his head back into his hands, then vomited.

AT SEVEN THE NEXT MORNING I was transported to Queens Central Booking and put in a holding cell with about forty other legally-challenged men, most of whom spent the night cramped in the cell. The place was ripe.

One of the prisoners told me the Queens Arraignment Court closed shop at 1 o'clock in the morning, so the unlucky souls who didn't make the cut had to hang out overnight to be processed.

Most of my companions were either black or Hispanic, plus a handful of Koreans and an Indian sprinkled in for flavor. In Queens, the justice system had a decidedly dark hue.

There were no benches, so the trick was to find a little piece of real estate and sit or just hang on to the bars. A toilet was off in a corner, and the space around it was the least desirable. Guys just walked over, whipped it out, and started pissing, most of it ending up on the floor. Fortunately, no one took a dump.

I stepped over a few bodies and squeezed in next to a

couple of guys lounging against the bars discussing their legal situation.

"You look like a smart brother," one of them said to me.

I shrugged.

"Fucking five-oh stopped me for DWB. That profiling shit's against the Constitution, or somethin' man. Yo, I know my motherfuckin' rights."

"Far's I know, DWB's not a traffic violation," I said.

"I was muling a trunk fulla shit."

And on it went.

The prisoner to my right asked, "Yo, whatcha in for, man?"

He looked like he belonged inside about as much as I did. Slight, maybe a hundred twenty pounds, Hispanic, a muscle nowhere to be found. If I had to rumble with anybody in the cell, I wanted him to be my dance partner.

"Jaywalking," I said.

"You clowning me, right?"

"Yeah. Double homicide."

"Say what?" he said, gave me a wide-eyed stare, then moved to the other side of the cell.

At some point during the night, I'd decided to use a Legal Aid lawyer to handle the arraignment, figuring the procedure was pretty basic stuff. Might as well save up for the trial. Just take the next lawyer on deck, as I passed through the system.

Figured I had nothing else to lose.

49

MY COURT-APPOINTED ATTORNEY met me in one of the eight-by-ten interview rooms. I knew the room's size because I counted the dingy two-foot ceiling tiles, and did the math. No view. A table and a couple of chairs against the far wall. A two-way mirror cut into the door.

The attorney looked green, probably in his late twenties or early thirties, with none of the battle scars of a beaten-down public defender. He wore a black double-breasted jacket and black slacks with a blue shirt, blue-and-yellow power tie. I took him for a clown. Obviously, he hadn't read *Dressing for Success.*

"Hello, Mr. Benson. I'm Josh Strickland, Legal Aid."

He handed me his business card, shook my hand. Scraped the chair across the linoleum floor, sat and scooted over to me.

"I've been assigned by the court to represent you until you're able to secure other representation, if you should choose to."

"Lucky you."

"You got a problem with me representing you, Mr. Benson?"

"You'll have to excuse my cynicism, Mr. Strickland—"

"Please call me Josh."

"Okay, Josh. But I've just spent the worst few hours of my life in a tiny cell with about fifty other guys, half of them puking their guts out, the other half screaming about one thing or the other. And to top it all off, I haven't taken a dump in almost two days and it feels like I have a brick up my ass. But, hey. Other than that, I'm feeling just peachy."

"Understandable, Mr. Benson—"

"Tony."

"Tony, sorry 'bout that, but take it easy, okay? I hope you haven't been talking to anyone in here. No jailhouse confessions."

"Hell, no. I saw that movie. I don't know anybody, and they sure as hell don't know me. These are not exactly the kind of people I hang out with."

"All right, here's the deal. You're going to be arraigned later this afternoon. It's a relatively simple procedure, and it'll only take about five minutes. The People will state the charges against you, then recommend a bail amount. I think it's going to be quite high. Can't beat up on a member of the tribe, Tony."

"I'm a lawyer, too. No member discount?"

Strickland looked at me like I had a few screws loose and said, "This is serious business, Tony. I figure at least a one-hundred-thousand-dollar cash bond, maybe more. You have access to that kind of money?"

"No way. I'm a hired hand, or at least I was. My house's underwater, the wife's going to divorce me, and you just know she'll get her pound of whatever's left of my flesh. At this point, I don't have the proverbial pot to piss in."

"I'll argue for a lower, more reasonable bail, but I'm not holding out much hope for the judge granting my request."

I noticed the thick stack of case folders on the table in front of him, and said, "Looks like you've got a full plate."

"Yeah, I'm overworked and underpaid. Most of these are petty, though. Driving with a suspended license, public drunkenness, squeegee guys, stuff like that. The mayor's been keeping me busy with his quality of life initiative, but you're my number-one priority."

He thumbed through my thin case folder.

"A coupla other things. From what I can tell, this will definitely go to the grand jury for an indictment. You said you're an attorney—"

"More like a desk jockey," I said.

"Then I'm sure you've heard the saying that a DA can indict a ham sandwich."

I nodded.

"Well in your case the DA's got the whole friggin' pig. It's a slam-dunk. Now you're entitled to a speedy trial, meaning the DA has to take his case to the grand jury in less than six days. That's a lot of trouble for them, seeing how this sewer's backed up. So, they'll ask you to waive your right to a speedy trial, giving them up to thirty days to go to the grand jury."

"Why the hell would I do that?"

"Because that gives us a little more time to work out a plea bargain. In this county there are no deals once the grand jury hands down an indictment."

"So?"

"You should sign the waiver."

"Anything else I ought to know?"

"Protocol in the courtroom. Court officers don't have a sense of humor, and they run a pretty tight ship. You don't speak to the judge. If you have something to say, you say it to me. I talk to the judge. No gum chewing, stand up straight, be respectful. We need all the goodwill we can get. Just sit tight, you'll be called soon."

"Aren't you going to ask me if I did it?" I asked.

"Does it matter?"

I HAD A GOOD FEELING ABOUT Strickland. He seemed competent, but unless I told him about Muertens, I didn't know what he'd be able do.

When one of the guards told me I had a visitor, I was expecting Strickland, but was surprised to see Detective Riley enter the interview room. He was dressed in his usual GQ-style, but his face was puffy, dark half-moon circles under his eyes.

"Still looking for those tickets to Vegas, Riley?"

Riley stomped across the floor, grabbed me by the collar with both hands, and pushed me up against the wall.

"Don't say another word," he said. "You open your pie hole when I say you can, get it?"

His face was so close to mine, I could've kissed him on his beaked nose.

"You blackmailing me, Benson?" Riley said, spraying spittle onto my face. "Trying to weasel out a deal with the DA, you little prick?"

I wiped my cheek and just stared at him.

Riley tapped me on the forehead with his knuckles and said, "Hello. You can speak now."

"In case you hadn't noticed, Detective, I'm in jail. Locked up. Behind steel bars. I have no idea what you're talking about."

He let go of my collar, took a step back and made a big production out of smoothing out my shirt, then took a photograph from an inside coat pocket and handed it to me.

"Don't play games with me, asshole. You're telling me this isn't your secretary's handiwork?"

It was the photograph I *wanted* Ma to take that night at the Fog—me handing over the thick wad of bills to Riley.

"You think you're smart enough to pull this shit off?" he said, then snatched the photo back and stuck it inside his jacket.

"You're not thinking straight, Detective, because if you were, you'd know that you took the camera away from me *before* I gave you the cash, remember?"

He raised an eyebrow, then his eyes went quizzical.

"Shit," he said, "you had backup," and came at me again.

I knew someone on the other side of the door was watching us through the glass, so I felt free to ward him off. "You lay a hand on me, and I'm calling in the cavalry. No way your buddies are going to give you another free crack at me. I suspect professional courtesy only goes so far."

He stopped short, then slammed his fist into an open palm. "I got almost twenty-five years on the job. I can't let it go to shit because of a dumb fuck like you."

"Shoulda thought about that before—"

Riley took a step towards the door, but stopped when I asked, "Where'd you get the photo?"

"You some kinda wiseguy? Your buddy Muertens had the balls to corner me in my own home, saying he was working on your behalf. Yeah, that's how he said it, 'I'm working on Mr. Benson's behalf.' I should've shot his crippled old ass right there on the spot."

"Muertens is *not* my pal. He's the reason I'm in here, and you're not going to like what I'm going to tell you about him."

I ran the story down for him—how Muertens killed Leo to collect on the insurance payout. Luke Skillman, the Wall Street broker hiding out in a Long Island sanitarium so Muertens couldn't kill him, too. And of course, my sordid tale.

"Muertens thinks he's some kinda of big game hunter," I said. "He stalks his prey until they're dead."

"You're full of shit, Benson."

It was much easier for him to believe I was using blackmail to work out a deal with the DA than an implausible story about some mystery man who killed for fun and profit.

"Suit yourself," I said. "Hey, you ever find out who killed Eddie Hambrick?"

"Yeah. Some lowlife drug dealer."

Riley knocked on the glass, impatient for the guard to unlock the door. Before he left, he turned to me and said, "Fish like you don't last a week in the joint."

I OFFERED A SILENT HOSANNA TO THE heavens. "Thank you, Muertens."

Riley was going to be my get-out-of-jail-free card. Way I had it figured, all I needed to do was point the DA in Riley's direction, let internal affairs break him down, leaving Riley no choice but to implicate Muertens to save his own ass. Then with blackmail charges pending against Muertens, I'd be free to feed the cops information into Muertens' insurance scam, and Schoolkraft's role in facilitating Muertens' scheme. And as the next victim queued up on the psychopath's to-do list, the DA would see me laying a beating on Schoolkraft as being more than reasonable under the circumstances. Hell, even a hack like Josh Strickland could sell that. Probation with a few hours of community service thrown in would likely be the stiffest sentence I'd receive, and that's if the case ever went to trial.

AN HOUR AFTER RILEY LEFT, Josh Strickland showed up. "You're not going to believe what happened. Some cop ate his gun. Pulled out his weapon, and just blew the top of his head off right here in the courthouse."

My stomach sank, and I was overcome with a wave of nausea.

"A cop? Suicide in the courthouse?"

"It happened just before I got here, but I heard somebody say he was a Nassau County detective here to visit an inmate."

"Shit." He had to be talking about Riley. "You get a name?"

"Naw, just some cop. Hey, you don't look so good."

I didn't feel so good, either. Riley had literally blown my plan all to hell.

50

THIRTY-SIX HOURS AFTER I was arrested, an officer led me from the holding cell into the courtroom. Strickland was already there standing before the judge. Court officers hung on the walls like paintings from Picasso's Blue Period.

"Stand there and face the judge," an officer barked, directing me to an orange arrow on the floor next to a sign that commanded DEFENDANT STAND HERE.

I'd driven past the courthouse hundreds of times, and had seen the long lines of people queued up to get in, not once wondering or caring what went on inside. I never imagined I'd be standing on the tip of an orange arrow, very much giving a shit.

The courtroom was small and claustrophobic with a low-hanging waffled ceiling. A few spectators sat on the benches behind me. With the mood lighting, it looked like the bridge on the Enterprise, and I was waiting to get beamed up the river to Sing Sing.

The judge, a thirty-something female, hovered above me behind a large desk, so I had to crane my neck to follow the proceedings. Strickland stood three or four feet to my left, and the distance was strictly monitored by the court officer who escorted me in.

"Keep quiet and move back to the arrow," the officer said when I'd drifted towards Strickland.

The aphorism IN GOD WE TRUST was chiseled into the granite wall behind the judge. I wondered who the trusting *We* was — the judge or the defendants. At that moment, I didn't trust God or the justice system. Muertens had taken care of that.

Another court officer who resembled Mr. Big, a character on HBO's popular *Sex and the City* franchise, approached the bench and handed file folders to the judge.

"File number 1534967, defendant Anthony Benson is duly charged with violation of New York Penal Code." Then he rattled off the sections I'd violated.

For the uninitiated, the charges included the assault on Schoolkraft and the cops who arrested me, reckless endangerment for firing the SIG, unlawful imprisonment for holding Schoolkraft in his office at gunpoint, and attempted murder when I put the slug into him. I'm sure there were some other handgun violations in there as well, but I lost track.

Mr. Big passed a copy of the pleadings to the judge, and everyone waited while she looked over the paperwork.

An infant in the spectator station started crying, and a court officer, in no uncertain terms, commanded the kid's mother to keep her quiet or leave the courtroom.

"Do you waive a reading of the charges, Mr. Strickland?" the judge asked.

"If it pleases the court, Your Honor, the defendant would like to be made aware of the charges against him," Strickland responded.

The judge, clearly annoyed, finally nodded to the ADA.

"People serve a demand for alibi," the ADA said. "The defendant, Anthony Benson, on October 15th did enter the office of David Schoolkraft, located at 80-10 Queens Boulevard, and there held the complaining witness at gunpoint and delivered terroristic threats to said complaining witness. Thereafter, defendant assaulted and committed bodily harm to the complaining witness' person. The People are requesting bail in the amount of $100,000 cash. Further, the People wish to convert this supporting deposition to information. There are no further notices in this matter, Your Honor."

"What is the extent of the complaining witness's injuries?" the judge asked.

"He's in serious-but-stable condition, Your Honor. He sustained a gunshot wound to the shoulder, severe head lacerations and multiple bruises on his arms, and two broken fingers."

"Judge," Strickland finally joined the proceedings. This guy was proving to be worth the nothing I paid him. "I respectfully request that the court grant a more reasonable bail. The defendant's a member of the bar, has lived in the community at the same address for over fifteen years, and has no prior criminal record, Your Honor."

"Thank you, Mr. Strickland. However, in light of the viciousness of the defendant's attack on the complaining witness, I'm going to grant the prosecutor's request for bail in the amount requested. Bail is set at $100,000. Can the defendant make bail, Mr. Strickland?"

"No, Your Honor."

"Has the defendant signed a waiver?" the judge asked the ADA.

"Yes, Your Honor. The People will be serving a grand jury notice."

The judge banged the gavel, then said, "Okay, that's it. Bailiff, please escort the defendant from the court."

Strickland was right about one thing—the proceedings took less than five minutes.

51

THREE DAYS LATER I sat in an interview room on Riker's Island waiting for Strickland to arrive. Immediately after I'd failed to make bail, I'd been transferred to the George Motchan Detention Center (GMDC), one of the ten mini-jails on the island.

Riker's sits in the East River between Queens and the Bronx. Urban legend has it that no inmate ever successfully escaped off the Rock, as the inmates called the hell hole, because of the killer currents—even though LaGuardia Airport, to the south is so close I could hit a pitching wedge to the north runway.

The sign at the entrance to the mile-long causeway connecting Riker's to Queens ominously announced the Rock is the home of "The Boldest Correction Officers in the World." As the creaky old Department of Corrections bus rattled over the causeway's speed bumps toward the processing center, I wished it had gone on forever, or at least until it stopped in Europe somewhere.

Riker's, with its 400-plus acres, was the world's largest penal colony. In a lot of ways, it was like Anytown USA. It had schools, athletic fields, gyms, medical facilities, chapels, a drug rehab center, grocery stores, barbershops, tailor shop, bakery, laundromat, power plant, print shop, bus depot, even a car wash. But that's where the comparison ended.

Anytown USA doesn't have more than 15,000 inmates housed within its borders.

GMDC, also known as C-73, served mostly as a detention facility for men awaiting trial, and didn't have the level of inmate violence the maximum-security George R. Vierno Center had. Nevertheless, it wasn't like I was lounging around in a suite at the Waldorf.

A lot of the inmates were gang members, and they were always trawling for new recruits, or fresh meat to prey on. I just stayed in my cell, kept my mouth shut, and tried to avoid all the drama.

I woke up that first morning, mistakenly thinking I was home, but the loud music, screaming inmates, and the sharp smell of disinfectant, quickly dissuaded me of that notion.

While I waited for Strickland, I studied the crude graffiti etched into the well-chiseled bench I sat on to pass the time. There was the ordinary—*Jose and Marie Forever* carved inside two interlocking hearts. And the edgy—*NYPD = KKK*. I should have been surprised that inmates could get their hands on the sharp instruments needed to scratch out their messages, but I wasn't. I'd read the stories about the cuttings and stabbings that, all too frequently, happened behind the razor-wire. These guys were geniuses when it came to developing weapons of singular destruction. Hell, on my second day, I watched an inmate slash another across the face with a shiv that looked like a toothbrush.

When Strickland finally showed up, I couldn't have been more surprised. It was as if he'd just stepped off the cover of GQ—a complete makeover, decked out in a stylish, silk shirt, expensive well-cut slacks, a pair of Ferragamo loafers. His dark hair was jelled and swept back off his forehead. I even caught a whiff of cologne.

He held out his arms and said, "A little something I was working on the side came through."

I shrugged, shook my head in wonderment.

"Any word on bail?" I asked before he'd closed the door behind him.

"Don't worry about that. This thing'll be over before that ever happens. So, how you getting along in here?"

I thought about what Riley had said to me—*Fish like you don't last a week in the joint*—and said, "It's only been a few days, but I'm bored and scared shitless at the same time. I keep my head down, mind my own business. Besides, I don't have anything anybody wants."

"Hang in there, buddy."

"For what, ten years? Out in eight if I'm lucky?" I said. "You talking to the DA?"

"Am I ever. Boy, you've been on a virtual rollercoaster ride, my friend—from deep shit to deeper shit, barely bobbed back to the surface, then back to deep shit again. The good thing? You didn't know anything about it. Know why? Because I'm on the case, my friend," he said, jabbing his thumbs into his chest.

"Virtual rollercoaster ride. That a new legal term?"

"You almost killed Dave Schoolkraft, Tony."

"Wait a minute. I just smacked him around a little."

"With a gun, and you shot him!"

"A flesh wound—nothing serious." *Yeah, deep shit to deeper shit.*

"Try selling that to the DA," Strickland said. "Remember the proximate cause doctrine from law school?"

"Vaguely."

"Schoolkraft had an allergic reaction to one of the medications he got in the ER and went into anaphylactic shock. Of course, since you'd rendered him senseless, he couldn't tell the doctors what drugs he *might* be allergic to."

Before I could protest, Strickland added, "Thankfully, he recovered. But if he'd died, the DA could have charged you with murder, even though the beating Schoolkraft took wouldn't have been what killed him."

"But before it got that far, seeing how you're on the case, I'm sure you would've argued Schoolkraft died from an intervening act, right?"

"Hey look, Tony, I'm not here to engage in a moot court debate with you," he said, his face the petulant mask of a five-year-old.

I backed off and started pacing around the room. It was twice as large as the interview rooms at County, and gave me plenty of room to stretch my legs. Two corrections officers standing in the hallway watched through the Plexiglas as I made my rounds.

"He dies, that could earn you the needle," Strickland said, feeling the necessity to get in the last word. Then he planted a black size-ten loafer on the bench, leaned forward and rested his forearms on his thigh. "The DA knows that dead cop, Riley, visited you."

He paused to let that sink in, then said, "And you were the guy in the photo handing over the payoff."

That caught me off guard, and I was sure Strickland noticed it.

"What? You think nobody would figure that out? It's in the log, Tony. And on top of everything else, Nassau wanted to throw a bribery charge at you."

"Bribery? For Christ sake, Riley was blackmailing me. *I was the fucking victim.*"

"And when were you going to tell me about that?"

I stopped pacing, felt my legs go weak, and sat on the bench that ran the length of the back wall.

"I hate surprises," Strickland said. "So, why was Riley blackmailing you?"

"He was working a case and found out I was fooling around. He threatened to tell my wife unless I got him a pair of first class plane tickets to Vegas."

"Well, it's your word against a dead cop's, so why pile on with more sordid allegations. Anyway, that's what I told the DA, and she saw my point. You dodged another bullet, my man."

"Guess it's my lucky day. I oughta run right out and buy a lottery ticket. Oh, I almost forgot. I'm locked up."

One of the corrections officers rapped on the glass and held up five fingers, signaling we had to wrap it up.

Finally I just said, "Muertens."

"Who is Muertens?"

"He's the guy that killed my friend, Leo, and I'm certain he tried to kill Dave Schoolkraft."

"I'm going to need more than some half-assed allegation like that," he said, unimpressed. "So?"

"It's a long story."

"We're running out of time, Tony. If I am going to represent you properly, I have to know everything you're *not* telling me. Get it?"

"What about the tape?"

"The tape's a laugh track for a bad sitcom that never made it to primetime. Besides, most of it's unintelligible."

"I guess I had it shoved down too deep in my pocket."

I started pacing, again.

"Didn't matter. Schoolkraft's confession, if you want to call it that, was sketchy at best. And you shooting and beating the crap out of him coerced even that. So, if your big plan was to get some kind of admission of guilt, it didn't work."

"Shit," then I sat back down.

"But *your* intentions sure as hell came through loud and clear."

Now it was Strickland's turn to pace.

"Guess I didn't have it shoved down far enough," I said.

"Okay, quick. Tell me about this Muertens character."

Like a busted up piñata, I spilled out the whole thing.

I have no idea how long I took, but when I finally ended the tale with the cops hauling my ass out of Schoolkraft's office, Strickland merely shook his head and said, "You're shittin' me, right?"

"That another legal term?"

"Sorry."

"I thought it was nonsense myself when Leo told me. He said no one would believe him until he was dead. He's dead, so now I'm a believer."

Strickland actually chuckled, then said, "Ah, earth to Tony. No offense, but that's got to be the craziest yarn I've ever heard, and I've heard some pretty wild ones. Why the hell would this guy Muertens go to all that trouble to kill your friend Leo, and then go after you?"

"That's exactly what I asked Leo, and what he said didn't make any damn sense either. Way I figure it, Muertens is just a crazy fuck who likes to control and manipulate people. It's all about money. He forced me to sign over a life insurance policy and execute a codicil to my will, leaving him everything I've got. Not that it's a whole lot. It's all a big game to him."

Strickland sat next to me, put his hand on my forearm and said, "I'm going to make a motion for a psych evaluation."

"What, you think I'm crazy?"

"No, it's just procedure, and it'll buy us some time to work out a deal."

"You talk to my wife about this?"

"No. By the way, is she pissed at you because of your little fling or because you're in jail?"

"She threw me out after Muertens e-mailed her some incriminating photos."

Strickland got up, locked his steel gray eyes on mine and said, "I don't do divorces."

I don't do divorces. One of Leo's crazy codes. Muertens' code to indicate a lawyer's been bought and paid for.

"What'd you say?" I asked, reeling.

"Guard!" Strickland shouted, knocking on the door. Then he smiled at me and said, "I'll be in touch, Tony."

I snapped and lunged after him, swinging wildly, trying to dislodge his head from his shoulders.

"You cocksucker! Muertens bought you off? Why you mother—"

The next thing I knew, a burly arm jerked my head back, a fist slamming against my temple. I couldn't breathe. The guards wrestled me to the floor, pinning my arms, then getting in a couple more shots for their trouble.

Strickland leaned in and popped me a good one, too.

Two more officers ran into the room, grabbed Strickland's arms, tied him up in a bear hug and escorted him out.

"Asshole!" Strickland's parting shot.

I COULD FEEL THE FIGHT draining out of me as I was being hauled off to the punitive segregation unit in full restraints, like some Hannibal Lecter character, and thrown into a dark cell the size of a coat closet.

Invisible inmates greeted me with hoots and howls, yelling out stuff I couldn't understand over the din, like I was a war hero returning home from the war in Afghanistan.

One of the two corrections officers escorting me quieted the men down, then said to me, "Try pulling any that Wild West shit in my cell block . . ." He popped me in the forehead with the butt of his baton, hinting at the consequences of me pulling some Wild West shit in his cell block. I had a good imagination.

Once the door clanged shut, I plopped onto the bed pushed up against the wall and took stock of my surroundings.

The cell was spartan. A stainless steel sink-and-toilet combination faced the cell door less than an arms-length from where I lay. That was it. The toilet must have backed up recently, because the smell of raw sewage permeated the cell. I quickly got used to it. There was a window in the door with perforations cut in the Plexiglas, giving the COs a full view of what was going on inside.

I checked my face in the shiny metal mirror welded to the wall above the sink. There was a knot in the middle of my forehead. My left eye was swollen and starting to discolor. A spot of blood bloomed on the bridge of my nose.

As near as I could tell, it was around one o'clock when a CO slipped a white Styrofoam tray of food through a slot in the door. The vegetables were overcooked, the meat patty buried in an unidentifiable gelatinous brown sauce. I wolfed everything down like I hadn't eaten in a week.

Later, word must have gotten around about my tussle with Strickland, because my actions seemed to have earned the inmates' respect.

"Lawyer telling you what to do and you want somethin' different, right?" the jailbird in the adjoining cell said.

"Motherfuckers always wanting you to cop to somethin' you don't know nothin' about."

A few shouts of encouragement, then from another cell, "Cocksucking lawyers. They just the grease to make it easy for the man to fuck you in the ass," this followed by a chorus of, "Right on, brother."

SEGREGATION TURNED OUT TO BE my good fortune—locked in the cell 23 hours of the day, the other hour spent alone in the gym shooting hoops. It felt good to be safely away from the madness that was GMHC.

Right after lunch on my third day in the hole, I was once again secured in restraints and taken from the cell. When I asked the officers where they were taking me, they answered with stony silence.

Newfound reputation or not, I was fearful they were hauling me back to gen-pop, but instead was taken to the administrative area, where I was surprised to see Rick Meyerson, my friend from Telecom Structures, straddling a chair.

The room was painted the same puke green that seemed to cover every flat surface in the joint, and was empty except for a dozen or so folding chairs. It might have been a training room.

Rick gestured to the chair next to him, and said, "Grab a seat," then to the guards, "You can take those off," meaning the restraints.

They looked doubtful, but when Rick, wearing a strained smile, said, "I can handle this badass," they reluctantly complied.

"Jesus, Rick, it's good to see you," I said, rubbing my wrists.

Rick merely stared through me, not at me, with eyes void of compassion—dead eyes, like those of a shark. No smile, no hint of recognition. He looked haggard like he'd battled New York traffic to get here.

Finally, after what seemed like an eternity, he said, "So you're a tough guy, now? Some shyster lawyer overcharges you for services rendered, so you shoot his ass?"

I wanted to interrupt, clarify that *Strickland* was my lawyer, not *Schoolkraft*, the weasel I shot. But surprised by his sharp reaction, I clammed up. Didn't expect him to be impressed, but he *was* a man who understood violence.

"Tell you what, Tony. I'm either your friend, or I'm not. You've got about two seconds to make up your mind."

I didn't hesitate. "It's complicated, Rick."

"Try me. I'm a smart guy."

"Damnit, Rick. Other lives are at stake," I stammered. "I can't—"

"Can't? You almost killed a man—"

"It was an accident. I just meant to scare him. Besides, he's a fucking lawyer."

"Now you're a comedian? That's your best defense? You're going to jail for a very long time, my friend. Let's see if you're still cracking wise a month from now, and to be honest, I don't see you making it."

"You're an optimist."

Rick rocked back, balancing the chair.

"What's that supposed to mean?" he said.

"I was told I wouldn't last a week."

That said, Rick squeezed my knee. I saw another flash of the murderous intent he'd displayed that afternoon at the Metro Tech. After a beat, he released his grip and said, "A little friendly advice. Learn the rules fast, because life hasn't prepared you for what you're going to have to deal with inside."

He stood, pushed the chair back and signaled to the guards he was ready to leave.

"Don't get punked, even if it means you gotta take a beating, 'cause if you don't, you're going to wind up being somebody's little bitch. And believe me, these guys ain't the pussy lawyers you been beating up on."

Rick extended his hand, which I reluctantly grabbed. "One last thing, Tony. If and when you finally pull your head outta your ass and decide to trust me with whatever the hell's really going on, give me a call."

"Rick, I didn't ask for any of this," I said.

"You know anybody who does?"

AFTER RICK LEFT, the officers led me into an adjoining room.

"What's going on?" I said.

"Strip search," one of the officers said. "Take your clothes off."

"You've got to be kidding me. You guys were watching the whole time. Did it look like we were passing shit back and forth?"

They weren't kidding. I piled my clothes at my feet and stood naked before the officers.

I couldn't have imagined all the places where one could hide a weapon or contraband. The officers made a visual inspection of my entire body. From the top of my head to the bottom of my feet. Shining a flashlight in my ears, nose, mouth; directing me to lift my arms; pulling and tugging my lips, tongue, ear lobes, genitals.

And the final indignity—bending over and touching my toes.

"Now, cough."

52

THE JUDGE GRANTED Strickland's motion to have me sent for observation and I was committed to a minimum security residential treatment center in the middle of a leafy suburban neighborhood in Bayside, Queens. I was sure that when Strickland petitioned the court even the DA thought I was nuts.

The van pulled into the circular driveway in front of a large two-story red brick chateau-styled building that could have easily been mistaken for a nursing home or an assisted living condo.

My DOC escort led me into the building. A mural of a meadow at sunset dominated the lobby. The security station, manned by two armed guards, was to the right and I shuffled across the marble floor towards them. Several people in the visitors' lounge to the left watched me being processed.

"Welcome to Shady Grove. I'm Dr. Redmond, and I'll be your attending therapist over the next however-long you're here with us, Mr. Benson."

Redmond cut a Lincolnesque figure—tall, rail-thin, a gaunt face with high cheek bones and a shaggy beard over a bobbing Adam's apple. A tweed jacket gave him a professorial look.

Redmond took me through the registration process, then signed the release and handed it over to my escort, who then unlocked my handcuffs.

"Come on, let me help you get settled in," Redmond said.

I followed him through a metal detector to the elevator bank. Redmond produced a barrel key, opened the doors, then used the same key to activate the floor-selection buttons. We got off on the second floor. Redmond introduced me as if I was an old friend to the guards at another security station, and he did the same with staff we met as he gave me a tour of the floor.

The furnishings throughout Shady Grove were shabby. The rooms were equally drab and much in need of a fresh coat of paint. There were lots of windows looking out on the grounds, but all were sealed and had shatterproof glass. Escape—not that I had any idea of trying to—would be loud and difficult.

As near as I could tell, there were only about forty residents, most of whom looked damn near comatose.

"Relax the rest of the day," Redmond said. "We'll get started tomorrow."

53

THE NEXT DAY, I was given the Minnesota Multiphasic Personality Inventory test, MMPI for short. Redmond told me the results would be used to determine my competency to stand trial.

"You have to be capable of assisting your legal team with the criminal defense," he said.

"Legal team?" I laughed, thinking of Josh Strickland and Muertens as my trusty legal defense team.

The test had 567 true-false statements. One statement was "Evil spirits possess me." I answered, *false*, but I'm sure my false to number twenty-eight—"When someone does me a wrong I feel I should pay him back if I can, just for the principle of the thing"—had the clinicians scratching their heads.

So, the test bought me some extra time at Shady Grove while the shrinks tried to figure me out.

My days revolved around forty-five-minute group sessions—one in the morning, one in the afternoon. With breakfast, lunch, and dinner sandwiched in, it was a pretty full day. The sessions covered everything from current events, to movies and sports. Occasionally, someone would actually try to talk about the shit that really ailed them, but no one was interested and that discussion ended pretty quick.

Dr. Redmond, usually dropped by in the afternoons for five minutes to treat me. I spent the rest of the time either in my room lounging around, or in the day room reading a book or watching TV.

My roommate was a zombie. He didn't say a word to me when I arrived, nor since. A real nutcase, but that was okay with me because I didn't want to know anybody, and I certainly didn't want anyone to know anything about me. I made no friends, and for the most part, kept to myself.

I was playing solitaire when Redmond came up behind me.

"How are you feeling today?" asked the upbeat shrink.

"Fine, Doc. How 'bout yourself?"

"Good, thanks." He tapped on a digital notepad, then said, "You been taking your meds?"

"You bet, Doc." In fact, I'd stopped taking the antipsychotic drugs prescribed to help subdue my twin demons, Muertens and Schoolkraft. But since I was totally sane, taking it gave me all of the side effects—lethargy, dry mouth, upset stomach and constipation—and none of the benefits. With my stomach problems, the little white pill came back as a sour deposit in my mouth.

Oh, I almost forgot—decreased libido. But what the hell. I wasn't getting laid at Shady Grove.

"So, you feel they're helping you?" Redmond said.

"Most definitely. I feel great."

I wasn't sure if he picked up on my gee-whiz sarcasm, because he plowed right on.

"Let's talk about Dave Schoolkraft."

Ah, *the* question—which actually began as "Why? Why would an otherwise responsible, sane and rational person do what you did? And you're a lawyer sworn to uphold the law," which eventually was shortened to "What motivated you, Tony?"

My response never varied: "Schoolkraft and Muertens killed my friend, Leo. And now they . . . well, Schoolkraft's in the hospital. Anyway, they're dead set on killing me. I was protecting myself. But I've told you all this before. Story's not going to change, Doc."

"Okay. Why do they want to kill you?"

"Because Muertens is a crazy motherfucker and Schoolkraft is just a go-along—a spineless jellyfish."

"You had a tape recorder. You said last time we talked that you wanted Schoolkraft to confess. Were you intending to kill him if the police hadn't intervened?"

Truth is, I didn't know. Nonetheless, I said, "He tried to kill me, so I was only protecting myself, no matter how it came out."

Redmond tapped out some more notes, then said, "I might have to adjust your meds."

"Okay. You're the doctor, Doctor."

That was my therapy, such as it was. Five minutes tops on a slow day.

I WAS IN THE DAY ROOM playing a video football game with a fellow patient when she walked in.

"Hello, Tony."

Distracted, I threw an interception, and then turned towards the voice.

"Trudy! I'll be damned," then to my opponent, "Let's save the game. We'll finish later, okay?"

The patient eyed Trudy, then got up and walked away.

"I never expected to see you again," I said. "You look great."

No bull. She did. A pair of jeans—tight, but not too tight—her brown hair with straw highlights swept back off her face and pulled into a ponytail.

"Howya doing?" I said.

"Good. Not bad. Keeping busy."

"The kids missing their father?"

"Leo was an asshole. They're doing just fine, thank you very much."

That got my attention.

"Not exactly the grieving widow, I see."

An awkward silence. Trudy fidgeted. I sensed she had something to tell me, but was reluctant to get it out. Finally, she took a deep breath and with an icy indifference, said, "You remember Leo's crazy story about the code?"

I nodded. Didn't like where this seemed to be heading.

"*I don't do divorces*, for Dave Schoolkraft."

"How'd you know about Schoolkraft?"

"Leo ever tell you the code for the betrayed wife or mistress?"

"What was that?" I asked, but didn't really want to know.

"*Hit the road, Jack.*"

"*Hit the road, Jack*, the old Ray Charles song?"

As Trudy smiled, a woman I'd never known before quipped, "So, Tony, it's time for you to hit the road."

Too stunned to move, I stammered before managing to say, "You and Muertens? Right from the start?"

"Not from the start. I came in later."

"How could you be so fucking cold to Leo! You knew Muertens was going to kill him."

"How could I do that to Leo? Fuck Leo! He didn't give a shit about me or the kids. When Muertens showed me the photos of that weirdo at a peep show, it was over. Muertens offered me a little proposition, and I jumped at it."

I squirmed in the chair. "How much blood money you get?"

"Let's just say me and the kids have nothing to worry about. Ever. Muertens did okay, too."

"And I was just a pawn in your little game."

"Leo used you first, trying to escape. Muertens couldn't have that. You put yourself into play."

"But why Leo?"

"You don't steal anything from Muertens."

"What about me and you?"

Again, she smiled. "I enjoyed our time together, Tony. I really did, but there was no me and you. It was fun, but it was never more than sex. Things were really tough and I needed someone. You happened to be there. No big deal."

"You really know how to hurt a guy."

I felt like a total fucking jerk. Everybody got a piece of me. Then again, it was my own damn fault. Like Muertens said, pussy was the ruin of many a good man.

"It was nothing against you."

"Well, Trudy, why don't you tell me who it *was* against?"

"Sorry, Tony."

"All right, all right. You certainly didn't hold a gun to my head. But tell me one thing. Your little plan would have gone up in smoke if Leo had killed himself before all the paperwork cleared. What then?"

"Muertens is a great judge of character. He knew Leo didn't have the balls to kill himself. It was always take care of Number One with Leo. He was a selfish little prick."

I started to pace.

"But what about all of those pills Leo took? If you hadn't showed up when you did, he'd be dead. He commits suicide and no money."

"You didn't really believe that little prank, did you?"

Shit, I don't know what to believe any more.

Dr. Redmond approached from across the room, and asked, "How's the new prescription working out, Tony?"

"Great, Doc."

He smiled. I didn't know if it was because I actually had a visitor or that Trudy looked so good.

We were quiet for a moment, then seeing I had no inclination to engage him further, he said, "Don't let me disturb you. Carry on."

After he left, I said, "I know you didn't just come here to cheer me up."

Trudy was patient, as frigid as a cold-hearted bitch could be. She watched me struggle, trying to fathom the purpose of her mission, then finally tired of the game said, "Muertens wanted me to put a deal on the table for you."

"He's got the DA in his pocket, too?"

That damn smile of hers again.

"Just go through this thing quietly, don't make waves, and stop throwing his name around. You and Leo aren't good for his image."

"And what's in this for me?" I hissed.

"You know what he can do."

"I know Muertens was right about one thing. He said you were a filthy whore."

She winced, but continued, "You're going to be offered a plea bargain by the district attorney."

I stared hard at her, ran my hands over my face.

"You'll be sent to a psychiatric treatment facility, evaluated every six months, and when you're judged to be recovered, you'll be released. That shouldn't be a problem for you."

"And the DA is going to go along with this?" I asked, incredulously.

"Muertens can make it happen. All you have to do is take the deal, do the time, and walk away."

"What's the catch? What's in this for Muertens?"

"You'd have to ask him, but I think you can guess he's no philanthropist."

I chewed on my lower lip. With the very real possibility of a felony conviction hanging over my head, I didn't really have much of a choice.

"If I don't take the *deal*, then what?"

She stared past me, then shrugged.

"End up like Leo?" I said.

"That's up to you, Tony. So do I tell him we got a deal, or not?"

54

I TOOK THE DEAL.
Strickland, my Armani-wearing, Legal Aid prick, brokered the plea agreement with the DA just like Trudy said he would. I needed all of my self-control not to go after the bastard, especially when he had the balls to wish me good luck as I was being led from the courtroom.

The judge sent me to Pilgrim State, the same state psychiatric facility out on Long Island where Leo had been. But now my perspective was entirely different. Unlike Shady Grove, where I spent a month for evaluation, Pilgrim's patients had major problems—real hard-ass cases. We're talking criminally insane killers and rapists. They're on another floor, but still . . .

Generally, I kept to myself, mostly in my room, reading or exercising, and oddly enough I'm in the best shape I've been in for quite awhile—mentally and physically. Too bad I had to be stuck in a fun house to say that. If I were on the outside, I'd probably be just fat and disgruntled.

I resided in a four-bed unit that I usually shared with two or three other guys. So far it's been a revolving door with a new crew of roomies every couple of weeks. I don't say much to any of them and they don't say much to me, and that's the way I like it. I don't want to know their personal history, or their favorite ice cream. Strictly hello and goodbye, and most of the time even that's too much conversation.

Hey, most of the guys in here even think professional wrestling's the real deal.

"You know that stuff's not real," I said to my roomie, Smitty one night, while we watched Body Slam II or whatever it was called, on TV.

"Is this?" Smitty said, looking around the room.

"Got me there, dude."

"If you think it's so phony, why don't you let Black Samurai grab *you* in his sleeper hold. Rock-a-bye baby," one of the patients said.

MY DAYS WERE STRUCTURED around group therapy and individual sessions, just like at Shady Grove. Group's a joke, but the one-on-one therapy really allowed me to touch on emotions I'd buried deep inside. I've been able to examine that "me" who emerged during the whole sordid Leo-Trudy mess, and understand the professional and personal malaise that made me weak and vulnerable. I know that sounds like psychobabble, but it's true.

No mention of Muertens, though. His tentacles extend everywhere, and around here you can't tell who might be checking you out. Certainly didn't want that madman taking any more notice in me than he already had. Oh yeah, he still kept tabs on me. Just this past December I received a package. Plain brown wrapper, no return address, postmarked Flushing, New York; addressed to Mr. Tony Benson, c/o Pilgrim State Hospital, Long Island, New York. It was a copy of Time Magazine, the cover story *Why Do Men Cheat*. "Woe to those who are led by their dicks," read the note attached.

The crazy fuck. *He* should be in here, not me.

Occasionally, I'd wander out into the day room and play cards. Sometimes the guys and I actually played Go Fish, and I'll flash back to that night I first saw Leo after his breakdown. Me, Diana, Trudy and the dearly departed Eddie Hambrick, sitting around the table playing that silly card game.

"*Leo, you got a jack?*"

"*No, go fish . . .*"

Boy, if I knew then what I know now.

Diana divorced me a *minute* after the judge read the verdict. It's kind of difficult to remember when, exactly. If time had a color, in here it would be gray. I suppose I could have fought her, but why bother?

My first six-month evaluation came and went. After my petition was denied, one of the doctors told me, "Can't have the judge thinking you pulled a fast one with some bogus insanity defense, now can we?"

So, I just bided my time, and waited for my next evaluation—a silent clock tick-tocking away in my head until I could re-enter society as a fine upstanding citizen.

But everything changed almost a year into my "bit," as my fellow patients call it in here.

It started with a familiar voice sounding over my right shoulder. "Hello, Mr. Benson." I turned and was astonished to see Dr. Redmond, my shrink from Shady Grove. He shook my hand.

"Doc? What're you doing here?"

Redmond's clothes hung loosely on his scarecrow frame. He looked tired and worn down. Picture old Abe Lincoln towards the end of the Civil War—gaunt, the weight of the world bearing down on his shoulders.

He twitched as he said, "Working on a consult. How have you been?"

A curious question.

"Uh . . . I'm in a mental institution, Doc."

He looked around at my sorry surroundings and said, "Yeah, but you shouldn't be here. That's what I want to talk to you about. To make amends. I'm sorry."

"Amends for what?"

Redmond glanced around the room, then handed me some folded sheets of paper. "This will explain some of it."

"What's this?"

"Call me after you've read it. Anytime. Day or night, and please understand—I had no choice."

And then he squeezed a business card into my hand, and limped towards the exit.

I RETREATED TO MY ROOM. I had three roommates, but only Smitty was there, sprawled on his bed. The room was twice as long as it was wide, and the large mirror on the back of the door made it look infinitely longer. Four beds were aligned along one wall, a small three-drawer bureau opposite each bed for our meager belongings.

I was in the back near the room's only window—the privilege of seniority.

My bunkmates had photographs of loved ones on top their bureaus, indicative of their tenuous ties to the world outside Pilgrim. There was nothing on mine.

I sat on the edge of my bed and read through the three pages. They were photocopies, and some of the text was smudged. A coffee stain blotted the top corner of the first page. It took me two minutes to finish reading, but less than a second to realize I wasn't getting out of Pilgrim State anytime soon.

SHADY GROVE RESIDENTIAL Treatment Facility
   Dr. Barry Redmond
   Patient: Anthony Benson, Case # 02-321
   Admitted: July 24, 2009
   Date of this report: August 28th

   Background: Mr. Benson was remanded to this facility in November and was in our care for one month, as ordered by the court. Starting in early 2009, Mr. Benson suffered a series of personal and financial setbacks that ultimately resulted in the breakup of his marriage of fifteen years, being fired from his position of Chief Legal Officer at Telecom Structures, and major stock market losses. For reasons unknown at this time, Mr. Benson fixated upon Hezekiah Muertens as the cause of these setbacks. Also, sometime during this period, Mr. Benson took on the persona of an avenging angel, we believe triggered by his friend Leo Radigan's suicide.
   Thereafter, Mr. Benson began to harass and stalk Mr. Muertens to the point where Mr. Muertens, fearing for his safety, obtained a full order of protection against Mr. Benson, a copy of which is attached hereto.
   On or about July 15, Mr. Benson burst into the law office of Dave Schoolkraft, an associate of Mr. Muertens, beat and shot

him, leaving him in critical condition.

Prior to standing trial for the assault on Dave Schoolkraft, Mr. Benson was sent to Shady Grove for observation. After thirty days of clinical study performed by Dr. Barry Redmond, PhD, Dr. Redmond concluded that Mr. Benson had diminished capacity, and therefore was incapable of assisting in his own defense. Further, Dr. Redmond recommended that Mr. Benson be remanded to Pilgrim State and treated until such time as he was able to do so. The Supreme Court, Queens County, ruled to accept Dr. Redmond's recommendation and transferred Mr. Benson to Pilgrim State for treatment until such time as Mr. Benson is capable of understanding the charges against him and fully participates in his own defense, or be released, as the findings may dictate. A complete copy of Dr. Redmond's report is included herewith as part of Mr. Benson's medical file.

A preliminary diagnosis of acute paranoid schizophrenia was made at this facility. Although this diagnosis is extremely rare in male adults in their 30s, Mr. Benson's medical history indicates that he exhibited symptoms of mental illness prior to 2009. However, Mr. Benson was able to mask these symptoms and carry on a meaningful and productive life until he was overcome by the personal and financial setbacks mentioned herein above.

Mr. Benson's therapy at Shady Grove has included a regimen of anti-psychotic drugs, including Risperidone and Depakote. A complete list of drugs, their dosage and the length of time prescribed, is included herewith as part of Mr. Benson's medical file. To date, neither of these medications has proven to be successful and Mr. Benson continues his decline, perhaps to a fully catatonic state.

<u>Prognosis:</u> Mr. Benson will likely continue to worsen in the near-term and in that event he will likely become a danger to himself and others. Therefore, Mr. Benson should be closely monitored and restrained and kept separated from the general population if he doesn't respond to medication.

<u>Therapy:</u> Continue with current medications, increasing the dosage to the levels prescribed in the medical file attached herewith.

THE PLEA AGREEMENT had just been a carrot that Muertens dangled in front of me, and it wasn't hard for me to fathom his motive. Short of getting the charges against me dropped, a close-by mental institution with minimal security was the best place for me to be, so he could keep an eye on me.

I gave Redmond an hour to get back to his office before I called him. Normally, there'd be half-dozen guys waiting for the phone, but luckily, there was no one there.

Redmond snatched up the receiver before I heard a single ring tone.

"Redmond!" he yelled.

"Why, Doc?"

"I had no choice, Mr. Benson. He—"

"Muertens?"

"Yes. He threatened me and my wife. She's dead now. Cancer. And my daughter's off in Africa somewhere doing missionary work, so she's out of reach. I don't care what he does to me."

"Why don't you go to the police?"

"Hell. Best case scenario? I'd lose my license. Or the alternative, wind up in jail. You probably couldn't tell it from the report, but psychotherapy's my life. Helping people resolve their issues. If I couldn't practice, I might as well be dead."

"What's to say I won't go to the police myself?"

"Honestly? Who'd believe you, Mr. Benson?"

"So what now, Doc?"

"It's Muertens' intention to keep you safely warehoused at Pilgrim State with more reports like the one you just read. But if we can show that you're not a threat . . ."

"And how do we do that?"

"I know a young local news reporter. Her name's Marcia Simpson and she's a friend of my daughter's. She's been doing a report on the downsizing of Pilgrim State, and how the Office of Mental Health's selling off the property to developers, putting desperate people on the streets. Watch the news tonight."

"What does that have to do with me?"

"She's been looking to get inside Pilgrim State and interview some patients. You'd be a great candidate."

"No way OMH's going to allow some news reporter to

come waltzing in here with a camera crew."

"You're right, at least not officially. Don't worry, she's quite clever."

"She could make my situation worse."

"I don't believe so. This could be win-win for you and the State."

"How so?"

"You get to show the evaluating committee that you're not some raving lunatic, and the State gets to show the public that they're not releasing raving lunatics. You see? Win-win all the way round."

I COMMANDEERED THE TV in the day room from six to seven. It took some doing, though. I had to barter a few personal items—an old watch, a new deck of playing cards, a pair of socks Smitty took a liking to.

No one was interested in watching the local news, so I had the room all to myself. Marcia Simpson came on at the bottom of the hour, right out of a commercial break.

She wasn't the typical TV eye candy with long blond hair, a toothy smile, and legs that wouldn't quit. Not that she was unattractive, but somehow I imagined she had to work twice as hard as her competition to make it to the networks.

The piece began with an aerial view of Pilgrim State's two giant buildings looming on the horizon, peeking out above a row of pine trees. As the camera zoomed in and cleared the trees, the broad expanse of a campus littered with the rubble of demolished and abandoned buildings came into full view. A hawk circled the grounds, and the camera followed it as it descended in a graceful spiral to a perch upon a stack of discarded bricks.

Behind and to Simpson's right, several patients played basketball on an outdoor court cocooned within the confines of a chain-link fence.

"This," Marcia Simpson said to the camera, pointing to the large art deco brick building behind her, "was once the largest mental health care facility in the world and at its peak in the 1950s, it housed more than 20,000 patients. But in the 70s, health care professionals began moving away from supersized facilities such as this, instead emphasizing smaller drug therapy and community-based treatment centers. Now the State, through its privatization initiative has sold off all but a few acres of this campus, leaving just a few buildings to accommodate less than two-hundred patients. The question some people are asking is, 'What will happen to the mentally ill?' And some health care advocates are worried."

The scene shifted to a raucous town hall meeting, where a representative from the department of health was being shouted down by the throng. He tried to gavel the unruly mob to order, but to no avail.

"They're tearing down facilities but I haven't seen any money being put into community-based centers," shouted a mental health care advocate, standing at the back of the hall. "Beds are hard to come by as it is, and it's going to get a whole lot worse. I'm telling you, a lot of sick people are going to end up living on the street."

Next, a typical suburban neighborhood of small box houses with white clapboard siding. Children riding bicycles, playing ball. The giant towers loomed over the scene.

"They got child molesters and murderers in there," said a local homeowner. "Our kids, nobody'll be safe. I'm a taxpayer just like the fat cats, but they always get what they want at our expense."

The camera shifted back to Marcia Simpson standing in front of one of Pilgrim's derelict buildings.

"Who are the nameless, faceless people still inside these massive walls? Watch part two of this three-part series where we'll go inside and find out. This is Marcia Simpson reporting from the grounds of Pilgrim State Hospital."

Later, I couldn't sleep what with Redmond's report replaying over and over in my mind. My six-month evaluation had been invisible leg irons—I wasn't going anywhere. But in an odd way, Muertens had done me a favor by getting me sent to Pilgrim State.

After all, Rick Meyerson's and Detective Riley's prognosis was that I couldn't survive in a maximum security prison.

55

VISITING HOURS WERE almost over when Marcia Simpson, accompanied by a man who appeared twice her age, entered the day room. One of the orderlies pointed them towards me and Simpson strode confidently across the carpeted floor, the man trailing a couple of paces behind.

Seeing Simpson in the flesh confirmed my initial impression of her as an overachiever, clawing her way to the top. She was about five-six. Her short dark hair was cut in a style more suited for an older woman, but the 'do complemented her round face. A small scar beneath her right eye was the only blemish on an otherwise unremarkable visage.

She wore a faded blue Nike T-shirt and distressed jeans with a jagged tear on the right knee. All in all, not the glam reporter on network TV, more like the visitors passing through here every day.

Simpson's companion had a beer belly, his wrinkled white shirttails tented around his ample waist. Shaggy, gray mutton-chop sideburns covered his puffy cheeks, and age lines criss-crossed around his eyes. A pair of Ben Franklin glasses hung precariously on the tip of his nose.

"Mr. Benson?" Simpson said.

When I nodded, she extended a slim hand, shook mine with a muscular grip, and introduced herself and her assistant, Roger Lanier, who looked as if he'd rather be anyplace other than Pilgrim State. He waved, kept his head down, ignoring my proffered hand.

Picking up on Roger's reticence, Simpson whispered, "Hey look, Roger . . . I know you think this is a shit assignment."

"They're all shit assignments, Marcia," Roger whispered

back.

Simpson brushed loose strands of hair away from her forehead, and glared at Lanier. "What?" she said through pursed lips.

"Don't worry, Marcia. Got you covered," Roger said.

Directing her attention back to me, Simpson said, "Thanks for seeing us, Tony."

I nodded.

"You know why we're here?"

"I've got a pretty good idea, Ms. Simpson."

"Please call me Marcia. Our mutual friend, Doctor Redmond, thought we might be able to help each other out."

I liked that, her getting right down to business.

Most of the day's visitors had come and gone, but a group sat clustered around one of the staff doctors. Another of my roommates—everyone called him Tattoo Man—was taking his customary laps around the room. By the time Simpson arrived, he'd already been at it for over an hour.

"Let's go sit by the window," Simpson said. "A little more privacy, all right?"

She spoke to me as though I was a child that needed to be coddled, or else I'd explode into a tantrum.

"This," the reporter said, wagging her finger back and forth between us, "is guerilla reporting." She spoke with a sense of glee, radiating at the thought of the clandestine interview. "So remember to speak clearly, and always keep your eyes on me."

"Okay, Marcia. Did Dr. Redmond tell you anything about my situation?"

"Doctor Redmond respects his patient's confidentiality, Tony."

Not, "yes," but not quite "no," either. Didn't matter, because I didn't believe her. It was the way she said it. Too practiced. Besides, if she'd read Redmond's report she'd know better.

"He thought you might be able to help me with this story I'm working on," she said.

"Which is?"

"The State's mental health system is broken, and I want to shine a big Hollywood opening night spotlight on it."

"An exposé."

"Yes, and Dr. Redmond thought you'd get some therapeutic benefit out of sharing some of your experiences."

"Win-win," I said.

"Win-win."

Simpson handed me a piece of paper and a pen, then said, "Would you mind signing this? It's a standard waiver agreement giving the station permission to use your image and comments for broadcast."

Since I'd been judged mentally impaired, I seriously doubted the waiver would stand up in court. Nonetheless I signed it and slid it across the table to her.

"You don't have to walk on egg shells, Marcia," I said. "I won't break."

"Sorry about that, Tony." She laughed, then said, "Just a few questions. Ready to get started?"

"That's why you're here."

Simpson waggled her fingers, presumably the signal for Roger to start recording. I wondered where they were hiding the equipment. One thing I'd learned at Riker's was there were plenty of places on and in the human body to hide just about anything.

"How long have you been at Pilgrim State?" she asked.

"Going on close to a year."

Then I proceeded to tell her the how, but not the why of my unfortunate circumstances. Mostly things she could've learned, and probably had, by checking the public record. She struck me as someone who did her homework.

"You're a lawyer?" Simpson said.

"Until I get disbarred."

"What practice area?"

"Corporate."

She paused, then said, "You get many visitors?"

"Not anymore." I turned and looked at Roger. "Seems

people are afraid of mental illness. It's like they think it's contagious or something."

Simpson leaned in closer. I could smell her perfume; the first touch of femininity in a very long time.

"So, what's a typical day like for you?" she asked.

"Well, there's therapy—"

"What kind of therapy? Within the scope of confidentiality, of course."

"Group, mostly. Not so much private. There's plenty of down time, too. I read, play cards with some of the guys. Watch television. By the way, saw your report the other night."

"What did you think?"

"Informative."

Simpson sat back and gave me a long stare, then said, "Thanks, I guess."

My roommate Smitty shuffled over from the other side of the floor, pushing past Lanier, then hovered over Simpson.

"You're the gal on TV," he said to her.

Simpson recoiled.

"Can't you see we're talking here, Smitty," I said.

He mumbled something unintelligible, stepped back a few feet, then pointed at Simpson. "I know I seen you on TV," Smitty said, lingered for a moment, then joined the patients in front of the television.

Simpson seemed to shrink in the chair as she checked out the room. Satisfied that no one was paying attention to us, she said, "Please go on, Tony. A typical day—"

"Am I giving you what you need?"

"You're doing fine."

"They let us walk around the grounds for about an hour every morning, weather permitting. Chaperoned, naturally. They certainly don't want us crazies roaming around scaring the locals. But the saving grace is we're in the midst of a pine forest and the air is just saturated with the aroma of all those tall trees. It's intoxicating. And for that hour I'm out there, I almost feel like the person I thought I was before I got thrown into this place."

"That's quite poetic, Tony. Do you write?"

"Not really."

She leaned in closer. "You should. I can tell you've really got talent."

"Stroking the crazy guy, eh, Marcia?"

"No, I mean it," she said, none too convincing. "So, what's your next step in here?"

"Well, I'll be evaluated by the medical board, shortly, and if I pass their inspection, I'll get the chance to re-start my life."

"Then what'll you do?"

"That depends on the bar association. I'd like to go into private practice. Maybe even work with people in my situation. I think I've learned a few things about myself that could be useful in that regard."

"Like what?"

"That information's privileged, Marcia."

She laughed. Even Roger cracked a smile.

"Do you think you're ready to be released, Tony?"

"Absolutely."

IT WAS WELL into the wee hours and my dorm mates were sound asleep. I should have been, but was wound way too tight, my encounter with Marcia Simpson pushing aside my dreams. I thought the whole thing went well, and the board would have a difficult time justifying keeping me locked up.

I was beginning to believe I could make it on the outside, Muertens be damned.

One of my mates, probably Smitty, snored softly. He stopped when the door creaked open, momentarily illuminating the room just enough for me to see a man enter. It was a little late for staff to be making their rounds, so I assumed it was Tattoo Man, who usually got up at least once during the night to roam the hallways. The guy was a shark, having to constantly stay in motion.

Tattoo Man bumped into a bed, and stopped mid-stride. The room stirred, and he stood statuesque for a beat, waited for the sleeping men to settle. Then, inexplicably, he clicked on a flashlight and followed its tight, meandering beam further into the room.

It definitely was not Tattoo Man.

I watched the intruder tiptoe across the floor toward me, stop at the foot of the bed. The light touched my face for an instant, then was switched off.

Alarmed now, I said, "What the hell you want?" then rolled away from him, tumbling between the bed and the wall. When the man's fist smacked against the mattress, I pushed hard on the bed, knocking him back against the bureau.

"What the fuck's going on?" a startled Smitty yelled.

The intruder momentarily entangled in the bedding, quickly freed himself, and fled from the room. But the commotion set off the newest roommate, and he started wailing like a firehouse siren.

Ponder, the night orderly, switched on the overhead lights and burst into the room. The lights flickered, then brightened.

"Somebody shut him up," Ponder said.

I crawled out from behind the bed and tried to calm the newbie down, but to no avail, his wailing getting higher.

"What the hell's going on in here?" Ponder shouted.

None of us responded.

"You know we don't tolerate no horsing around." Ponder said.

Another orderly entered the room, restrained the screamer and hauled him away, his shrieking echoing down the hall.

Then Ponder said, "Okay, Benson, what happened?"

"I don't know. The guy just started screaming for no reason. Bad dream, I guess."

Ponder was slim, just like the dude who attacked me. I tried to remember something else about the intruder, but couldn't come up with any other clues as to his identity. So,

Ponder may, or may not have been the guy.

We stood around like Madame Tussaud's wax figures until Smitty finally said, "Somebody came in the room."

After a long side-long glance at Smitty, Ponder looked at me and said, "Straighten this place up, Benson, and stay the fuck in your own bed."

He pointed his flashlight at me, and I nodded.

"You got five minutes before I turn the damn lights out," he said.

CONSIDERING THAT SOMEONE had tried to kill me, I slept reasonably well the rest of the night. I figured the assailant, whoever he was, wouldn't try anything again, at least not right away.

By the time morning rolled around, something Leo once said struck me—his crazy tale about AIDS, and how he believed Muertens would infect him. Of course, my response at the time was "You're fucking nuts, man," or something to that effect.

But now, was there a better explanation for what had happened? I hadn't made any enemies. Didn't piss anybody off, at least not that I knew of. This had to be Muertens' doing.

I checked the bed for slashed sheets or puncture marks, but there was nothing to indicate the weapon I'd been attacked with or if there was a weapon.

I needed help, and there was only one person I could turn to. I went to the phone, dialed, then said, "Hey, Rick—"

I was cut short by Rick's flat greeting on his answering machine. "You know the drill."

"Tony here. We gotta talk, buddy. It's important, maybe life-or-death important. Call me. I'm still in the same place." I hesitated, then added, "If you don't know, that's Pilgrim State out on Long Island." I gave him the building and ward number. "It's time I told you everything."

56

"DR. PATTERSON, YOUR two o'clock's here."

It was my regularly-scheduled therapy session the following day with Dr. Patterson, and as usual I was sitting in front of his secretary Susan's desk, waiting for him to wake up from his lunchtime nap.

"Who's the patient?" Patterson said, sounding groggy.

"Anthony Benson," she said.

"Oh, yes. Give me a minute before you escort him back, and would you bring his file? Thanks."

Susan shrugged, giving me a wan smile. I smiled back, crossed my legs and waited.

"I better get his pick-me-up tea before he complains," she said, then left.

My thoughts wandered to Ma. She would have been appalled by the secretary's drab work space. The old wooden desk, the dim ceiling light fixture, a phone with old Lucite pickup buttons. And, of course, Patterson for a boss. I hoped Ma still held me in some regard.

After about ten minutes, Patterson buzzed the ancient squawk box, indicating he was ready. Susan, who'd already delivered his tea and returned to her sanctuary, escorted me into his office, dropped the file on top of a magazine Patterson was reading, then spun on her heels and left.

Patterson slid the folder aside, fixed his gaze on me for a beat before turning back to the magazine. "Almost finished," he mumbled.

The weekly sessions with Patterson had long outlived their usefulness and I could've just as easily stayed in my room, watched a replay of any one of the previous sessions and gotten just as much feedback. Clearly, Patterson's heart wasn't in mental health anymore, and he should have retired a long time ago.

For the umpteenth time I took in the bastard's face. He appeared to be in his late sixties. His pale face sagged and loose skin gathered at a bulbous double chin. Patterson gave off an air of poor health.

A pair of rimless glasses was perched on the end of his ski-slope nose. He wore a buttoned-down white shirt, the long sleeves rolled up around his elbows. A suit jacket was carelessly thrown over the back of his chair.

Signaling the charade was over, Patterson concluded with, "Very interesting."

He poured steaming hot water from an ornate ceramic tea pot into a matching mug, dunked a tea bag a couple of times, stirred in a packet of sugar, and then took a tentative sip.

I stood with my hands clasped behind my back while he went through this high-tea ritual.

Suddenly revived, Patterson began whistling some vaguely familiar Broadway show tune between pursed lips, and seemed almost jaunty. Perhaps he'd just remembered that he won the doctors' football pool.

Finally, I thought, *screw it*, sat down and took in the diplomas and certificates hanging on the walls and pictures of his grandchildren prominently placed on the desk. A small gold-plated plastic trophy proclaiming Patterson WORLD'S BEST GRANDPA was huddled among the grandchildren. That must have been a new addition, because I hadn't seen it during our last session. A large green leather couch with red seat cushions opposite the desk near the door completed the cramped office's furnishings.

Patterson closed the magazine, threw it aside, looked at me and said, "Perhaps you'd be more comfortable on the couch, Mr. Benson." When I didn't move, he said, "Suit yourself."

Patterson peered over his glasses. "I understand you had a situation in your room last night," he said.

"No big deal. One of my roommates is having a hard

time adjusting."

Patterson removed the glasses and stuck them in his shirt's ink-stained breast pocket.

"You sure that's all it was?" he said.

"Doctor, if I could get into the heads of everybody stuck in here, I'd be sitting in *your* seat."

"Humph," Patterson said. He picked up my file and started poking through it. I didn't know why, nothing had changed in the week since I'd last seen him.

"It's almost time for your evaluation, Mr. Benson."

"In two weeks, but who's counting?"

"But," he took a dramatic sigh, "before the medical board completes its review, we want to factor in how you'll adjust to living on the outside. We wouldn't want to not do our homework and have you running around menacing the locals, now would we?"

It was my turn to peer at him. He parroted what I'd said during the clandestine Simpson interview.

"How do you determine my fitness, Doctor?"

"We'll release you to your spouse or some other sponsor for a weekend, and monitor how you're doing."

Patterson blew on the hot tea and took another sip.

"I'm divorced, Doctor."

"There must be someone else you can stay with."

He placed the mug on the tray.

"I'll make some calls."

"Good. Do that. You'll see Dr. Redmond in the morning and he'll explain everything to you, okay?"

LATER THAT NIGHT, I WATCHED Simpson's exposé in the game room. The piece had been edited down to about five minutes, and Simpson interviewed at least two other patients and several anonymous staff members for the story. Both patients raged against the institution, surely sounding quite insane to the casual viewer. I knew a lot of what they said was true. But the volume was way too loud, and Simpson certainly didn't do me any favors by sandwiching my *crazies running around threatening the locals* comment between the madmen's rants.

My face was a mosaic of pixilated pastels, my voice had been run through a filter and I sounded like a robot from one of those cheesy old science fiction movies before George Lucas came along with *Star Wars*. Probably my paranoia, but I felt even a casual acquaintance would have known I was underneath that rainbow of colors. Fortunately, none of the other patients were watching.

Simpson did cut me a break, though, by using the footage where I pontificated about "helping people in my situation once I got out," but her report was not quite the win-win I'd hoped for or what she had promised. I gave it a C-Plus.

Would it be enough?

THE NEXT MORNING, I was transported in a hospital van to Doctor Redmond's office. I sprawled on the bench behind a wire mesh partition separating me from the driver, luxuriating in the fact this was the first time I'd been off the grounds since I was institutionalized.

The world seemed foreign to me as I watched ordinary people doing ordinary things—things I'd been denied for almost a year.

The driver pulled the van into a parking space at the front of the building designated for official vehicles, got out and unlocked the rear door.

"Here we go, pal," he said.

"I didn't know Dr. Redmond had an office in Huntington," I said.

The man, a middle-aged Hispanic, flipped through some papers on a clipboard.

"This where they told me to take you," he said. "Mid-Island Medical Center, first floor, room one-oh-three." He extracted a cell phone from a pocket in his oversized blue Pilgrim State Hospital jump suit and said, "You want I should call and check it out?"

"I guess."

After a series of head-nods and uh-huhs, he dropped the call, and said, "Doctor Patterson say it's okay. I wait for you here."

I'll be damned. The air seemed crisper, the sweet smell of freedom.

I pressed the handicap entry button and the double doors swung open with a whoosh. I checked the building's directory, verified Dr. Redmond's suite number, and followed the arrow down the vinyl-tiled hallway to Room 103.

I opened the door and entered a small dimly-lit vestibule. Two chairs flanked a round table with a Tensor lamp and a stack of magazines on top. A sound spa was on the floor near the door to Redmond's office preventing anyone in the waiting room from eavesdropping. Other than the gentle digital rainfall, all was quiet.

I took a seat and waited. After about fifteen minutes, I got up and put my ear to the door, but heard nothing. I knocked lightly. No response. The knob turned easily in my hand, and I slowly opened the door.

"Dr. Redmond?" I said, poking my head into the room—

And saw the blood. Redmond was slumped over, his face planted in the middle of the desk. His arms dangled at his sides, both wrists slit. A box cutter lay in a pool of blood.

I closed the door, moved to his side and checked his pulse. He was dead.

Panic momentarily immobilized me. My first thought—wrong place, wrong time. My second—Muertens had put me there. And then I ran out of the building, downshifting to a slow-yet-nervous walk as I neared the van.

The driver leaned against the vehicle, puffing on a cigarette, headphones over his ears.

"Finished so soon?" he asked, smiling.

"Doctor's not feeling well."

He took off the headphones, the smile vanishing as his eyes locked on my hands. "Hold up, mistah. You got blood—"

I didn't hesitate, clipping him with a roundhouse right to

the temple, stunning him. Slipped behind him, and grabbed him in a choke hold just like the wrestler Black Samurai executed on television. The guy struggled, desperately trying to peel my arm from around his neck, not knowing the harder he struggled the quicker he'd pass out. It took about ten seconds. I eased him to the ground, wiped my bloody hands on his coveralls. Emptied his pockets, cleaned out his wallet, and took his cell phone, then jumped in the van, buckled up, and drove to the exit.

As I sped away, I saw the black Crown Vic pull out behind me.

MUTT WAS SO CLOSE ON MY TAIL, I could make out the red pimples on his passenger's sunken cheeks.

Back when I was a rebellious teenager, my buddies and I used to pile into my old Chevy Corvair and cruise around Suffolk County looking for mischief. One of our little pranks was to cut in front of old geezers tooling around town in a big Buick or Caddy, then turn the Chevy's parking lights on and off real quick. Invariably, the old guys would jam on the brakes thinking they'd just barely avoided rear-ending us.

It usually took two or three times before the old geezers got wise. We'd get a big laugh out of watching their faces turn from panic stricken to feral snarl, followed by an angry outburst of obscenities. Thinking back, it's lucky for us none of those old-timers suffered a heart attack.

Just like the geezers, Mutt jammed on the brakes when I switched the parking lights on-and-off. Unlike the geezers, though, he didn't slow down the next time I did it. So, I sped up to put a little distance between us, then braked hard. The Crown Vic rear-ended me, then ricocheted into a line of parked cars.

57

I DROVE THE VAN to the Cold Spring Harbor, Long Island Railroad Station, about five minutes from Mutt's wreck in Huntington. A sign at the entrance to the parking lot warned that vehicles without a town permit would be towed away at the interlopers' expense.

After a couple of turns around the parking lot, I found a spot a long walk from the station's waiting room, locked the van, then skipped the keys across the pavement where they wound up beneath a car an aisle over.

Tucking my blood-dyed hands in my pockets, I headed to the waiting room, looking to get cleaned up.

The station was painted the same institutional green as the cell block at Riker's, and was probably smaller than most of the master bedroom suites in upscale Cold Spring Harbor. The ticket booth was to my right, restrooms to the left. Two red-stained benches faced each other across the worn, tiled floor. Other than the man in the ticket booth and a young couple sitting on the bench facing me, the room was empty.

After I cleaned up, I checked the timetable and bought a ticket to New York Penn Station even though I had no intention of riding all the way into the city. If the cops were able to track the ticket, they'd have a good time trying to figure out which of a half-dozen stops along the Port Jeff-New York line I might've gotten off at.

The next train was scheduled to arrive in fifteen minutes. Just enough time for me to set in motion a plan I'd been devising to extricate myself from the mess I found myself in.

I used the van driver's cell phone to call Rick. Got his answering machine again. Didn't have his cell, so I tried Telecom Structures, but disconnected when I got bounced to his secretary's voice mail.

I dug Marcia Simpson's business card out of my wallet and dialed her. When she answered, I said, "I think I might be able to help you with your mental health exposé," my voice muffled in the crook of my arm.

"Who is this?"

"You can call me Leo, but who I am is not important. I have some e-mails you'll want to see, Ms. Simpson."

"How did you get this number?"

"You gave me your business card."

"I give out lots of business cards."

I started walking westward, away from the waiting room, and said, "At Pilgrim State."

When Simpson didn't respond, I said, "Don't worry, I'm not talking patient records. It's mostly interoffice memos, and there's no expectancy of privacy with e-mail correspondences."

"You sound like a lawyer. Is this on the record?"

"Yeah. You can fact-check everything I give you. Believe me, it'll all pan out."

"Why're you doing this?"

Playing the pity card, I said, "I have a brother—"

"So, how do I get a look at these e-mails?"

"Why don't we meet up?"

"Sounds good. I'll bring my technical guy along, if that's okay by you."

I pivoted and started back towards the waiting room.

"You mean Roger? No problem."

"How do you know Roger?"

"Told you. Pilgrim State. I saw you talking to Tony Benson."

"You're an orderly?"

"You want what I got or not?"

"Okay. Where do we meet, and how will I spot you?"

"You know the Roman Eagle in Hicksville?"

"Yeah. A Roman eagle once urban is now in Hicksville quite suburban."

"What?"

"The inscription on the statue. Every kid on the Island knows about it. It sat on top of the original Penn Station, and was moved to Hicksville in the '60s when that old Beaux-Arts masterpiece was demolished to make room for some drab high-rise office buildings and the new Madison Square Garden."

"Thanks for the history lesson. One o'clock."

"That's less than thirty minutes."

"Then you'd better get going."

A man in a silver BMW convertible pulled up to the front of the waiting room, stopped, popped the trunk and stepped out of the car. I must have been in his way because he hit me when he opened the door. No, "excuse me," no nothing. But I didn't say anything. Couldn't afford the unwanted attention.

A young woman jumped out on the passenger side, hurried around the back of the car, and stood next to the man while he retrieved an overnight bag from the trunk. When they embraced ("Have fun, dear," the guy said) I took a quick look around, then dropped the cell phone on the floor behind the driver's seat. Let the cops follow the arrogant prick all over the North Shore.

"The 12:33 to Manhattan is on time, and will be arriving in five minutes," the announcement boomed over the public address system.

I went to the front of the platform and waited.

58

THE RIDE TO HICKSVILLE station took less than fifteen minutes. I rode the escalator down to the street level, then headed for the eagle at the west end of the station's parking lot.

A teacher standing at the base of the statue lectured a group of bored grade-school children on the eagle's history.

I stood a few paces behind them, as close as I dared without being mistaken for a pedophile.

"The old girl's beak's broken," I overheard the teacher say.

"Maybe she needs a facelift," one of the kids yelled out, prompting raucous laughter until the teacher quieted the kids down.

A female voice coming from behind me said, "Leo?"

I turned and faced Marcia Simpson, my tired face reflecting in the dark lenses of her designer sunglasses. Unlike the first time we met, she was dressed in casual business attire—a three-piece pantsuit with an aqua, short-sleeve jacket, black pants, and a print blouse. She carried a laptop computer. A Bluetooth headphone was stuck in her left ear.

Roger Lanier tagged along behind her, loaded down like a Sherpa. He almost dropped the equipment bags slung over his shoulders when he saw me.

"Wait a minute. You're Tony Benson, the guy I interviewed at Pilgrim State a few days ago," Simpson blurted out, then removed the sunglasses. I hadn't recalled her eyes being so dazzlingly blue. "What are you doing here?"

"Weekend pass."

"It's Wednesday," she said.

"Figure of speech."

"Marcia," Roger Lanier, the cameraman, said, his voice cracking, "I didn't tell you, but I heard on the police scanner that the cops are looking for this guy. Maybe we should get out of here."

An eastbound train rumbled into the station.

"I didn't kill Dr. Redmond, but I know who did." Didn't know what else Lanier heard on the scanner, but thought it wise to mention it now if I was to gain Simpson's confidence.

Simpson gasped. "Dr. Redmond's dead?"

She took a cell phone from her bag. Before she could dial, I said, "I was supposed to see him this morning. Found him dead, instead, his wrists slashed." I held my hands out, palms up, and shook my head. "I'm sure I left all sorts of incriminating evidence behind."

"Yeah, like a dead doctor," Lanier said.

"Hey, numbnuts. Would I have called you if I killed him? I need your help, Marcia."

Simpson didn't run, and at that point I felt she could go either way—stay and hear what I had to say, then call the cops, or split, and call the cops. I counted the obvious dilemma playing out across her face as *having a chance*.

She put the cell phone away, then said, "Let's see the e-mails." Cold, efficient.

Roger pleaded. "Marcia?"

"I don't have any e-mails . . ."

"Then why am I here?"

"Because what I do have will get you that big job you covet with the networks."

"You don't know me," Simpson blustered.

"Just hear me out," I said. "You don't like what I have to say, call the cops."

She turned to Lanier—for assurance? "Let's hear it, Benson."

Lanier looked like he was getting ready to bolt. But I knew he wouldn't run. He couldn't. Not without Simpson. Wouldn't be good for his "man creds" if he left a colleague—especially a woman—alone with a *killer*. He had to let this play out.

I led them a few steps away from the kids, then said, "Usually it's the disgruntled employee who goes postal. Walks into the office, shoots the boss, then kills himself. Except with my friend Leo Radigan, it was the psycho boss who killed the employee."

I told her about Muertens and his murder-for-fun-and-profit scheme; how I got sucked into the vortex and was the next victim on his hit list.

After I'd finished, she said, "That's the craziest damned thing I've ever heard."

"Hello!" Lanier said loud enough for a few of the kids to turn around. "He is *cray-zie*."

Simpson held out a restraining hand, then said, "I can't run a story like that. It's pure speculation at best. Where's your proof? Plus you're telling me this Muertens character's a big muckety-muck in the community? He'll sue my ass off. I want to build a career, not destroy it before it ever gets off the ground."

"You're all of, what—twenty-five? Thirty, maybe?"

"Thirty-six, and it seems the closer I get to making it to the big time, the longer it takes," she said.

Agonizing moments of hesitation before her shoulders slumped, telling me she was "all in." She'd follow the story wherever it went.

"Look," I said, "I appreciate you trying to help those poor schmucks at Pilgrim State. God knows they need an advocate like you. But the public doesn't give a shit about them. They'd just as soon keep 'em locked up and throw away the key. What they want is their nightly news filled with heavy doses of murder, mayhem, and Kim Kardashian."

"Boy, are you cynical."

"What do you expect? I've been locked up for a year."

Two girls from the school group ran past us. One of them bumped into Roger, and he petulantly brushed the kid aside.

"Asshole," the girl said.

I smiled at the girl. Wanted to tell her how observant she was, but—

"I can get you the proof you need, Marcia. I'm your personalized, gold-plated ticket to the big time."

"Why should I believe you?"

"Let me answer your question with a question. Why'd Redmond falsify my psych evaluation?"

She didn't answer, but Lanier did. "Sounds like the perfect motive for murder to me."

I had the floor and I wasn't about to let Lanier nudge me aside. "Come on, Marcia, I know he told you."

She nodded a silent admission.

"This is bullshit," Lanier again.

"He never said why," Marcia said. "But I can tell you, he wasn't proud of what he did. It really ate at him," then offered a rueful smile.

That makes me feel better.

"He told me he had no choice. Muertens threatened his wife," I said. "You don't believe me, check out the circumstances surrounding my friend Leo Radigan's death, and there's a broker out in Breezeway Terrace, a sanatorium on the North Shore, in a similar situation. Name's Luke Skillman. If what you find doesn't convince you I'm on to something, I'm done."

"Got that right," the cameraman said.

"Can you find out where Muertens is hanging out today?" I said.

Simpson punched some notes into her smart phone, then said, "How do we nail this bastard?"

"He's going to confess. To everything."

I WAS IN THE END GAME, and as every good chess player knows, to navigate the myriad of combinations that can play out on those sixty-four squares, it calls for slow and thoughtful deliberation.

But I was on the clock and had to make a move—fast.

While Simpson went back to her car to contemplate if

taking a chance on me was worth blowing up her career (not to mention going to jail), I found a payphone and tried Rick again. This time I got through. He didn't seem surprised to hear from me. Pretty blasé, actually.

"Finally got your head outta your ass, huh?"

A train's air horn sounded twice as it pulled into the station.

"Yeah, and then I stepped into another pile of shit. I had an appointment this morning with my shrink. Problem is when I got there, he was dead. Murdered, and now I'm on the run."

I watched a steady stream of cars moving in and out of the station, passengers dropped off, others picked up, as I recounted the entire story—Leo's initial plea for help, my involvement with Trudy, Muertens' role in all of it—all the time keeping a wary eye out just in case my assessment of Simpson's motivation was off the mark.

"Muertens had one of the staff try to off me a couple nights ago. And I'm pretty sure he killed my doctor this morning to set me up."

"Sure you know how crazy this sounds, right?"

I did indeed.

"And Muertens needs you dead to collect on the insurance?"

I agreed.

"Shit, no one's been executed in New York in forever. And, on the off chance the death penalty comes up, any asshole lawyer can plead you out with a diminished capacity defense. Maybe your doctor just committed suicide."

"I didn't consider that. I understand he was pretty depressed."

But Muertens was the boogieman. The cause of every bad thing that had happened to me in the past year. Couldn't completely let him off the hook.

Silence on the other end of the line, then Rick said, "This Muertens character. Isn't he the guy you had me look into a while back? You thought he had a GPS tracker on your car?"

"Yeah, and he's a psycho with his fingers dug into everyone, including that lawyer Schoolkraft. That's why I went after him. Figured he was the weak link. Thought I could break him and get a confession."

"And how'd that work out for you?"

Rick being Rick. By the tone in his voice, I could hear the unspoken word at the end of his question—*asshole*.

"Why didn't you tell me all this before?"

"Like I said, Muertens is a psycho."

"I specialize in psycho."

"He'd go after your family. I don't want to be responsible for what he might end up doing to you and yours."

Another long pause, and for a second I thought Rick had dropped off. But then he said, "This reporter, what's her deal?"

"Young, but she's sharp. And she's hungry."

"Seems to me like she's already got a story that'll get her on the evening news. Calling the cops is a hell of a lot easier than chasing after this Muertens with some idiot who just escaped off the funny farm and is running from the law."

Again, Rick being Rick. So, I swallowed his put-down, instead saying, "But my story won't get her to the networks. Muertens' will."

Rick actually laughed. "Hey, she sounds as crazy as you," he said, then hesitated before adding, "Okay, what's your play?"

I explained my plan, and when I'd finished, Rick said, "Sounds like it can work. Let me get what I need. Where do we meet up?"

Before I could answer, out of the corner of my eye I caught Simpson running towards me. She pulled up short, tugged at my arm and said, "We've got to get moving."

"Hold on, Rick," then to Simpson, "What's the matter?"

She tried to catch her breath, then blurted, "Roger's run off to the cops, so we got to get out of here before they show up." Before I could respond, she took another deep breath, then told me where Muertens was.

"Liberty Avenue in Queens. You know the area?" I said to Rick.

"Sorta."

"There's a pizza parlor on the southeast corner of Liberty and Lefferts. Meet us there."

"I'm on my way."

"ASAP. I'm running out of time."

The school group started dispersing and some of the kids wandered off towards a line of school busses parked in front of the station entrance.

Spotting a kid about a head taller than his classmates, wearing a Yankee baseball cap, I asked Simpson if I could borrow her cell phone. She handed it to me and I jogged after the kid. When I reached him, I said, "Trade you this phone for your cap."

"For real?" he said, eyes wide.

"For real."

"Cool."

I took the cap and the kid hurried off to tell his friends how he'd snookered some old fool.

"What the hell did you do?" Simpson said. "How am I going to explain to management I lost a phone."

"Cops can track the GPS. And thanks to Roger, I might need a disguise. A cap and sunglasses can do wonders in changing a guy's appearance."

"Oh, no, you don't," she said, clutching her glasses.

I FOLLOWED SIMPSON back to a late model Saturn sedan. I didn't have any statistical data to back me up, but I was willing to bet most Saturn owners were women. The car's interior still had a little of that new-car smell and I guessed she'd bought it within the last six months. A digital tape recorder, paperback book, and a FedEx envelope were scattered on the passenger seat.

"Just throw that stuff in the back," she said.

When I asked Simpson if she knew Queens, she said, "I had a cousin who lived in Bayside, but no, not really."

"Okay. Get on Northern State and take it to the 168th Street exit. I'll give you the directions from there."

Simpson fingered a white plastic cross on a chain hanging from the rearview mirror, and then off we went. We had a jump on the rush-hour, so traffic on the parkway was light. In another hour it would be bumper-to-bumper in both directions.

"Does Lanier know where we're headed?" I asked.

"I had him looking into that broker, Skillman, who, by the way, is dead."

I wasn't surprised. "Suicide?"

"Street mugging."

"Dollars to donuts," a phrase my grandfather used often, "Muertens just cashed in on another big payday."

Simpson looked puzzled.

"Dollars to donuts. A sure thing," I explained.

"Insurance scam?"

I nodded.

"Roger knows you're going after Muertens. He's no rocket scientist, but he'll figure out where we're headed soon enough."

"Yeah, and tell the cops. We'd better hurry."

Traffic slowed at the Northern State-LIE interconnection, and then sped up again after we got past Mineola Boulevard. The drive felt a lot like the trip I took to Philly with Leo. He was lost that day, but hopeful his troubles would soon be over. Although I now felt hopeful, my optimism came with two big questions—would the cops be waiting for me when I arrived at Muertens' office? Would Rick come through?

We drove in silence for a couple of exits, lost in our thoughts.

Simpson was the first to voice her misgivings. "And you're absolutely sure about Muertens?"

"Absolutely. Not having second thoughts, are we?"

"Did you know he presided over a ribbon-cutting ceremony at the opening of a new youth center this morning?"

"Even black has different shades," I said, then told her

about the plaques and photos chronicling his good deeds covering the walls in his Flushing office. "Two-faced? This guy's a hydra, and believe me you don't want to see the face I've seen."

But rather than reinforcing her crumbling resolve, my words had the opposite effect. She flipped on the turn signal, pulled over onto the shoulder, and stopped the car.

"What's the matter?"

"I don't know if I can go through with this," Simpson said.

"Sure you can."

She glanced at me.

"Look, I understand," I said, then reached for her.

She shrugged my hand away.

"I know what I've told you is hard to believe, but it's all true, and I know you feel it in your gut. That's why you're here."

She sat still for a beat, then slumped forward and draped herself over the steering wheel.

"Can you at least drop me off in Queens? You could always say I had a gun to your head. After all, I am nuts, remember?"

My forced laughter didn't get a response.

She fluted the cross, and I imagine said a silent prayer, then without a word, got back on the Parkway.

I sighed, then said, "Thanks."

When we reached 168th Street, she said, "How do you propose getting Muertens to confess?"

"I have a friend with some very special skills."

"The guy you were talking to on the phone?"

"Yeah. At the fourth light, turn left onto Main Street. I'm banking on Muertens not expecting me. His arrogance will take care of the rest."

I told her my plan, and after I'd laid it out, she said, "This doesn't work, you know you're dead."

"It might work and I could still end up dead."

"Just like my career."

When she put it that way, I didn't feel so confident anymore.

59

I CHECKED THE TIME.
"Rick should've been here by now."

Simpson and I were sitting at a table by the window at the rendezvous spot with a good view of Muertens' office half a block away.

The aroma of garlic and tomato sauce was heavy in the small store. I watched the pizza chef, like a rhythmic gymnast, artfully spin the pie-dough over his head, throwing off clouds of flour. The two customers sitting at the counter beneath a mural of the Amalfi coastline oohed and aahed at his performance, and when the chef had finished his routine, they gave him a rousing ovation.

"Where's this guy coming from?" Simpson said.

"Rick? He was in the office, but he had to make a stop before meeting us here."

"Maybe he got stuck in traffic."

I looked at my watch, again. Only a couple of minutes had ticked off.

"Not exactly the neighborhood I'd expect a heavy hitter to have an office," Simpson said.

"Don't let that fool you. It's just camouflage."

I took a bite out of my third slice of pizza, then said, "I'm gonna take a walk. Make sure Muertens is still in the office."

I put on her sunglasses and pulled the Yankee cap low on my forehead.

"How do I look?"

Simpson didn't return my attempt at lightheartedness. Probably wondering why she hadn't thrown me out of the car when she had the chance.

"Make sure you bring 'em back," she said pointing to her

shades, then flashed a thousand-watt smile.

A jaunty two-finger salute and I was out the door and onto the street. I hung by the traffic light, staying a few steps behind a dreadlocked Rasta man. Didn't see any obvious signs of trouble, so maybe NYPD hadn't received the BOLO (be on the lookout) from the Nassau County cops. I could only hope.

Thanks to Billy Strayhorn's famous song, everybody knows the A-Train stops in Harlem, but the train's journey begins at the elevated Lefferts Boulevard station in the far lesser-known borough of Queens. An outsized billboard featuring Muertens' ten-foot high mug stretched across Liberty Avenue, trumpeting a half-dozen of the businesses he owned in Brooklyn and Queens.

As I made my way to Muertens' office, the Rasta man turned left, so I tried to blend in with the multiethnic crowd, hanging close to two women dressed in colorful saris, keeping my head down, my eyes open.

Liberty Avenue is lined with mom-and-pop stores on the street level, with two floors of residential apartments above. Shafts of mote-filled sunlight cut through the shadows beneath the elevated tracks. Park a few Model-T's along the street and it could have been the set for a Roaring '20s-themed Hollywood movie.

Muertens' storefront real estate office was sandwiched between a fruit and vegetable stand and a Punjabi convenience store.

The fragrance of exotic spices from the restaurant further up the street drifted on the early afternoon breeze. I stopped at a souvenir shop and feigned interest in a rack of *tchotchkes*, all the while checking out Muertens' office on the other side of the street.

But it was difficult to tell what was going on inside. Trusting my disguise, I decided to go take a closer look.

As far as I could tell, Muertens and his two goons, Mutt and Jeff, were the only ones inside. Muertens was removing papers from one of the file cabinets lining the back wall, and stuffing them into a briefcase.

Shit, he was preparing to leave. But wasn't he supposed to be in a wheelchair?

I decided I couldn't wait for Rick. Couldn't blow the only shot I was likely to get to unmask this homicidal maniac and take my life back. I clicked on the recorder, and pushed open the door.

OKAY, TOUGH GUY. *Now what?*

I knew it was crazy borne out of desperation. I didn't have a plan, but I was banking on Muertens not having one either. So maybe we were even, and by forcing his hand I'd catch him off guard and somehow be able to get in and get out with his recorded confession in my pocket.

The office had four desks, one in each quadrant of the open space. Office chairs were scattered around the desks. Posters with slogans to motivate the sales staff were spaced haphazardly around the walls.

Mutt and Jeff sat in front of a desk, their backs to me, Jeff reading a newspaper, Mutt leaning back in his chair, feet propped atop the desk.

An elevated subway rumbled overhead, shaking the windows and rattling the "Closed" sign against the glass.

"Can't you see we're not open?" Jeff shouted.

I took off Simpson's sunglasses and wedged them down over the bill of the ball cap.

Jeff didn't turn around, but Mutt did.

He had a large bandage across his forehead, both lips swollen. "Oh, shit. It's him."

As if a starter's pistol had been fired, they jumped up in unison, and ran to me, each grabbing an arm, and roughly shoving me towards Muertens, who stopped my forward progress by jabbing an ornately carved cane into my chest.

"How's the market?" I said.

Muertens, seemingly bemused by the commotion around him, removed the cane and said, "Well, if it isn't Mr. Benson. I heard they'd let you out."

"Guess your boy Mutt told you. He ought to learn how to drive."

I didn't get a chance to smirk because Mutt responded with a quick jab to my ribs.

Fortunately, Muertens called him off before he could slug me again, and said, "Good of you to drop by," a grin from ear to ear, a cat playing with a mouse.

Classical music sounded from the ceiling speaker above my head. I recognized the powerful last movement of Beethoven's, 9th *Symphony*, the full-throated chorus singing the text of the German poet, Friedrich Schiller's, *Ode to Joy*.

Playing for time, I said, "Where's the wheelchair? In the shop?"

Muertens got into my face, his nose brushing my chin. His teeth were yellowish, the incisors recessed.

"I see you're still a wiseass. Check him out."

Jeff patted me down, dug the recorder out of my right pants pocket and, holding it up, said "Lookee, lookee. Numbnuts has got a tape recorder."

Muertens snatched the recorder. "You think I'm a fucking idiot?" he said, then threw it onto the floor, smashing it beneath his heel, before kicking it aside. He slapped me, knocking Simpson's designer sunglasses and the Yankee cap to the floor.

Mutt stepped on the glasses, mangling them. "Oops."

Simpson won't be happy.

"You got anything else on you, smart guy?" Muertens said. Before I could answer, he back-handed me again. Blood was warm liquid copper on my tongue. "You wired?"

Turning his wrath on Mutt and Jeff, he shouted, "Didn't I tell you two morons to lock the fucking door when the office's closed?" then smacked me again, and ordered Mutt to pat me down. "This time like you got half a fucking brain."

But when Mutt didn't move fast enough, Muertens yelled, "Strip his ass. I wanna see his nuts."

Mutt unbuckled my pants jerking them down around my

ankles, then ripped my shirt open, sending buttons flying to the floor.

Muertens slammed the briefcase shut, and said, "Well, this changes everything. Eliminate this problem."

Both goons smiled. They were going to enjoy this assignment.

Where the hell was Rick?

"What, another good old fashioned street mugging?" I asked, spitting blood.

Muertens' quizzical expression told me I'd surprised him.

"Yeah, I know all about Luke Skillman," I said. "How much am I worth?"

He hesitated, then said, "Enough." He turned to Jeff, "Check out front. See if this clown's brought company."

Jeff disappeared.

I pulled my pants up, buttoned my shirt as best I could. Thought about trying to somehow maneuver past Mutt and escape, but suddenly he had a gun pointed at my head.

Muertens tapped the cane on the floor and stared at me, trying to divine, I'm sure, what I knew and how I came to know it.

He hummed along with the classical music. "You like Beethoven, Benson? Man was a giant."

"He was a slave to tone-deaf patrons."

"Everybody's a slave to someone, or something," Muertens said.

"And who's your master, Hike?"

"Money and power, of course." Again the cartoonish laughter.

Jeff returned after a quick reconnaissance. "Don't see anyone, boss."

"Then you really are stupid, Benson." I couldn't have agreed more. "Here's Plan B. You're a freaking psycho, right? An escaped psycho at that. Overpowered a guard. Beat the shit outta your lawyer. Came here threatening to kill me out of some paranoid delusion that I murdered your friend, which, I did."

He paused, enjoying the sound of his voice, laughed, then added, "Ruined your life, or some such shit, which I did. Sound good so far?"

When I didn't respond, Muertens said, "Too bad Joe here," pointing to Mutt, "had to shoot you in self-defense. Tell you what. This hip's acting up on me today. I need the exercise, so I'm going to pick up MetroCards for that volunteer appreciation dinner tonight over at the Legion Hall. Call me after you've finished cleaning this shit up."

Mutt shoved me in the back and I stumbled forward, bumping into one of the desks.

"Nobody's gonna be playing violins for this guy, boss," Jeff said.

Mutt and Muertens shared a laugh, then Muertens said, "And make sure you lock the damn door this time."

"Sure thing, boss," Jeff said.

Muertens hobbled out, the "Closed" sign rattling against the glass.

"Show time," Mutt said.

I raised my hands in defense. "How much you guys getting paid to do *his* dirty work?"

"Like the boss said, enough," Jeff said.

"Hell, I'm insured for five million and my estate's worth another two mil."

Which was bullshit, but they didn't know that. They looked at each other in something like awe, and I followed up with, "I think you guys are underpaid."

"Shut the fuck up," Jeff yelled, then turned to Mutt and said, "Shoot him already, will ya."

THE SIGN BANGED against the glass and then, just like in the movies, Superman stepped through the door, or rather his alter ego, Clark Kent.

Dressed in dark slacks, a white shirt casually open at the collar, Rick had rolled up the sleeves to his elbows, his tie askew, the knot loose.

"Can't you people around here read?" Mutt said, then, lowering his weapon, said, "What the hell you doing here?"

"I forgot that damn code again. You know. The one that's supposed to tell our boy Tony, here, that I've gone over to the dark side."

I almost slumped to the floor. "Not you, too, Rick?" I stammered.

Mutt and Jeff snickered.

Another betrayal. First Trudy, then lawyers, shrinks, and now Rick, my savior turned assassin.

"What you guys doing?" Rick said.

"Boss wants us to take care of this mess," Jeff said, jabbing a stubby finger at me, then rubbing it and his thumb together. I was just another payday.

But something is off. Rick's got that electric swagger.

"So, again, what're you doing here?" Mutt asked, again, raising his gun toward my chest.

"I was in the neighborhood. Thought I'd drop in and say hey."

Rick's playful banter. Just like at Metro Tech when he took out those two punks.

He extended his hand to shake Mutt's, and when Mutt lowered the weapon to his side, Rick delivered a front kick to his forearm. "What the fu—" Mutt screamed in pain, the gun sliding across the floor.

Rick followed with a round kick to Mutt's temple, knocking him across the desk. The goon rolled onto the floor, landing with a dull thud.

Jeff scrambled, grabbed Rick from behind and lifted him off the floor. Big mistake. Rick snapped his head back, crushing the guy's nose with a sickening crack of bone and a spray of blood. Jeff let Rick go, clutching at his nose. then Rick spun, and spiked him in the groin. Jeff crumbled to his knees, clutching his nuts. Rick finished him off with a rapid-fire three-punch combination to the head, unleashing a geyser of blood.

I picked up the gun, awed once again at the sight of Rick

unleashing the animal within. The massacre couldn't have taken more than five seconds. The Karate Kid on steroids.

"How—?"

"I'll explain later," Rick said. "Go find Muertens and let's finish this thing. I'll babysit these assholes." But before I reached the door, Rick added, "You better leave the gun. Don't want you to hurt yourself."

Yeah, it pissed me off when he sold me short like that, but he had a point. So I handed the gun over, and hurried for the exit, feeling lucky to be alive.

Out on the street, I took a quick glance up and down Liberty Avenue. No Muertens.

"Tony!" It was Simpson. She was set up across the street, standing behind what looked like a pair of binoculars on a tripod. A few curious onlookers surrounded her.

"Where did he go?" I yelled.

She gestured to the tracks above.

I had forgotten. That's where Muertens said he was going—to pick up MetroCards for a volunteer appreciation dinner. I just hoped I hadn't missed him. I didn't. When I got to the foot of the stairwell at the northeast corner of Liberty and Lefferts, I spotted him. Ever the good citizen, he was helping a young mother carry a stroller down the stairs.

As I angled my way through the descending mob, I yelled, "Muertens!"

Startled, he looked up, and when he saw me dropped his end of the stroller, the mother struggling to stop the toddler from bouncing down the stairs. Muertens threw a handful of MetroCards at me, then turned and hobbled back up.

I tripped over an elderly man reaching for a card, quickly regained my balance, then charged after Muertens. Clear now, I took the steps two at a time, yelled for him to stop, but when I made it to the mezzanine, he'd already made it to the train platform, another flight up.

I didn't pick up one of Muertens' transit cards, so I jumped the turnstile and continued the chase, dodging riders pouring down the stairs. The train that had just arrived was on my left, a Manhattan-bound train to the right. Didn't see Muertens, though.

The smart move would have been to get on the Manhattan train. I ducked my head into the last car. It was about three-quarters full, but no Muertens. I ran along the platform to the next car. There were fewer people, but again, no Muertens.

I heard the signal indicating the train was about to leave.

"Watch the closing doors," the conductor announced over the train's speaker system.

I hurried inside the third car. Muertens was standing near the door at the far end, looking like a cornered animal, one foot inside the car, the other on the platform.

We played peek-a-boo, but Muertens slipped out of the car just as the doors closed. I reacted a split second too late and got stuck. I pushed back and the doors released me from its viselike grip. The train began to slowly pull away.

Muertens staggered towards the exit at the far end of the platform. He was a car ahead of me when he tried to force his way back onto the train, but couldn't do it.

When I got closer, he screamed, "I'm being robbed," and swung the cane to keep me at bay.

I danced out of reach, then pressed forward.

"It's over, Muertens."

Someone yelled for me to leave him alone. Understandable, because it looked like a physical mismatch—a younger man pouncing on an old guy with a cane.

"It's not the way it looks, folks," I shouted. But to no avail. I was grabbed, then pulled away by a beefy construction worker.

"Take it easy, man," the guy said. He smelled of sweat and sawdust, and the pizza he'd had for lunch.

Another onlooker yelled for the cops, as a crowd pressed in on me. That's when Muertens took another swipe at my head, missed and hit a spectator on the shoulder. The guy was gassed, but had enough strength to throw the cane at me. I dodged it, and it skittered harmlessly along the platform and onto the tracks.

Muertens turned to run away, and bumped into a vendor pushing a cart. Losing his balance, he teeter-tottered at the edge of the platform for a second, then with an ear-piercing scream, he toppled over the edge and onto the tracks.

The rest remains a blur, a cacophony of sounds—the whistle of a two-car maintenance train filled with track workers sliding into the station; its brakes screeching; the shrieks and screams from onlookers; and Muertens.

I imagined—heard?—him screaming, "It's not supposed to happen this way." Of him reaching out for me in a silent call for help. The swirling air raising the hairs on the back of my hands as I stared down at him.

I'm not sure, but I believe I smiled.

THE MOTORMAN REPEATEDLY blasted the distress signal calling for police assistance.

Two uniformed officers jumped onto the tracks and disappeared beneath the platform.

No sense in making a run for it. Cops were closing in from both ends of the platform. At least a half-dozen riders motioned them towards me, so it was easy for them to figure out who to zero in on.

"He pushed the old guy," some loudmouth cried out.

I held my hands out shoulder-high as if to ward off the officers now surrounding me and said, "It didn't happen like that. Ask that man over there," pointing at the construction worker.

"On your knees, lock your fingers behind your head," one of the patrolmen shouted.

I did as he commanded. His partner yanked my arms behind my back, and cuffed me.

When he ordered me to stand, I struggled to my feet and came face-to-face with another cop, who identified himself as Sergeant Johnston.

"You got any ID, pal?" he said.

I shook my head, no.

"How 'bout a name?"

"Tony Benson. The guy on the track's Hike Muertens, and he's trying to kill me."

Another cop stepped forward and said, "Didn't we hear something about this asshole? Escaped nutcase? There's a Nassau BOLO out for him."

The sergeant grinned, said, "Well, chalk one up for the good guys," then turned away and yelled to the men on the tracks, "How's it going down there?"

"EMS—"

"Or a priest—"

"—better get here fast, or this guy's a goner."

"He'll need more than a priest to save his murdering ass," I said.

The sergeant gave me a long cold stare, then said to the cop who'd cuffed me, "Smith, better read Mr. Remorseful here his rights."

"I know the drill," I said.

"Bet you do," Smith said, then recited the Miranda warning in a dull, flat voice. A sudden sense of panic swept over me, and my knees almost buckled. *Muertens is as good as dead and he's still screwing me.*

I hadn't practiced criminal law, but I remembered a little from law school. The perpetrator was liable for the injuries, or death, suffered by a fleeing victim. And I was the *perp*, unless I could prove that *I* was the victim.

But I failed to get Muertens' recorded confession, so what's the word of an escaped mental patient with a history of violence worth?

The sergeant's two-way crackled.

"Got another hot one, boys. Some Rambo just called in a citizen's arrest. Smith, you and Rollins take it. You won't have far to go. Our hero's downstairs, outside the real estate office next to the convenience store."

After the cops hurried off, I pleaded, "I told you I *didn't* shove Muertens onto the tracks."

"Officer, he's right about that," the construction worker

said. "The old guy tried to brain him with a cane, missed, and hit me instead. But he sure enough was chasing after him."

Sergeant Johnston ordered the two remaining officers to escort me to the precinct.

As they led me away, four EMS technicians lugging emergency gear charged up the stairs.

The intersection at Liberty Avenue and Lefferts Boulevard was cordoned off. Police, fire and emergency vehicles, their light bars flashing, were parked haphazardly.

A large crowd had gathered behind the yellow police tape to watch my personal train wreck. Additional officers manned the perimeter keeping the onlookers back.

I spotted Marcia Simpson in the throng. She waved her arms and bounced up and down, her body charged with excitement.

"We got him, Tony," she called out, her delicate fists extended, thumbs-up.

60

"TODAY, NEW YORK CITY POLICE, working with federal investigators, arrested prominent New York City businessman and community activist, Hezekiah "Hike" Muertens, and two associates, charging them with a long list of felonies ranging from racketeering to murder," Marcia Simpson said.

I watched her report on the monitor in the Green Room at Nassau Cable News. The so-called green room was actually a soothing beige. A couch with a floral-print and similar color palette faced the monitor on the opposite wall. A mahogany coffee table squatted in front of the couch. I'd brought a dozen red roses for Marcia and placed them on the table next to a bottle of champagne in a crystal ice bucket. A pitcher of water and glasses were on an end table next to the couch.

Simpson stood on the steps at the Queens County Court House. She wore a red ensemble and it had a slenderizing effect. She looked stunning, seeming to pop off the screen. With her talents and good looks, she was definitely ready for prime time.

Mutt and Jeff—heads bowed, and hands cuffed—were shown being led out of Muertens' Flushing office by uniformed police officers.

A file photograph of Muertens flashed on the screen while Simpson, doing the voiceover, said, "Mr. Muertens is in Jamaica Hospital recovering from serious injuries he sustained when he fell onto the tracks at the Lefferts Boulevard subway station, trying to elude Tony Benson, one of his alleged victims."

The picture my mother had taken at my college graduation flashed on the screen. I don't know why I gave it to Simpson for her report. Perhaps to show her I hadn't always been cynical and disaffected. Back then you could see hope in my eyes.

"As I reported here exclusively on Nassau Cable News," Simpson said, "Mr. Muertens is accused of masterminding a murder-for-profit scheme in which investigators allege he received millions of dollars in death benefits.

"I've personally combed through records of every homicide in New York City over the past five years, including the unsolved murder of my cousin who was gunned down on a Brooklyn Street, and cross-referenced them with death benefits paid out during that same period."

She paused a beat for dramatic effect and then said, "I believe there are several other instances where Mr. Muertens may have benefited."

Simpson went on to detail three suspicious deaths, including her cousin's and the broker, Luke Skillman, making a case for conspiracy against Muertens.

"The case was cracked wide open when this reporter gained access to an audio tape, a tape on which Mr. Muertens can be heard admitting to killing Leo Radigan, whose death was originally ruled a suicide. After I turned the tape over to the district attorney's office, Mr. Muertens and his accomplices were arrested today.

"On that same tape, Mr. Muertens directs an associate to kill Tony Benson, the alleged victim he was fleeing from when he fell onto the subway tracks."

Another dramatic pause, then, "Mr. Muertens, through his attorney, vehemently denies the charges against him."

Muertens' attorney stood in front of Jamaica Hospital, ringed by microphones, and said, "Mr. Muertens is innocent of all of these sordid allegations. This fiction has been concocted by Mr. Muertens' political and professional enemies. We'll have our day in court, and when all the facts are presented, Mr. Muertens will be completely exonerated of all these scurrilous charges."

"SO, WHAT'D YOU THINK?" Simpson asked, back in the Green Room after the newscast. She was a bundle of nervous energy.

"I thought you were great," I said. "You're on your way now."

She ran across the room, wrapped her arms around my neck, squeezed hard, then kissed me on the cheek.

"I couldn't have done it without you, Tony."

After she let go, I handed her the roses.

She smelled them, and said, "They're lovely. Thank you."

"Read the card."

She took a moment, then said, "That's beautiful."

"I appreciate you believing in me, Marcia. I'd run out of options. If not for you—"

"Being hungry?"

We both laughed. She'd blasted me when I'd accused her of coveting a big job with the networks.

"Champagne?" I said.

She nodded. I poured her a glass, and, back on the wagon again, water for me.

"None for you?"

"It's a long, sordid story. Anyway, here's to bringing down Muertens." I raised my glass.

"And to you getting your life back," she said, returning my toast.

"Amen to that. So, what's next for you?"

I perched on one end of the couch.

Simpson sitting opposite me in the wing chair, said, "My agent's looking at a couple of things, but they're out of town."

"Got to start somewhere, even it's in Podunk."

She shrugged. "I suppose."

An awkward silence settled between us. We really didn't have much in common. Our interests intersected and ended at Muertens.

Simpson sipped from her glass, then said, "This is good stuff."

"What's the latest on Muertens?"

"He lost an arm, but he'll recover, and with Rick's tape and Muertens' boys rolling on him, he'll be going away forever."

"Murdering bastard should get the needle."

I watched the weatherman on the monitor pointing out the high and low fronts on the weather map.

"This is just the tip of the spear, Tony." She wrung her hands. "I didn't report it, but it's going to come out in the next couple of days that the DA will be looking real hard at Leo's wife, Trudy."

"I hope not. Leo and I didn't exactly do right by her."

"That's no excuse for accessory to murder."

"I suppose you're right, but still . . ."

61

RICK HAD A LARGE HOUSE on a sprawling two-acre plot in Dix Hills. The expansive yard was landscaped with shrubs and colorful flowers. A brick path meandered through a stand of bushes with pink flowers, from the split-level house down to the pool.

He offered me a place to stay while I got myself together, and I'd gladly accepted.

We sat in the Florida room overlooking the pool, Rick working on a six-pack, munching chips and salsa while I sipped a club soda. Having been released by a Nassau County judge, I was thoroughly enjoying my first few days of emotional freedom in well over a year.

"Big place for just two people," I said.

"You see anybody else?"

An orange tabby ran into the room and jumped up on Rick's lap.

"I thought you were married?"

Rick didn't say anything, just scratched the cat behind the ears, the tabby purring like a well-tuned sports car.

The man was an enigma. He kept some rooms locked and others were off limits to me. What was he hiding?

Finally, he said, "An old spy's got to have some secrets."

"Like working for Hike Muertens?"

He gave me a sly wink. "Yeah."

"That's all you got to say?"

The room turned frosty.

"Muertens and his boys visited me awhile back. I'm a mercenary, right? Isn't that how you viewed me? Muscle, but not worthy of your trust? Anyway, Muertens told me you and your buddy Leo stole from him—"

"That's bullshit. I didn't steal anything from anybody."

Rick shrugged. "I asked you to tell me what was up. You wouldn't say shit, so I assumed he was telling the truth."

"Like I said, I didn't want to drag you into my mess."

"Whether you wanted to or not, you did. More to the point, I'm offended you thought I couldn't take care of those guys."

"My mistake."

"Could've saved yourself a whole lot of trouble, son."

The cat jumped back onto the floor, sniffed at my shoes, then ambled out of the room.

"That tape saved my ass, though," I said. "How'd you record it?"

"Laser audio microphone. Damn thing can pick up conversations half-a-mile away. Had to call in a few favors to get my hands on that kinda hardware, though."

"Well, I owe you big time, Rick."

I'd given Leo the same IOU, oh so many years ago. A lot a good it did him.

As if he read my mind, Rick nodded. "Your girlfriend told me where you ran off to."

"Marcia's not my girlfriend."

Rick smiled. "Whatever. Got her set up just in time to catch Muertens going all confessional."

"I knew I'd get him to talk. Just didn't know if I'd be around to see him pay for what he did to Leo."

Rick popped open another beer.

"How's that attorney I turned you on to working out?" he said.

"Good old Marty. He's been great."

"So, now what's your legal status?"

I drained my club soda, crushed the can, and then ran through an abbreviated version of what had transpired since I was dragged off the subway platform.

"The only thing hanging over me is an assault charge in Nassau for choking out that hospital driver, but with all that's gone on, Marty thinks worst case scenario, I'll get probation and a few hours of community service."

"Told you Marty's the best."

"And I'm sure the pointy-heads at Pilgrim released me because they didn't want me inside pissing all over them."

Rick nodded. "What's next? Back to Telecom Structures?"

"Nah. By the way, how's Ted Strickland doing?"

Rick raised his bottle in a mock toast and allowed himself a tight smile.

"Okay. But let's face it, a trained monkey could do that job. On second thought, I'm not even sure the monkey's gotta be trained."

"Gee, thanks." I said. "Anyway, Marty thinks I've got a nice lawsuit against the Mental Health Department. Says the case could be worth millions."

"Don't lawyers always tell you that?"

He had a point.

272 **Ronald Aiken**

Acknowledgements

Thanks to all the people who have made this journey possible:

My friends, Tony and Sylvia Cristiano, thanks for taking me to Italy. Its beauty and timeless art so overwhelmed my senses I just had to chronicle what turned out to be the starting point of my writing career.

Susan Breen at Gotham Writers' Group encouraged me to expand my first short story into a novel. At the time, I had no idea how to accomplish that, but that initial offering became *Death Has Its Benefits*.

To my sister Penda Aiken who introduced me to Arthur Flowers, an Associate Professor of English at Syracuse University. Arthur led my very first critique group, and his tough-love approach, stressing craft, craft, craft, still resonates with me.

To Marty Aftewicz, Clay Ramsey, George Weinstein and the Atlanta Writers' Group for providing me with everything I needed to reach my goals.

To my Atlanta critique group and friends, Leanna Adams, Ralph Ellis, Chris Rapalje, and Cynthia Tolbert . . . thanks for your support and always speaking your minds. *DHIB* is so much better because of you.

David Fulmer, who taught me so much about writing and the business of writing, and encouraged me not to be the great college performer who couldn't make it to the pros.

My mentor, editor and friend, Jedwin Smith. I thought I had all I needed to complete the journey until I met you. Mere words cannot express my gratitude.

Jeff Dennis, my publisher, and the staff at Nightbird Publishing; working with you was a pleasure.

Thanks, Kerry for bringing me up to speed on the strip club scene.

And to all of my readers—Sandy Baker, Lora Egans, Sue Harden and Joe Lazzaro, my friend for over 40 years, Karen Sparer, my cleanup hitter—thanks for your help. Any errors are mine alone.

Lastly, to my wife, Herma, my first reader and toughest critic. Thanks for checking me when I'm trying too hard to be a writer. I still hear her admonition to "keep it clean." When you like something I know I have a winner.

About the Author

Ronald Aiken is a retired attorney from New York City. He currently lives in the metro Atlanta area with his wife, Herma, and their three cats. This is his first novel.

You can learn more about the author at his website: www.ronald-aiken.com